WONDER WC SUPERGIRL

SEX AND CHAOS

WRITTEN BY
VERA SIMS

VERA SIMS

Copyright © Vera Sims, 2023

SEX AND CHAOS

Copyright © 2023 by Vera Sims.
All rights reserved. This book or any portion thereof may not be reproduced or used in any manner whatsoever without the express written permission of the publisher except for the use of brief quotations in a book review.
Printed in the United States of America
First Printing, 2023
ISBN: 979-8857610848
Vera Sims.
51 S Cicero Ave
Matteson, IL 60443, USA
lifeisg00d@gmx.us

VERA SIMS

CONTENTS

CHAPTER 01

   Kidnapped And Enslaved

CHAPTER 02

   Kara's True Desire

CHAPTER 03

   Circe's Invasion

CHAPTER 04

   Circe's Reign

CHAPTER 05

   The Kryptonian Queen

CHAPTER 06

   The Hunt for Lena

CHAPTER 07

   Enslaved by Roulette

CHAPTER 08

   Lena's Mental Manipulation

CHAPTER 09

   Circe's Bargain

CHAPTER 10

SEX AND CHAOS

   Pleasure Games

CHAPTER 11

   The Queen's Lie

CHAPTER 12

   Betrayal

CHAPTER 13

   Desire for Submission

CHAPTER 14

   The Queen's Education

CHAPTER 15

   The Imposter

AUTHOR NOTE

VERA SIMS

CHAPTER 01

Kidnapped And Enslaved

Wonder Woman kidnaps Kara and Lena and makes them her pleasure slaves.

"AMAZONS ATTACK!" Lena Luthor let out a small laugh and shook her head at the headline of the newspaper as she tossed it down on her bedside table. It was true that Themyscira was on the brink of war with the rest of the world but the newspaper was clearly just trying to have a catchy headline. It was a problem she would worry about tomorrow, it had already been a long day for her and the only thing she was focused on was getting some sleep. She knew that there was a strong possibility she would be drawn into whatever conflict would arise from Wonder Woman's decision to kill Maxwell Lord. As the smartest being on Earth, she regularly was called upon to assist the government when they faced a threat beyond their capabilities. For all the time Wonder Woman had spent in "Man's World," so little was still known about her people: the Amazons. Their culture, their magic, just what they were hiding on that island; it all remained a mystery, even to Wonder Woman's allies in the Justice League. Lena could already imagine getting a call tomorrow, begging her to assist in putting together some kind of defense plan against an invasion by the Amazons of Themyscira.

She reached back and unzipped her black business dress, trying to stop the gears in her head from turning already, her mind already eagerly wanting to tackle the problem. The fabric loosened around her sensual form then she slipped it off of her shoulders and let it fall to the ground. She stepped out of it in only her black bra and panties, sitting on the edge of the bed to slip off her high heels. She then walked over to her dresser, sliding it open and retrieving a silk chemise nightdress. Her slender arms arced back as she found the strap to her bra, her fingers pinching down on the clasp and releasing it from her chest. She slipped the bra off and set it aside, her perky breasts barely needing the support as they rested so firmly on her chest. She then slid her panties down from the curve of her hips, pulling them down her long legs. She remained nude for only a moment, taking the nightdress and lifting it above her head then letting the fabric flutter down and settle on her feminine form nicely, the straps resting on her slender shoulders as the silk aligned to the curves of her figure.

The hem of the nightdress swished alongside her upper thighs as she walked to the bed, her bare feet padding softly on the ground. She tossed her bedsheets open then slid under the covers, settling into their warm embrace as she let her eyes close. The phrase 'Amazons Attack' flashed across her mind one final time before she dismissed the words from her thoughts, letting out a small sigh at what tomorrow would bring. But her involvement in this coming conflict would arrive far sooner than she realised...

As Lena drifted off to sleep, a figure stood on the rooftop of a building opposite her high rise apartment. The dark shadows of the night clung to her red and blue outfit, making her go unnoticed which was rare. The heroine known as Wonder Woman usually garnered attention wherever she went, but tonight she intended to remain quiet, her eyes narrowing as she calmly waited for enough time to pass.

She was wearing her standard onepiece outfit, the blue stars on the lower half with the red on top, the golden lining of her belt across her waist and the W that went across the top, running along the plunging line of her cleavage. In one hand she held a black bag full of items she would soon need, the firm muscles in her arm tensed as she kept a grip on it. Her flowing black hair rested between her shoulders, her beautiful features had a serious expression as she remained focused on her plan. She waited for another hour just to be sure that Lena would be asleep then she took a step toward the edge of the rooftop, the muscles in her long legs tensing before she leapt forward. She sailed through the air then her red boots touched down on the balcony outside Lena's room. Her hand reached for the door then, with a firm crack, she forced it open with her incredible strength. The

night air made the curtains ruffle as the door opened, then she stepped through into the room. Walking through the darkness of Lena's bedroom she approached the sleeping woman, standing over her and looking down at her peaceful expression. She looked even more beautiful asleep, her feminine features taking on an almost angelic quality; her plump lips parting ever so slightly as she took slow breaths.

SEX AND CHAOS

Wonder Woman reached down carefully and peeled the bedcovers up, revealing Lena's body beneath, the chemise having slipped even higher on her supple thighs. The heroine then set the bag down on the bed next to her prey and opened it. She reached in and first pulled out a white cloth and a small brown bottle, unscrewing the lid and pouring out a few drops of the liquid onto the cloth. Lena's head turned to the side and she made a soft mewling sound, her brow furrowing as she seemed to react to the presence in the room. She was beginning to stir but it was far too late, Wonder Woman had the cloth ready and she began crawling up the bed toward her. One hand rested next to Lena's head as she settled herself into position, the the other hand brought the cloth slowly forward. The cloth hovered by her mouth for a moment then in one swift movement she brought it clamping down, making a tight seal over the womans lips.

Lena's body shifted as she felt this pressure weighing on her, then her eyes snapped open and she made a loud muffled moan of shock. Wonder Woman let herself rest down fully on top of her to keep her in place, letting her weight pin down the waking woman. Lena began wriggling under her captor, her shock at seeing Wonder Woman giving way to a desperate struggle. Her body grinded against the firm form pressing down on top of her, their breasts rubbing as her chest shifted and wriggled side to side. Her legs were a little harder, wriggling and kicking up and down until Wonder Woman hooked her legs against Lena's, trapping them in a simple hold she had learnt on Themyscira. Lena moaned desperately as she felt the scent from the cloth filling her lungs, Wonder Woman keeping it constantly against her mouth and nose no matter how hard she struggled. Her hands tried to weakly push at Wonder Womans wrist, but using her free hand the heroine grabbed Lena's wrist and slammed it down to the bed beside her. Lena's free hand continued pushing but it grew weaker every second, her eyes starting to show a glassy dazed look. With every breath she could feel a numbness washing over her, the chloroform making her feel weak and listless. She made another moan through the cloth, this one of distress as she felt herself fading.

Wonder Woman watched intently as Lena started making long slow blinks, the hand that had been pushing at her flopping down on the bed. She loosened her grip on Lena's wrist, letting her arm lay there beside her head as she calmly brushed a strand of her dark brown hair out of her eyes and said "Just relax Ms Luthor. No harm will come to you" the words barely reached Lena's drug-muddled brain, drifting past her ears and bringing her little comfort. She made another few long slow blinks, her eyes getting closer and closer to being closed every time. Her expression softened along with the rest of her body, Wonder Woman feeling the woman going limp beneath her, sinking just a little deeper into the bed as her muscles lost any tension. Only the smallest sliver of white was visible now, then her eyelids snapped shut, her chest rising and falling as she let out a soft sigh and her consciousness faded away. Wonder Woman kept the cloth pressed over her mouth and nose for a few more moments then cautiously peeled it up, the damp cloth lifting from her plump lips. She observed Lena's peaceful features for a moment then leaned in and kissed her, their lips pressing together as the heroine let out a moan of pleasure from the delicious taste of her captive.

She remained in the passionate kiss for a few moments, her hands sliding down to squeeze Lena's breasts through the nightdress. Then she removed her mouth and smiled, seeing just how helpless Lena was. This was only the first part of her plan though; she would have time to enjoy her new slave later. She put the cloth away and retrieved the items she needed to ensure Lena remained her helpless captive. She pulled out multiple lengths of silk rope and a silk cloth, all made from the finest materials in Themyscira. She started with her gorgeous captive's long, luscious legs, planting a kiss on the smooth skin of Lena's soft, bare soles before binding her ankles. She tied the silk

tightly as she secured the knot, the soft material pressing into Lena's supple form and squeezing her legs together. With silk ropes tied to her ankles and above and below her knees, Wonder Woman was satisfied she could move higher. She took Lena's shoulders and carefully turned her over, letting her limp form slump onto her front. She then took her wrists and let them flop down on the small of her back. Wonder Woman was skilled with the rope and quickly tied up Lena's wrists, the silk becoming like handcuffs as she cinched them in the middle and made an inescapable knot.

She tied another length just above Lena's elbows and around her torso - above and below her perfect breasts -, pinning Lena's arms to her shapely body, then turned her back over, smiling down at her bound captive. She gave her breasts another firm squeeze then her hands ran down along her silky chemise nightdress, slowly lifting her own body off of that of her prize as she turned to pick up the silk cloth. Wonder Woman carefully straightened out the cloth, turning it into a long rectangular strip which she pressed tightly over Lena's lips. The soft silk covered the lower half of the woman's face, from just under her nose to her chin. When she awoke any sounds she made would be muffled by the fabric, and to ensure it stayed that way Wonder Woman tied it as tightly as she could behind her head. Lena was now helplessly bound and gagged, although she remained completely unaware of it, taking soft breaths through her nose as she lay still. Wonder Woman ran her hands along Lena's legs, stroking her soft skin before moving back to her breasts. For all her intelligence she had been so easy to defeat and the princess of Themyscira was already wondering how easy it would be to make her submit and accept her new status as the prized pleasure slave and concubine of Diana and all of her Amazon sisters.

Her eyes flickered from her captive to the bedside table, seeing Lena's phone sitting there "Perfect"

Wonder Woman smiled as she reached for the phone and picked it up, tossing it into the bag. It was time to go and Lena was coming with her. She carefully turned Lena around so her long legs draped off of the bed, then she leaned her forward so she could take her waist and hoist her up over her shoulder. With Lena's weight nicely settled she wrapped an arm around her upper thighs, unable to stop herself from giving her captive's lusciously plump behind a quick squeeze. As quietly as she entered the room she walked back to the balcony, Lena slumped over her shoulder with her legs draped down in front of her chest, the nightdress doing little to cover her rump as it stuck up in the air. Wonder Woman tensed her legs then leapt into the night, kidnapping Lena without raising a single alarm.

The CatCo news offices were buzzing with the seemingly inevitable war between Themyscira and the rest of the world. No one had seen Wonder Woman since the murder of Maxwell Lord but his killing wouldn't go unanswered. Kara was trying to stay out of it, most were anticipating how many papers this would sell but she was more concerned with the ramifications this would have for her superheroine identity. The last thing she wanted was to fight the Amazons but if they started a war it might have to come to that. She especially wasn't looking forward to facing Wonder

Woman; she had never had any reason to test her strength against the Amazon princess but the thought frightened her. She walked past all the fervour as people ran amongst the desks, all trying to compile as much information on the Amazons as possible. She made it to her desk and sat down, tapping the power button on her computer just as she heard the phone in her purse buzz.

She was still focused on her computer as she absent-mindedly reached for her phone, her eyes glancing toward the screen. Her brow furrowed with confusion as she saw someone had sent her co-ordinates along with an image attachment. She focused on her phone as she unlocked it and opened the attachment, her eyes going wide as she made a shocked gasp. The image was of a clearly kidnapped Lena Luthor! She was kneeling, bound and gagged, in a silky nightdress on a beach somewhere and it looked completely deserted, only Lena and whoever took the picture were

there. Kara could feel her heart beating hard in her chest, her mind racing with a million questions as her trembling hand continued holding the phone. Whoever had sent the image was clearly trying to lure her there and yet she knew she had to go. Lena wasn't just a close friend to Kara, the young heroine had strong feelings for her which might even be described as a crush. She wondered if the person sending her the photo knew about how she felt, if they knew that seeing Lena in danger would light a fire in her that couldn't be put out. She had so many questions and no way to answer them, they would all have to wait; saving Lena came first. She shot up from her chair, hurrying across the office and into the elevator. She was so focused on Lena she didn't even bother to tell anyone where she was going.

Moments later she was shooting through the air having quickly changed into her outfit on the roof of CatCo. Her red pleated skirt fluttered in the breeze as she rocketed forward, the air rushing all around her. She had a determined expression on her face and her mind was filled with thoughts of Lena. There were few people she cared about as much as Lena and rescuing her was all she could focus on. Following the co-ordinates that had been sent, she made her way to a deserted tropical island, her eyes narrowing as she saw Lena on the beach far below her. She flew down with great speed, only stopping when she was just above the sand, her red boots touching down as she made the last few steps to Lena. She was still on her knees and she looked weakened, her head limply lolling up to look at Kara with a hazy stare. She let out a small moan through her silk gag as Kara got closer and said "It's okay I'm going to..." But before she could finish a golden lasso flew through the air and lowered perfectly around the heroines torso, tightening at her elbows and pinning her arms to her side. Lena moaned softly again but it was far too late, Supergirl had already been caught.

She immediately tensed her arms to try and break free, a look of frustration crossing her face as she found the rope seemingly unbreakable. With all her strength she couldn't understand why the rope wouldn't break, her shoulders wriggling side to side as she groaned angrily. She then shot up into the air, planning to loop round and fly right at whoever was doing this to her. She only barely made it off the ground before a firm yank on the other end of the lasso brought her crashing down into the sand. With a pained groan she stumbled up messily, wobbling from the inability to use her arms as she got to her feet. As she did she finally saw who was holding the end of the lasso, a look of shock coming across her face as she stared at Wonder Woman striding confidently toward her on the beach. "Wh... What? Diana? What are you doing?" Kara asked with a confused look, the momentary distraction giving the Amazon princess more than enough time to pull the lasso again, yanking Kara off of her feet and bring her to the ground right in front of her.

Wonder Woman was upon her immediately, spinning her onto her back and straddling her as she pinned her to the ground. She reached behind her where she had tucked a cloth into her golden belt, already damp with a special type of chloroform made on Themyscira. She whipped the cloth round then pressed it down over Kara's mouth as she replied "I'm doing what I have to for my people" Kara moaned as she felt the cloth pressing firmly over her lips, her body wriggling under the Amazon as she tried to get free. She may have been trapped but she wasn't as helpless as Lena had been, her shocked look turned into a hard stare as her eyes glowed red and she shot out her heat beams. Wonder Woman quickly raised her other arm, using her gauntlet to deflect the beams off into the ocean. She held her arm there until Kara realised it was pointless and let the beams die down. Once that tactic was foiled she found herself at a loss for what to do, with all her powers she couldn't find any way to get Wonder Woman off of her and every second more of this strange scent filled her lungs.

She tried flying up but Wonder Woman pressed down on her harder, the heroines form soft yet so strong as she kept her trapped on the floor. Kara moaned desperately through the cloth, an indignant look on her face as her legs wriggled and kicked in the sand. Her efforts only made her take deeper breaths and soon Wonder Woman felt the younger heroine begin to soften, her

struggles becoming more listless. Her hips made a final few jerking motions then she settled down, her angry look sinking into a weak expressionless stare. Her eyelids fluttered then with a soft sigh they closed, her shoulders sagging as her body lost any tension. Wonder Woman smiled as she peeled the cloth up from her lips, looking down at Supergirl's unconscious form with a satisfied expression. She tucked the cloth back into her belt then stood up, standing over Supergirl in a dominant pose.

She stepped to the side of her, then moved to her boots, kneeling down and calmly taking Supergirl's ankle. She wriggled off the bright red boot and let Supergirl's leg flop down, then she reached for the other ankle and removed that boot as well. The blonde's legs and feet were now completely bare and Wonder Woman couldn't help stroke her hand up from her ankle to her supple inner thigh. Her fingers pressed down firmly then she moved higher to her torso. She carefully unwrapped her lasso to give her better access to Supergirl's costume. She then had to move behind her to lift her up a little and peel the upper half of her costume off. The tight fitting fabric lifted up over her head and off her arms, leaving her in just the blue bra she wore underneath. She let Supergirl rest back down as she tossed the upper half of her costume aside, she looked so cute and helpless in just her bra and skirt that the Amazon couldn't help fondling her breasts for a few moments, testing how firm they were as her fingers squeezed down around them.

Supergirl would be out for hours so she had plenty of time to gather up her boots and outfit then calmly walk the few steps down the beach to her invisible jet. It had shielded her from detection when Supergirl had landed on the beach and it would soon be departing with both of her beautiful captives. She tossed the items inside, then picked up a silk cloth she had left on one of the seats. She came back to Supergirl and rolled her over, taking her arms and moving them behind her back then binding her wrists together with her golden lasso. She wrapped the rest of the lasso up her arms and above her elbows, trapping her arms behind her back. She then carefully rolled Supergirl back over and took the silk cloth, pulling it tight over her lips and tying it behind her head. Wonder Woman ran her fingers along the gag to make sure it was smoothly against the blond heroines mouth, then her hand slid lower and she took a firm hold around her waist. She hoisted her up, the amazons incredible strength allowing her to sling Supergirl over her shoulder like she weighed nothing at all.

Lena was still on her knees, bleary-eyed, as she watched Supergirl being carried toward her. Wonder Woman walked up to her, then retrieved the cloth she had tucked in her belt. Lena weakly shook her head and whimpered for mercy, but Diana ignored the pleas of her gorgeous captive and, once again, calmly pressed the drugged cloth against Lena's gagged mouth and nose and held it there until the already groggy kidnap victim's eyelids fluttered closed. Lena slumped forward against the Amazon as she tucked the cloth away and Diana grabbed her round the waist with her free arm. In one smooth motion she hoisted Lena up, settling her on the shoulder opposite Supergirl. Both their rumps - Lena's lusciously plump and spankable; Kara's more muscular and firm, but no less enticing to behold - stuck up in the air as Wonder Woman wrapped her arms around their curvaceous bare thighs to keep them in place. Her hands stroked up and down their soft and smooth legs as she triumphantly carried them to her jet, sat them in separate seats facing across from each other, and buckled the two kidnapped damsels in securely for the long ride. They would soon be taken to Themyscira where their new lives of captivity would begin.

ONE MONTH LATER

Diana smiled as she lay on her side in bed, her hand stroked along Lena's shoulder then down to the curve of her hips, slipping between her thighs then back up to firmly squeeze her breasts. Lena was dressed in a silky white nightdress, similar to the one she had been captured in, with an equally short hem that showed off her long legs. Diana was dressed in a white regal gown befitting her status as a princess but she would soon be stripping out of it, the more she played with her captive the more she could feel that passionate desire to ravish her growing again. Lena's time on Themyscira had mostly been spent in the Amazon's chambers, bound and gagged. She had been reduced from the smartest woman on the planet to a mere pleasure slave, albeit a cherished one.

Diana kept her busy most of the time but she was generous to her sisters as well, allowing them their own time to enjoy Lena's body.

She rolled on top of Lena and began grinding her body into hers, delighting in the soft moans and wriggling Lena made under her. She could feel the heat in her growing and she moaned deeply as she kissed her neck then worked her way down to her breasts. She kissed lower until she found her inner thigh, making Lena shudder with every teasing kiss as she worked her way up between her legs. Then she heard a knock on the door, a sad sigh escaping her lips as she raised her head and declared "Enter!" She gave Lena's thighs a final kiss then rolled off the bed to address the Amazon that came in, standing to attention as she said "Princess, you asked to be informed when Supergirl returned from her mission" Diana nodded and smiled at the Amazon as she replied "Yes, thank you sister, I'll go out to greet her"

Diana walked through the halls of the royal palace then down the marble steps. Supergirl was already waiting for her at the bottom and Diana smiled warmly at her as she approached and said "How did it go? I trust their boats were all destroyed?" Kara looked clearly uncomfortable being controlled like this and she let out a small sigh before replying. "Yes. We left them with one to take back the crew from the other boats. But they won't be trying to invade by sea again" Diana walked right up to her and stroked a hand along her cheek as she smiled and said "Very good, my slave." Her hand then turned to take Kara's chin a little more firmly, her other arm wrapping around her waist as she pulled their bodies against each other and kissed her deeply. Kara let out a muffled moan of shock against her lips but she didn't resist. She knew she had no choice and it wasn't the first time Diana or one of the other Amazons had treated her this way. They were either using her to help them win the war or using her body for their own desires. She had tried to resist at first but as long as they had Lena she had no choice but to submit.

Diana's hand slid down and went under Kara's pleated skirt, groping her ass firmly as she kissed her. Then with one last moan of pleasure she peeled her lips away, smiling at seeing Kara's submissive look of shame from the kiss. "Seeing as you did such a good job I think you deserve a reward" Diana said with a sultry smile as she motioned for Kara to join her then walked back up the stairs into the palace. She walked Kara back to her chambers and up to the door, stopping to say "The one you care so much for is in here. We will be having a ceremony for her tomorrow. Until then, she is yours to do with as you wish." The blonde heroine slowly pushed the door open and stepped inside, seeing Lena on the bed she hurried over as Diana closed the door and locked them both inside. She walked back down the hall with a smile on her face, knowing that the temptation would be too great for the more naive heroine.

"Lena! Are you okay?" It was the first time she had seen Lena since they had both been brought here and she could feel her heart racing as she rushed over. She came onto to the bed and knelt beside her, carefully reaching behind her head and removing the gag. She slipped the soft fabric off of her mouth then curled her arms around her, lifting her from the bed and hugging her tightly as Lena replied "I'm okay, I'm glad you're here Kara" they embraced for a few moments then Kara gently lay her down on the bed as she said "Let me see if I can get these off" the silk ropes ran all along Lena's body, the intricate knots hard to release. Her hands ran along Lena's soft, shapely body as she tried to get the ropes off and as she felt the supple skin beneath her fingers her heart began to beat harder. Diana's words rang in her head 'She is yours to do with as you wish' and she looked down at Lena's sensual form. She would be lying if she said she hadn't imagined this very scenario multiple times: Lena Luthor, the woman she'd had a crush on for so long, completely at her mercy.

Her eyes glanced over to the silk cloth she had left beside Lena on the bed and she made her decision, reaching out and grabbing it. "What are you... mmmppphhh!!" Lena's words were quickly muffled by Kara pressing the gag over her lips and tying it tightly behind her head. As soon as it was in place she placed both hands on either side of Lena's head and pulled her toward her. She pressed her lips against the silk cloth, kissing Lena through the gag as she closed her eyes and enjoyed the romantic moment she had dreamed about for so long. Lena's eyes were still wide with shock and she moaned against the kiss, but there was nothing she could do against the stronger woman, held in the passionate embrace as she felt Kara's soft lips against her gag.

Kara didn't know if there was something about being on this island that was doing this to her but she didn't care. She could feel the blood pumping through her body now, the kiss had awakened a hunger in her that she needed to satisfy. She came out of the kiss then pushed Lena down on the bed with a heavy thump. She then reached down and took the top half of her costume and peeled it off, her hands rising above her head as she stripped down to her bra and tossed the blue material away. As soon as it was off she lunged down, pressing her body on top of Lena's and kissing her again. Her hands were all over her, squeezing and fondling as she lived out every sexual fantasy she had ever had. Her lips moved lower, kissing down to Lena's breasts then squeezing them firmly as she licked and nibbled at the two soft mounds. Lena's moans slowly turned from distressed to pleasurable as she was unable to control the sensations from Kara's mouth. She could feel every wet kiss on her skin, shuddering and moaning as she felt Kara's soft lips move lower and lower. Then she felt her between her legs and her head tilted back as she moaned loudly through her gag, her cheeks blushing a bright red as her whole body trembled with pleasure.

Kara made love to Lena long into the night, keeping her bound and gagged the entire time while she ravished her. When she finally tired and fell asleep, it was with Lena in her arms, curled up around her like a prized possession. Lena was slowly starting to get used to (and even enjoy) being a slave for the desires of other women and she had also passed out from sheer exhaustion. Their peaceful embrace was interrupted when the doors opened and Wonder Woman loudly declared "It's time for the ritual to commence!" Other Amazons filed in alongside Diana, lifted Lena up from the bed, and then carried her away. Diana walked over to Kara as she shuffled off the bed and got dressed with an embarrassed look "I see you enjoyed yourself last night. For every successful mission I will allow you another chance to enjoy Lena. Consider her your reward, do we have a deal?" Kara pulled her top back on and blushed as she replied "Okay... I'll do whatever you want"

Diana led Kara to where the ritual was starting, a large number of Amazons had gathered around a mystical pool of water deep amongst a wooded area on Themyscira. The trees cleared for a strange, circular hole in the ground that had water so pure it seemed to sparkle. As Kara arrived the Amazons still had Lena in their grasp beside the pool, waiting for Dianas arrival. They were all wearing skimpy white minidresses and leather sandals, their long toned legs bare as they gathered around the pool. Diana walked up alongside Lena who was still moaning and wriggling her shoulders side to side on her knees "Sisters! Today we bestow the great gift of immortality upon this mortal woman! After this ceremony is complete both she and the Kryptonian will be our slaves for all time!" The Amazons all cheered, even some applauding as Lena shook her head and moaned desperately through the gag.

There was nothing Kara could do except watch as the Amazons picked the bound and gagged Lena up and carried her into the magic pool of water, letting her sink down to her shoulders. They surrounded her in the water, kissing and fondling her from every angle as they let the magical properties of the pool take hold. Their bodies all pressed together in the wetness of the pool, Lena's

silky nightdress becoming practically see through as she was overwhelmed by the sensual assault. Wonder Woman watched over the erotic display in the water then she calmly walked beside Kara and whispered in her ear "Join them; the water will have no effect on a being like you" she then kissed her neck and gave her a small pat on the butt to usher her forward.

Kara let out a small gasp from the swat of Diana's hand on her backside. Then - as if she was in a trance - she slowly walked forward and lowered herself into the water. She was immediately pulled in amongst them, her body becoming one of the many writhing feminine forms. Diana smiled at Kara accepting her place as a pleasure slave on the island, the perfect weapon and the perfect submissive subject. Both her captives moaned and shuddered as the Amazons in the water with them kissed and squeezed their wet forms, using their bodies however they desired. Then when she was unable to control herself any longer the princess stepped down into the water and joined her subjects.

CHAPTER 02

Kara's True Desire

Chapter Summary: Lena and Kara's new lives as pleasure slaves are explored and Kara must confront a revelation about her true desires...

Her bare feet padded softly on the grass even though she was running as fast as she could. Her slender frame made the impact of her feet barely audible, the only sound was the heavy breaths she took as she ran amongst the trees. She was running through the forests of Themyscira, although where she was actually going she had no idea. Lena Luthor had been on the island for weeks now and this wasn't her first time running through these woods. She knew that escape was impossible, it was an island, there was nowhere to go. But if she didn't at least try to feign an escape attempt she would be placed across the lap of one of her captors and spanked til her rounded behind was a rosy red. At least this little game gave her a brief respite from the near constant sensual assaults upon her supple form. She was one of the many 'pleasure slaves' on the island, and with so many Amazons who lusted after her she rarely spent a waking moment not writhing and moaning in pleasure, wanted or not.

She was wearing a white skimpy nightdress, the hem of which fluttered up to show off her backside with every stride of her long legs, flashing a matching set of silk white panties that perfectly hugged the curve of her rear. She glanced over her shoulder nervously as she continued running, then she faced forward and nearly ran right into one of her captors. Lena came to a sudden halt as the Amazon put her hands on her hips and giggled "Going somewhere?" Like the others she was wearing a white dress with a fabric much thicker that the thin silk of Lena's, although the hem was almost just as short. She also wore a pair of leather sandals in contrast to Lena's bare feet. "I found her!" the blonde Amazon called out to the others who were pursuing her through the forest. But before they could arrive Lena darted to the left and kept running. "Over here!" she heard behind her as she took off, her luscious dark hair fluttering behind her back.

She barely saw the thin rope looping over her, then it travelled lower and the lasso tightened around her ankles. Her long legs snapped shut and her momentum came a quick stop, sending her tumbling forward, her breasts bouncing into the soft grass as she let out a breathless groan. While not magic like Wonder Woman's, the lasso was a common tool of the Amazons and this wasn't the first time it had been used to bring this game to an end and it most likely wouldn't be the last. "Got her!" the feminine tone came from behind her, it was full of joy and a girlish glee. Then three Amazons were upon her a second later. Their hands were all over her, holding her down and giggling as they tied her hands behind her back and groped her legs and behind. She knew by now to play the part of helpless captive, moaning and wriggling her hips, her backside jiggling to their delight as their hands squeezed and fondled it.

With her wrists and ankles bound she was promptly sat up, her long legs lying out in front of her as the Amazons closed in. One sat on her thighs facing and the other two knelt either side of her, each holding an arm to keep her up while getting so close their bodies became like two walls near squashing her with their soft bosoms. "Got you again" the one straddling her thighs said softly, her hand reaching out and gently tilting up Lena's chin to face her "You're completely helpless" she looked into Lena's wide eyes, seeing no hint of resistance. "Say it" she said as she leaned in closer, the warmth of her breath tickling Lena's lips. With a soft sigh Lena slowly opened her mouth and said the words she knew they loved to hear

"I'm completely helpless"

The words barely made it out of her lips as the Amazon immediately began kissing her, pressing their mouths together, the soft shape of their pillowy lips perfectly molding into a passionate embrace. As she kissed her the other two began fondling Lena's breasts, their hands sliding between the two women's bodies and squeezing down on the two malleable orbs. They also leaned in and began kissing and nibbling on either side of Lena's neck, sending shivers through her sensitive skin, her shoulders twitching upward in response. She moaned deeply from the overwhelming erotic assault, the sound muffled by the woman's mouth still locked against hers.

SEX AND CHAOS

The three amazons worked in unison to dominate their captive, kissing and fondling her as they slowly lowered her down to the ground, resting her head gently onto the grass.

The one kissing her began to kiss lower and lower, finding her breasts she kissed her nipples through the soft white silk, her wet tongue making the fabric near see through in how passionately she licked their soft shape. Lena's mouth wasn't left unattended for long, the other two now taking turns in forcing their tongues deep into her mouth, their hands gently turning Lena's head to one side for a long passionate kiss then to the other and back again over and over. As they kissed her the third continued her journey lower, kissing down to Lena's hips then carefully shimmying her night dress up to reveal her panties. Her hands raked up Lena's supple thighs, moving up to the curve of her hips and gripping the waistband of her silky white underwear. Then with a firm motion she pulled it down, jerking Lena's hips up from the floor as she pulled her panties down her long legs. As soon as they were off she buried her head between Lena's thighs and the gorgeous brunette let out a long shuddering moan.

A little while later, once the Amazons had sufficiently ravished Lena, they slid her panties back on and sat her up. They put her back in the same position, trapped between their bodies, her skin now glowing with the perspiration of her multiple orgasms. She was breathing heavily and had a dazed stare from the overwhelming sensual assault, her plump lips hanging ever so slightly open as the blonde straddled her thighs again and said "Awww our little pleasure slave is looking sleepy. Let's help her out" the other two giggled and began gently fondling Lena's breasts as the blonde reached between her own bosom and pulled out a white cloth she had prepared earlier. It had been soaked in the Amazons magical chloroform, the effects making the chemical never lose its potency, no matter how much time passed between its application on the cloth and its use.

The blonde leaned in and gave Lena one last long passionate kiss, then she peeled her lips away and replaced them with the cloth, her hand firmly pressing down over Lena's mouth and nose. Even though she had been chloroformed dozens of times now she still let out that same muffled moan of shock, her eyes snapping open wide then fluttering down to a glassy eyed stare. She could still feel the sensations of the other two groping her breasts, but those sensual tingles began to fade the further her eyelids drooped down. She made one final mewling moan against the cloth, a soft "mmmmppphhh..." barely audible from how weak she was. Then her eyelids slowly closed, the light behind her eyes fading away just before they snapped shut. The Amazon peeled the cloth away and said softly "So beautiful" then leaned in and gave her another quick kiss on the lips.

Once Lena was unconscious and sleeping peacefully she was slung across the blonde Amazon's shoulder and carried back toward the main city. She was so deep asleep she couldn't feel the grip of the arm around her upper thighs, the slight bounce of her hips against her captor's shoulder with every step, the cool air on her backside as it stuck up on her captor's shoulder. She also couldn't make out the sounds of the new training grounds as she was carried past those. The noise of swords clashing against shields and the grunts of the new recruits being trained in combat. Lena was the first to be taken to the island against her will but she hadn't been the last. Over the past few weeks Wonder Woman and her army of Amazons had been capturing dozens of beautiful women and bringing them here. The war in Man's World was raging on and the kidnapped women were given a choice: Join the Amazon army or become pleasure slaves as a reward for those that did fight. The ranks of their soldiers and their slaves had grown larger every day, the sounds of feminine moans now audible throughout the city at night.

The game that Lena had played and lost once again was quite common for her and the other pleasure slaves. The Amazons delighted in letting them try to escape then capturing them and making them their slaves all over again, bondage and chloroform always being used to subdue their captives once the game came to its inevitable conclusion. The Amazons walked down the cobbled streets of Themyscira, past a few other slaves being led on collars, toward a white stone building that had a lavish bedroom suitable for their prize. Before they could reach it they heard a loud "Hey! Put her down!" from above them. They paused and looked toward the sound, seeing Supergirl hovering down and landing in front of them. She was wearing her modified costume, the one that made it clear she was Wonder Woman's property. Over the S on her chest there was now a larger W, and the top itself had been amended to be sleeveless and cropped, showing off her toned stomach. Her skirt had been made shorter, the slightest ripple now showing off her blue panties and toned rump, and she was no longer allowed to wear boots, Wonder Woman preferring the look of her long legs when there was nothing on her feet.

Kara landed with an angry expression, her arms crossed as she blocked the Amazons path and said "I told you to put her down. She belongs to me!" The Amazons just smirked at her demand, her cute girlish features and her skimpy outfit made it hard to take her seriously. "I think someone's jealous" the Amazon to Lena's left giggled, the one to the right chiming in "Or maybe she just wants to join Lena. I've got space for you over my shoulder, Super-slave!" Kara glared at both of them, she was tired of being treated like this by every Amazon on the island. Since being captured she had become one of their greatest warriors, second only to Wonder Woman, yet between missions she was still treated like any other pleasure slave, knocked out, tied up and ravished by any woman who desired her. The blonde Amazon looked at her with a smug smile as she said "You forget your place Supergirl. Would you like it if your mistress was informed of your impudence?" While she could be used by other Amazons, she officially belonged to Wonder Woman, and the princess of Themyscira had trained her to be obedient through bondage, spankings, and rewarding her with access to Lena.

With a soft sigh Supergirl unfolded her arms and hung her head as she replied "No" the blonde Amazon's smile got a little wider as she said "That's what I thought." The other two slowly advanced on Supergirl, glancing toward each other with a devious twinkle in their eyes. "I think she needs to be reminded of her place" the one on the left said with the other nodding and replying "I agree" Supergirl saw their intent and began backing away with a nervous wobble in her legs. But they were too quick for her, one rushing round behind her and wrapping their arms around her chest to keep her in place, the other pulling out a white cloth from her bra and pressing it down on Supergirl's mouth. She had gone from demanding Lena's release to becoming just another helpless slave in moments, her eyes going wide as she made muffled moans.

The woman behind her gripped her tightly while the one in front pressed her body firmly into Supergirl, the two of them squashing her between their sensual forms. Her wide eyes soon took on a hazy stare, her eyelids slowly drooping down. Her body melted between them, their feminine forms squeezing into her as her legs trembled and went limp. They kept her on her feet, their hands groping and holding her up as they watched her eyelids flutter down over her wet eyes. Then, with a barely audible sigh, she sank down into unconsciousness, her limp form slumped forward over one of their shoulders and hoisted into the air. With another slave added to their collection the three Amazons resumed their path back to their living quarters, both Supergirl and Lena hanging limply on their shoulders.

Once they had Lena and Supergirl back in their bedroom they dropped them on the silk sheets of their large bed. There were many rooms like this, designed for the purpose of pleasure. The bed was large and the sheets silky and soft. They were a few candles lining the room and a rose scent in the air. Near the bed was a cabinet that had any items an Amazon might need to play with their slaves. As soon as Supergirl's limp form was deposited on the bed the Amazons retrieved some rope and smelling salts from the cabinet. They rolled Supergirl over and neatly crossed her wrists behind her back. Then they tied them together and carefully looped them round her chest, creating a harness that made an X shape between her breasts. They left her legs unbound for now so they could be spread apart, one of the Amazons kissing her inner thigh then sliding off her panties.

They used the smelling salts to wake Supergirl and Lena, then they immediately pushed the cloths over their mouths again to bring them down into a sleepy state. Both women moaned weakly under the cloths, the smelling salts giving them a brief moment of clarity before the chloroform once again subdued them. They were both used to this by now, being awakened only to be brought down to a more pliable state. Once they were sufficiently weakened, the Amazons slid the straps of their own white dresses off of their shoulders and let the fabric fall to the floor at their feet. Two made a sensual crawl across the bed to Supergirl while the third ravished Lena all over again, their bodies entwining as their soft moans grew louder and louder.

After the lengthy passionate lovemaking, Supergirl had once again been knocked out with chloroform. She was so exhausted she almost welcomed the peaceful slumber. When she woke she had been moved to a different bed, one that she was very familiar with. Her eyes fluttered open and she found she had been released from her bondage and her skimpy modified outfit put

SEX AND CHAOS

back in place. Her long legs stretched out on the bed and she moaned softly as she looked up with dazed eyes. She could hear a strange slapping sound and a muffled moan following every impact. It took a second for her head to clear but when it finally did she realized she had been taken to the room of her mistress, Wonder Woman. She groggily managed to sit up and saw that Wonder Woman was in the room with her, she was sitting on the end of the bed, and across her lap was Lena. Supergirl could see where the sound was coming from now, Lena's perfectly rounded behind was perched on Wonder Woman's knees and she was being spanked to a steady rhythm.

Lena was bound and as gagged as usual, a thick cloth was between her lips and her arms were secured in a boxtie so they wouldn't block the steady assault of Wonder Woman's firm hand. Supergirl could see Lena had been stripped to just her bra, her bare bottom having turned a light shade of red from her spanking. Supergirl wanted to yell at Wonder Woman to stop but she knew better than to defy her mistress. Instead, she scurried off the bed and came beside Wonder Woman to say "Mistress please... she didn't do anything wrong." Wonder Woman made one final smack to the supple skin of Lena's backside, her hand coming to a rest on the red mark she had created, then she looked up to Supergirl and replied "I heard about your little outburst, my pet. I know that spanking Lena is a much more effective way of getting you to behave. So, from now on, any disobedience by you to any Amazon will result in sweet, innocent Lena here being put over my knee" Wonder Woman stared into Supergirl's eyes, daring her to question her dominance. Kara's plump lips parted, remaining open for just a moment, then she sighed and said "Yes mistress..." Wonder Woman was just too powerful, and while Lena remained a slave here Kara had no choice but to comply.

"Good. You can kneel right there and watch me finish the spanking. Then, once it's done, you can both pleasure me to make up for being so impudent" Wonder Woman said in a firm commanding tone, to which Kara bowed her head and replied "Yes Mistress" and sank down to her knees.

Lowering down she came closer to Lena's face, seeing the woman she loved moaning through her gag as Wonder Woman resumed her spanking. Supergirl tried to hide it on her face but she was fuming on the inside. She had completed dozens of missions for the Amazons, helping them beat the military of Man's World and bringing them closer to winning the war. Yet, for all her efforts, she was still treated like a simple pleasure slave. After every mission she would be rewarded with Lena, given time to have the gorgeous brunette all to herself. But it wasn't enough. Being here with her had made Kara fall even more deeply in love with Lena and she wanted her all to herself. It was a revelation she had realized on her first night on Themyscira. That was when she had come to see that she wanted to be the one making Lena her slave...

That first night Wonder Woman had landed her invisible jet on the shores of Themyscira, Supergirl was only just starting to wake up after the ambush on the beach. The first sensations she felt were of her clothing being removed, her boots wriggled free from her feet and her top lifted up over her breasts. She made a soft mewling moan as her heavy eyelids tried to open, making it halfway on her sleepy expression, showing half of her wet eyes as as she was carefully rolled over onto her front. She felt her arms being placed behind her back then something being tied around them, she could feel it was some type of rope and whoever was tying it knew what they were doing. She remained in that sleepy state throughout her bondage, feeling the rope binding her arms then running up and around her neck in a type of collar, the long length of cord having just enough slack to bind her and leave a length long enough for a leash.

Finally her eyes opened a little wider, her plump lips trembling as she moaned "Wh... mmmpppphhh" her very first word was interrupted by a thick white cloth being pulled between her lips then tied behind her head, gagging her in her first waking moment. "Shhhh. Just stay right there" she heard from behind her as the gag was tightly tied in place. With her arms behind her back she could only weakly lift up to her knees, watching dizzily as Wonder Woman walked round in front of her. Across from Supergirl was Lena in that same skimpy nightdress Supergirl had seen her in on the beach. She was starting to wake too but Wonder Woman quickly retrieved a white cloth and firmly clamped it down over her mouth. "Mmmpphhh!" Supergirl moaned in their direction, her shoulders wriggling as she tried to free herself. But there was nothing she could do, it wasn't just ordinary rope, it was Wonder Woman's magical golden lasso binding her. She was forced to watch as Lena was brought down to the edge of consciousness, her eyelids fluttering near closed as her whole body melted down to a limp pliable state.

Supergirl continued watching as Lena was bound and gagged, the Amazon princess deftly restraining her captive with knowledge gained from a lifetime of experience in bondage. With Lena bound and gagged, Wonder Woman hoisted her up like she weighed nothing at all, settling her on her shoulder and wrapping an arm around her supple thighs to keep her in place. Wonder Woman then walked right in front of Supergirl still on her knees, displaying Lena to her as she picked up the other end of the leash and said "I've brought you to Themyscira, Kara. Both you and sweet, pretty little Lena here are now my personal pleasure slaves. I'll tell you what you'll be doing for me in my private chambers. For now all you have to do is..." Wonder Woman gave the leash a firm tug, pulling Kara to her feet as she said "Follow your mistress" Kara tried to glare at Wonder Woman but her eyes couldn't help but tremble. Not so much for herself but for the lithe form of Lena so limply hanging over the Amazon's shoulder. With a muffled whimper and a submissive nod she submitted to Wonder Woman's command, and she was promptly led out of the jet and toward the city.

In just her bra and skirt, Kara was led through the streets of Themyscira. The other Amazons had heard of Wonder Woman's conquest and had come out to welcome her home. There was cheers, laughter and applause as the beautiful women lined the streets to watch. Already there was excited chatter about capturing more slaves for the coming war. This first example so enticing that it began to light a fire in every Amazon that saw it. Lena had been reduced to a pair of long legs draped in front of her Wonder Woman's chest, her soft creamy skin making them deliciously sensual. Her behind stuck up on Wonder Woman's shoulder like a prized trophy, its perfectly plump shape garnering the attention of all Lena's future mistresses. Supergirl could hear Lena making embarrassed moans through her gag, they were weak and soft but showed that Lena was fully aware of what was happening to her. She made the smallest wriggle of her hips, the movement only making her behind more enticing as it shook side to side.

Lena was garnering a lot of attention but so too was the gorgeous barefoot blonde captive being led on the leash behind her. Supergirl tried to just focus on Lena as she was led amongst all the Amazons. But she couldn't help notice how they were ogling her, their eyes burning into her with a deep desire. A desire she would soon find herself subjected to over and over. In the distance, the large marble building of Wonder Woman's palace loomed over them, getting closer and closer as Supergirl's bare feet padded softly on the cobblestones. Supergirl looked toward it fearfully then back down to Lena, reminding herself that she had no choice but to submit. As she looked at her she felt a small tingle from the golden lasso binding her. Its magic forced her to accept a truth she had been trying to ignore. Her noble notions of protecting Lena weren't that noble at all. She didn't truly want to free her, what she wanted was to be the one with Lena over her shoulder, to be the one chloroforming her then making her a helpless prisoner. Kara's cheeks blushed as the lasso forced her to realize this. Another added humiliation that Wonder Woman wasn't even aware she was inflicting upon her. From that first night, what had been a strong crush had changed into a passionate desire. Supergirl wanted Lena to herself and there was only so long she could resist this urge.

After the thorough spanking, Wonder Woman lifted Lena up from her knees and placed her back on the bed. Kara could see an amorous look in Wonder Woman's eyes as she came toward her, grabbing her and pulling her into a deep passionate kiss. She was then pushed down to the bed next to Lena and Wonder Woman pounced on both of them. She was their true mistress, the superior woman who had defeated and enslaved them both. In bed she treated them like the slaves they were, making them submit to her desires as she stripped out of her outfit. Wonder Woman's feminine form was utterly magnificent, and both women were now used to worshipping it in every way she demanded, whether it was pleasuring her with their mouths all over her body, or allowing her to ravish them with a hungry lust. Wonder Woman only allowed Lena's gag to be briefly removed when she wished to make use of her mouth, or when she wanted her to call her 'mistress.' Other than that, she remained always gagged and in her tight bondage.

While being utterly dominated Kara found herself being bound as well, Wonder Woman enjoying to slowly pleasure her then tie her up and force her to return the favor. Wonder Woman had a more boundless energy than any other Amazon, she never seemed to tire or falter, her slaves chests heaving as she wore them out with her ravenous appetites. She had them squashed close together, bound and gagged while her nude form kissed and groped them at the same time. She might have kept going until they passed out from sheer exhaustion had there not been a knock at the door.

Wonder Woman sighed in annoyance while her two slaves sighed in relief, finally given a moment to recover, their bodies having been constantly forced to respond to the erotic assault, the continual shuddering and moaning wearing them down. Wonder Woman gave them each a final kiss on the thigh then slid off her bed and slipped into her outfit. She answered the door to one of her Amazon warriors. It was time for another mission in Man's World.

She left Lena bound and gagged on the bed but Kara was released so she could join her. Kara had come to look forward to these missions, it was upon their completion that she was rewarded with Lena, allowed to have her all to herself. Even on the missions, Wonder Woman kept her in the modified skimpy outfit, for all her powers she still looked like a slave even on the battlefield. The war in Man's World had predictably been going in the Amazons favor. With both Wonder Woman and Supergirl on their side there was little any military could do to oppose them. Kara always made sure that there were no casualties, once their tanks and weaponry had been disabled there was little they could do but retreat or surrender. She took one last look at Lena lying helplessly on the bed then she quickly took off, wanting to be back as soon as possible to retrieve her prize.

"Well done slave. You fought well" Wonder Woman said hours later as she stood with Supergirl at the steps to her private quarters. Kara was practically shaking with excitement but she managed to contain it as she submissively replied "Thank you mistress" Wonder Woman smiled at the submissive gesture and nodded toward the building as she said "You may take your prize" again Kara replied "Thank you mistress" then she hurriedly ascended the steps and rushed down the hall. She threw open the doors and her excited expression turned into a gasping look of shock as she saw three Amazons groping Lena as they knocked her out with chloroform, the three of them kissing and stroking her weakening form as they knelt beside her on the bed "Let her go! She belongs to me" Kara cried out as she entered the room and demanded Lena's release.

But one slave demanding the release of another meant little to the Amazons who just giggled and pulled Lena off of the bed, one of them slinging Lena's limp form over her shoulder as she replied "You can have her when we're done. We need to do some training for our next recruiting mission." She knew Wonder Woman would punish her for trying to stop the Amazons, so all Kara could do was tremble with rage as Lena was carried away, the Amazon holding the drugged brunette reaching up to give Lena's rump a spank and possessive squeeze intended to further tease and anger Kara just before they left. Being denied her reward for the mission was more than Kara could take and her fists clenched as she watched the Amazons once again kidnapping Lena in front of her. At that moment, Kara decided she had to escape. She was going to make Lena her slave and take her away from here to keep Lena all for herself.

Much later, Lena was returned to Kara's room. She was waiting by the door, taking Lena from the shoulder of the same smug Amazon who had whisked her away. She cradled Lena lovingly in her arms and slammed the doors closed, taking her to the bed and carefully laying her down. Kara had been waiting for her all day, the sun had set now and she finally had Lena all to herself. She had made the bed in preparation and she slowly let Lena's supple form rest on the crisp white sheets. Lena had been given to her bound and gagged, her long legs squeezed together, her wrists behind her back, a white cloth between her plump lips. Kara rested an elbow beside Lena's head, letting her rest on the bed and look down at Lena's wide helpless eyes. She carefully brushed a few strands of her dark brown hair out of her gorgeous blue-green eyes, Kara's fingers brushing against Lena's soft cheek.

She had ravished Lena many times after her missions but now she went a little slower. She leaned in and kissed her on her gagged lips, making a soft wet sound as she kissed lower and lower. She kissed her neck and along her shoulder, tasting Lena's smooth skin as she worked her way down to her long legs. She heard Lena let out a shuddering moan from the sensation of the gentle kisses on her thighs, the sound so feminine and passionate that Kara couldn't control herself any longer. She moved back up so she was face to face with her then to Lena's surprise she gently lifted her head up and untied her gag. A look of confusion went across Lena's face as the gag was pulled away, so rarely was she allowed to be ungagged that she remained silent even when it was removed. With her lips free Kara leaned in and kissed her again, and this time Lena responded, moving her mouth so it matched Kara's movements, their lips pressing together over and over as they kissed each other passionately.

From the way she had kissed her back, Kara already knew the answer, but she still had to ask, she pulled her mouth away and said in a breathless tone "You want this don't you? To be my slave? To belong to me and just me? Tell me I'm not imagining it. The only reason I've stayed here was for you, Lena" Kara watched as Lena took a few heaving breaths, her heart beating hard in her chest as she looked up into the eyes of Supergirl. Then she replied "Yes. I didn't know what to think at first but all this pleasure... It's like nothing I ever imagined. I love being so helpless, so overwhelmed with so may sensations. The others treat me like just a toy. But... I've always known how you felt about me Kara... and... I do want to belong to you. Just you. Please take me, Kara. Steal me away and make me all yours." Kara's eyes went wide with delight, a huge smile spreading across her lips as she immediately kissed Lena again, their bodies pressing together as she made a grinding motions that squashed Lena down into the soft bed.

As they kissed Kara reached over for the gag, smoothly picking it up and holding it in her hand. She so wanted to pleasure Lena right now but she wanted to get her far away from here first. With the gag in her hand she lifted her mouth, keeping her lips close to Lena's as she looked into her eyes and said "I'm going to gag you now... my slave" Lena smiled in response and replied in a soft tone "Yes mistress" Kara pushed the gag between her lips and tied it behind her head, kissing her on the mouth as the cloth pulled her lips open. She then reached behind her pillow where she had stashed another item, her day of waiting for Lena having given her the time to prepare everything she needed. She pulled out the cloth that she had earlier soaked with chloroform, bringing it in front of Lena's mouth and slowly clamping it down as she looked into her loving eyes. "Breathe in my pet. Take nice deep breaths. When you wake up it'll just be you and me" Kara said as she held the cloth in place, and in response Lena's chest rose and fell, obediently inhaling the chloroform.

As she chloroformed her, Kara's other hand gently fondled and groped Lena's breasts, squeezing the soft orbs as she felt Lena slowly going limp.

She peeled the cloth away to kiss her on the lips and whisper "Good slave" then she pushed it back down and continued knocking her out. "Everything's going to be okay. I'm going to take care of you from now on" Kara said soothingly as she watched the light begin to dim in Lena's eyes, a glassy stare settling over her expression as she melted beneath Kara. Lena's trusting look slowly faded as her eyelids fluttered closed, her wet eyes shining as the image of Kara faded to black. With a soft sigh, the now willing damsel passed out, her muscles losing any tension as her sensual form drifted into unconsciousness.

Kara's heart was beating harder than she thought possible, her body shaking with excitement as she peeled the cloth away and kissed Lena on her gagged lips once again. She then tucked the cloth into the waistband of her skirt and carefully scooped Lena up from the bed. Taking care with her limp form she lifted her up and let her weight settle on her shoulder. Kara stroked her hands up the soft legs that now rested in front of her chest, enjoying the smooth feeling of Lena's body. "You're all mine" Kara said with a breathless smile. Then she turned to the door and hurried away into the night, lifting up into the dark sky as soon as she was outside, taking her sleeping beloved with her.

CHAPTER 03

Circe's Invasion

Chapter Summary: *After Kara's bold and brazen escape, a vengeful Diana pursues her coveted pleasure slaves and leaves Themyscira unguarded...*

Three women lay around Diana on the silk sheets of the bed. They were all naked and their bodies were glowing with the perspiration of their passionate lovemaking. Two of them were so exhausted they just let their eyelids flutter closed, emitting soft sighs as they sunk down into sleep with smiles on their faces. The third noticed that Diana was staring at the ceiling with a troubled expression; she had been amorous in their lovemaking, pleasuring all three of them as they submitted to her completely, but now in the aftermath there was clearly something on her mind, while they were basking in the afterglow of their orgasms, she was lying in the centre of their bodies staring silently upward.

The Amazon that noticed this made small kisses on Diana's thigh, moving higher until she pressed her lips to the curve of her hip. She then looked up in awe of the magnificent body and said "What's wrong Diana? Did we not satisfy you? Perhaps you'd like to tie us up? Make us your helpless slaves?" Diana reached down and stroked her hand along the girl's head, running her fingers through her hair as she sighed "Not right now" Pretending to make them her bondage slaves would normally excite her, but she wasn't in the mood for games. Nothing could fill the hole of her most valued slaves that had escaped a few days ago; all Diana could think about was Lena and Kara.

There was something so satisfying about making a woman as powerful as Kara submit to her, as well as making a woman as intelligent and jaw-droppingly gorgeous as Lena completely helpless. The two of them together had made a potent combination for Diana to dominate and she was missing them greatly. She missed their beauty, how they would moan so desperately when she tied them up and gagged them, that helpless look in their eyes as she knocked them out with chloroform. She had been trying to use both the Amazons and the pleasure slaves on the island to fill that void but it wasn't working.

She wanted them back.

When they had first escaped, her mother had told her that she couldn't go after them. She had to focus on the ongoing war with Man's World. But her many victories in battle meant little when she returned home without Lena and Kara waiting bound and gagged for her pleasure. This malaise weighed heavily on her mind. She barely noticed as the young woman began kissing higher, up her toned stomach and to her chest, her tongue licking and nibbling at Diana's nipples as she tried to make her feel better. In one smooth move, Diana rolled over and pinned the woman to the bed, holding her down as she said "Perhaps I will make you my helpless slave"

Her hand slid under a pillow where she had hidden a chloroform-soaked cloth, she had left it in there to tempt herself to use it and forget all about the runaways. She retrieved it and firmly pushed it against the Amazon's mouth and nose. Their bodies remained pressed together as Diana held the cloth in place, she was in the dominant position, keeping her prey pinned to the bed, squashing her into its softness as she forced her to inhale the chloroform. The Amazon made a valiant effort to play the part of helpless damsel, making small writhing motions beneath Diana, moaning weakly and fluttering her eyes.

For a moment Diana did begin to enjoy herself. But then the Amazon's eyes snapped shut and that feeling faded, it still wasn't enough. She peeled off the cloth from the woman's lips and left her lying with the two others. She slipped off the bed and put on a white robe as she walked out onto the balcony of her bedroom. The cool night air tickled her bare legs as she leaned on the railing and looked out across Themyscira. She could feel a tension building inside of her, one she knew she wouldn't be able to control forever. Her fists clenched and she spun around, marching back into her bedroom and toward her armoury.

"Princess, where are you going?" One of the guards in front of Diana's door asked as she marched out. She was wearing her red and blue costume but with a shield strapped to her back and a sword by her side, the place she was planning on going wouldn't be easy to get into and she was prepared for a fight. "Out. I'll return soon, don't tell my mother" she replied sternly as she walked away.

There was another guard there and they looked to each other with matching worried expressions. They knew that Queen Hippolyta should be informed if her daughter was running off unannounced, but they also didn't want to disobey a direct order. One of them hurried behind her as she made her way toward the beach and asked "Are you... going anywhere in particular?"

Without turning around Diana replied "Yes. I'm going to retrieve what is mine. I will be back by tomorrow morning" The guard could see there was no stopping her, so she didn't follow her any further. Diana continued her purposeful strides until she reached the beaches of Themyscira, then she walked up to where she had parked her invisible jet. The stairway was already down and she walked right up it and boarded the plane. She took her seat in the cockpit and with the tap of a few buttons the jet rose into the air. It turned in the direction she was headed then shot through the night, cutting through the air like an arrow.

Diana knew she couldn't leave for too long. She only had time to check one location, but it was a place she was confident Kara would be hiding. Even at the high speeds of her advanced jet, it took over two hours to get there. Then she saw the white snowy plains of the Arctic far below her. No human life existed in these climates, it was the perfect place to hide. Only those who knew its location could find it, the white crystalline surface of the structure blending so perfectly with the huge blanket of snow all around it. Diana closed in and narrowed her eyes as it came into view: the Fortress of Solitude.

She landed outside and approached the door. She doubted Kal would be here due to the war, his efforts would be focused on protecting Man's World. She also knew that Kara didn't care about the war at all, she had taken Lena to keep her all for herself and Diana was betting this is where they were. She unsheathed her sword and took the shield from her back, stepping toward the impenetrable fortress as she prepared to break in by force.

Diana's quiet exit had gone mostly unnoticed as planned. Unfortunately, there was someone who had taken great interest in her leaving Themyscira so late in the night. Currently two Amazons were playing their favourite game in the woods. The game involved letting one of their pleasure slaves try to escape them, then chasing after them and capturing them all over again. There was no chance for them to really escape, but the game was no fun if they didn't try.

A young blonde woman in a skimpy silk nightdress was currently being pursued, running amongst the trees as she glanced over her shoulder nervously. Her hair fluttered behind her as her bare feet padded softly on the grass. She had played this game dozens of times already and it always ended the same way, with her bound, gagged and a chloroform-soaked rag pressed firmly over her mouth. They were so fast she rarely even saw them coming, and in the darkness amongst the trees, they could be anywhere.

As she ran she made another nervous glance over her shoulder, but that distraction caused her to stumble and fall to the floor. She made a small groan as her chest bumped down onto the grass, then she scrabbled to her hands and knees as she tried to catch her breath. She suddenly noticed there was a pair of feet right in front of her and with a scared gasp she looked up, expecting to see one of the Amazons with a cloth in her hand, ready to put her to sleep. But looming over her was a woman she didn't recognise. The woman who had been waiting for Wonder Woman to leave the island unguarded.

She wore a flowing green dress with two large slits on either side that left both her long legs exposed. At her midsection she wore a golden belt that cinched in the green fabric around her trim waist. On her torso the dress had a large V shape open at her chest, the material running along her breasts and stopping just above her belly button. That open section of her dress was connected with a few criss crossing gold chains, doing little to cover the soft supple skin on view. The gold motif was continued in her jewellery, on her neck she wore a large gold necklace, on her wrists and ankles she wore a series of gold bands. She had long, dark reddish hair that accentuated her naturally beautiful features. There was a calm confidence in her eyes, mixed with a sense of glee that frightened the helpless woman looking up at her.

The woman wore nothing on her feet and it seemed like she had appeared out of thin air. The woman on her knees continued looking up with a small tremble running down her spine. Her mouth opened and she said softly "Who... who are you?" the mysterious woman was delighted by the question, smiling and gesturing theatrically to herself as she said "I... am Circe. And you have the honour of being my first captive." Before the woman on her knees could ask what that meant, something suddenly came from the shadows and grabbed her, dragging her into the darkness as she let out a muffled moan of terror.

Deep in the Fortress of Solitude, Kara was passionately kissing her helpless slave. But Lena was no longer enslaved against her will, with every kiss she let out a deep moan of pleasure, her body shuddering in ecstasy. She was currently in just a pair of silky bra and panties, and she was tightly tied up with thin white ropes. Kara was lying on top of her, their bodies pressed against each other as their tongues danced against the other. Kara was only in her skirt and bra but her hands slowly moved from Lena's breasts to the slide the skirt off of her hips, wanting to feel more of Lena's skin against her own.

With her skirt off, her hands slid back up to find Lena's breasts and squeeze them firmly as they continued kissing. The last few days had been like a dream, they had barely left the bedroom, becoming even more deeply enraptured in their lustful desires. Kara felt like she could stay here forever, keeping Lena in bondage and pleasuring her whenever she wanted. She was filled with contentment at having Lena all to herself. Her lips lifted from Lena's and she kissed along her cheek then to her neck and up to her ear. Once she reached her ear she whispered softly "Tell me you belong to me" and Lena immediately replied in a breathless gasp "I belong to you"

Kara began kissing lower, moving along her collarbone and to her breasts, her plump lips pressing into their soft shape as she kissed and tasted them with her tongue. She kept moving down and her hands went to the ropes on Lena's legs, planning to undo them so she could spread them apart and bury her head between her thighs. But just as she started untying them the entire building shook, a sensation that was even more scary due to how secure this place was supposed to be. Then immediately the Kryptonian security system sounded with a loud 'BREACH. BREACH. BREACH.' repeating over and over again.

Kara's head lifted from Lena's soft legs and they looked to each other with matching worried expressions. They had both been worried about the Amazons coming after them, but this place was a fortress; it was right there in the name. Kara slid off of Lena and grabbed her skirt, sliding it back up her long legs as she said "Don't worry, I'm not going to let anyone take you" She then sat on the bed and put her boots on, then grabbed her blue top and her cape and settled them on her torso. She leaned over Lena and kissed her on the lips again and said "I'll be right back" taking one last loving look into her beautiful concubine's eyes, she rose from the bed and hurried out of the room.

All Lena could do was just lie on the bed and wait. She was so used to being in bondage now it barely registered to her, the ropes restraining her feminine form seeming completely natural. After a few minutes the building shook again. She could hear a loud booming sound as if a fight was going on. Her eyes widened with worry as more time passed, the heavy beating of her heart like a clock that went on and on. She could feel her breath catching in her throat as she stared at the door, hoping for Kara to come back and tell her everything was alright.

After what seemed like a long time the door finally opened. No-one came through it at first, leaving Lena in suspense for a few moments. Then Kara appeared, Lena was about to make a relieved smile but that instantly faded as she saw the state Kara was in. She stumbled through the door messily, her legs wobbling and making un-coordinated lurches forward. She had a glassy look in her eyes that Lena recognised from seeing other slaves be chloroformed on the island. Whoever had broken in here had clearly won the fight and Lena could hear their footsteps from hall outside as they approached to finish Kara off.

Kara let out a weak moan and she stumbled a little further into the room. Then Wonder Woman appeared in the doorway, striding confidently into the room she immediately wrapped on arm around Kara's waist and pulled her back so their bodies pressed together. With her other hand she clamped a cloth down over Kara's mouth and said "Thought you could get away from me did you?" Kara moaned into the cloth, her body wriggling in Wonder Woman's grip as she tried to get free. The arm around her waist was just too strong, and with every breath she took she felt weaker and weaker. She could feel the chloroform filling her lungs, easing the tension from her muscles as her body went limp. The harder she fought the weaker she became, the cloth so firmly pushed against her mouth there was nothing she could do to remove it.

"No!" Lena made a shocked gasp as began trying to wriggle out of the ropes binding her, but Kara had done too good of a job, her legs were too tightly squeezed together, her wrists bound securely behind her back. Moments ago she had been enjoying her bondage but now it was forcing her to lie there and watch Kara being knocked out. Kara's struggles had slowly died down to weak pushes at Wonder Woman's hands, moaning as she failed to get them off of her. Wonder Woman's hand slid slowly up from her waist and began groping her breasts, one then the other in slow firm squeezes. She was already enjoying having the beautiful blonde back under her control, unable to stop herself from fondling her soft breasts.

Kara's eyes slowly fluttered closed, coming down over her glassy eyed stare as her consciousness faded away. Her legs buckled and her knees turned inward, her arms flopping down by her sides. Her breathing became slow and heavy, that cloth on her mouth still forcing her to inhale chloroform with every long breath. Then her eyes snapped shut and she passed out, a barely audible muffled sigh coming from behind the cloth as she faded away in Wonder Woman's arms. The Amazon slid the cloth away from her, revealing her limp lips which remained ever so slightly parted. Then she took hold of her waist with both arms and dragged her toward the bed, her boots scraping listlessly on the floor as she was carried.

Wonder Woman released Kara's limp form and she fell forward. She bounced down on the bed next to Lena who let out a soft moan of fear. Kara's head rested to the side, facing Lena who could see her peaceful sleeping features. Lena's eyes flickered from Kara up to Wonder Woman who slowly advanced on her and said "I'm very disappointed in you, my slave" she crawled onto the bed, over Kara's unconscious form and on top of Lena who made a frightened whimper beneath her, her bound form trembling under the dominant Amazon warrior. Wonder Woman straddled her prize, her knees resting either side of her hips and giving her a small squeeze with her thighs as she said "No one is taking you from me. You're mine, forever" as she said this her hand with the cloth slid onto Lena's mouth and nose, forcing her to inhale the familiar scent of chloroform with her shuddering breaths. Soon that frightened look began to sink down into a hazy stare, everything going fuzzy as she stared up at Wonder Woman's satisfied smile looming over her.

"Where'd she go?" one of the Amazons asked the other, the two of them wandering around the forest as they looked for their slave. "You don't think she actually escaped?" One said as they continued trying to find her "We're on an island. There's nowhere for her to go." It was as if she had just disappeared but neither of them could figure out how. They kept walking for a few moments then heard a feminine tone behind them "Looking for someone?" They both turned to see a woman casually leaning against a tree with a sly smile on her face. They immediately recognised her and their fists clenched as one of them said "Circe"

She smiled at them and lifted out of her leaning pose as she said "The one and only. Now were you looking for that cute blonde girl? Allow me to reunite you with her" As she said this the two Amazons heard movement all around them, dark shapes twisting and slithering through the shadows. They took a scared step backward as they saw they were completely surrounded, then Circe's minions stepped out of the shadows and swarmed them.

Their skin was a scaly green and their eyes a bright yellow, they had a feminine shape, their chests pushing out in the form of breasts, but they were clearly something far from human. Their teeth were sharp and their expressions twisted into cruel seething smiles. Their hair was made of a series of tentacles that twisting around their monstrous faces like snakes.

Their endless number descended upon the two Amazons, holding them down to the floor and pushing cloths against their mouths that began knocking them out. There were so many of them the Amazons couldn't resist, their many hands pushing and holding them to the floor, every inch of the Amazons bodies firmly handled. Through the mass of snarling faces, the Amazons could see Circe standing over them and watching them being subdued. Then the chloroform forced them down into a deep sleep.

The two Amazons, along with their slave, were left tied to trees in the forest. Then Circe turned and addressed the yellow eyes dotted all around her "Very good my pets. Now, the rest" She began walking toward the city, coming out from under the shade of the trees and into the moonlight that beamed down on her. She emerged first, then from behind her came the

SEX AND CHAOS

swarm of her demonic minions, spilling out in a seemingly endless number as they ran toward the closest buildings.

Most of the Amazons were asleep, all they experienced of the invasion was to feel something pressing against their mouth, they opened their eyes to see a green snake like creature chloroforming them then their eyes simply fluttered shut again with a soft moan. The ones who were awake tried to fight or raise an alarm, but they were quickly overwhelmed by the creatures. As they moved through the city Circe walked in a straight line in the middle of the cobblestone streets, smiling at every knocked out and bound Amazon she saw her minions collecting.

As her minions broke into every building and subdued every Amazon, Circe just continued her casual stroll, walking straight toward the palace which sat at the highest point in Themyscira. She walked to the gleaming white steps then stopped. While the rest of the city had been caught unprepared the palace was always guarded. A dozen Amazons in full armour stood on the steps, their swords drawn and ready to fight off the evil sorceress.

"You will come no further, witch" one of them said as she glared at Circe with disdain. That look of disgust only made Circe smile even wider as she replied "That's no way to be talking to your future queen. Let me show you your true place" She made a flourish with her hands and a green flame burst across her fingers. The Amazons tensed as they prepared for whatever magical attack she was planning. Then with another flourish of her hands the green flames suddenly made circles around their feet. A few made gasps of shock but the flames weren't burning them, each one had a circle around their feet but even as the green fire licked at their ankles they felt no pain.

A second passed then out of the flames came lengths of rope, they began twisting and curling up the Amazons legs, snaking around them as if the ropes were alive. Circe laughed as she watched the Amazon guards try swiping at the ropes with their swords as they moaned angrily. Nothing they did could stop the ropes as they twisted out of the green portals of fire, slowly wrapping around each Amazon and binding them. The ropes found heir wrists and looped round them, pulling them behind their back, they slithered all over their bodies, restraining every limb and squeezing their feminine forms.

Swords and shields began to clatter to the floor as the Amazons were restrained, unable to hold onto them as their arms were pulled behind their backs. Their legs snapped together from the pull of the magical ropes, it threw their balance off and one by one they all fell to the ground at Circe's feet. She watched all of this with a delighted glee, letting out a villainous laugh at the Amazons writhing around in the ropes. One of them looked up and groaned at her "You won't get away with this!" but she just rolled her eyes and replied "Oh, be quiet" with a snap of her fingers green flames trailed around each of their mouths, when it faded away white cloths were tied between their lips, turning their protestations into muffled moans.

She walked up the steps, between the bound and gagged Amazons who moaned in her direction from the floor. Then she pushed open the large double doors and walked down the grand hallway to the throne room. She walked in to find Hippolyta sitting on the golden throne, her regal white robes and flowing blonde hair making her gleam in the light. Their eyes met as Circe stopped and put her hands on her hips, making a cocky smile as she said "You're in my seat"

Hippolyta glared at her and rose from the throne, taking two steps toward her as she said "If you want my throne, you'll have to best me in combat" Circe raised her eyes and put a finger to her chin as she mockingly considered the queen's proposal, then she said "Hmmmm... no, I don't think so" with a flourish of her hands the green flame suddenly consumed her and she disappeared.

Hippolyta was left alone in the throne room, looking at the spot Circe had just been in with a confused expression. However, she wasn't alone for long.

That same green flame appeared right behind her and Circe stepped out of it, surprising the queen as she grabbed her from behind and clamped down a cloth over her mouth. The queen immediately begin trying to throw her off, jerking her hips forward and trying to tear the hand away from her mouth. Their feet shuffled around as the struggle began, Circe clinging to the more statuesque woman and slowly wearing a down. A few times it seemed like she might get away, but each time Circe managed to get the cloth back in place to continue subduing the powerful woman.

SEX AND CHAOS

From behind the cloth Hippolyta made ferocious moans of frustration, her face scrunching up in anger as her muscles tensed and fought against the woman behind her. The more time that passed with the cloth on her mouth the more she began to soften. Her angered expression slowly losing tension as she began to feel weaker. Circe could feel it too, firming up her grip on the softening queen, delighting in overcoming her stronger opponent.

"That's it. Submit to your true queen" Circe whispered mockingly by Hippolyta's ear, elicting another moan from behind the cloth. Fully taking control, she dragged her back to the throne. Circe sat down and pulled Hippolyta onto her lap, tilting her back so she could keep the cloth pressing down on her mouth while she looked down at her sleepy expression. "I think you'd make a much better slave than a queen" she cooed softly as her free hand stroked along Hippolyta's neck and down to her chest.

She was so listless now, so helpless to stop Circe as she began firmly groping her breasts. Her hand came up to try and stop Circe but the sorceress simply pushed it away and it flopped back down.

She kept the cloth in place while she fondled and squeezed the queens breasts, humiliating her with the violating act on her own throne. Hippolyta's eyes stared upward, that heavy chloroform scent too overpowering for her to fight any longer. She could still feel the tingling sensations in her chest as she began to pass out, Circe's firm fingers the last thing she felt before her eyes closed.

The large doors to the Fortress of Solitude lay broken apart on the floor, beyond them were a series of destroyed robots that had tried to defend the fortress, smoke billowing out of them. Through the rubble, a figure began to slowly emerge; the shape of a woman walking out with two other shapes on her shoulders. Through the smoke Wonder Woman appeared, she had a pleased smile on her face as she walked confidently to her jet. On her left shoulder sat Supergirl's toned behind, her red skirt having lifted just enough to show a glimpse of her panties. On her right shoulder was Lena, her pleasantly plump and shapely rump was also perfectly perched, sticking up in just the right position for Wonder Woman to give the soft cheeks a firm squeeze whenever she wanted.

As she walked she stroked the legs of both her captives, enjoying the softness of their skin, sliding up to their behinds and squeezing those as well. She had missed the feeling of their helpless forms, her hands hungrily stroking and squeezing as she carried them up the stairs to her jet. With a small pat on their respective rumps, she deposited them on the floor. She had tied them both up and gagged them inside so they weren't going anywhere. She crouched in-between them, looking down at them sleeping peacefully. She couldn't help herself from groping and fondling them for a final time before leaving them there and going to the cockpit to return home.

She piloted the jet with a big smile on her face, feeling elated at having reacquired her most prized captives. She was already looking forward to their punishment for escaping, as soon as they awoke they would both be going over her knee for a firm spanking. She would need to be even more firm with them this time, clearly she hadn't trained them properly if they thought they could escape from her. Their training this time would be far more thorough, she would mould them into her willing slaves, her dominance would force them to obey her.

Her mind was racing with thoughts of taming her captives the entire flight, she couldn't wait to get started. She landed on the beach from where she had taken off earlier, the sun was just beginning to rise so she was sure her mother wouldn't have noticed her sneaking off in the night. Lena and Kara were still sleeping from the effects of the chloroform, so she hoisted them back over her shoulders, her enhanced strength allowing her to lift them like they weighed nothing all. With them back in place she gave their behinds another firm squeeze, then carried them down the steps.

It wasn't until she reached the city that she noticed something was wrong. The sun was still rising as it's light shined across the streets of the city Diana couldn't hear a single sound. Her footsteps were the only noise over the eerie silence, her head swivelling left and right as she walked amongst the buildings. She had planned to take her slaves home but now she didn't know what to do, it was as if all the Amazons had just disappeared.

She decided to go to her mother, if something bad was happening then the queen would know what to do. She didn't have time to drop Lena and Kara off, so she brought them with her, running down the streets with both of them making small bounces on her shoulder. The doors to the palace were wide open, which she knew was a bad sign. She hurried up the steps and began running toward the throne room. From behind the doors she heard the first few signs of life, a soft moaning sound that got louder as she approached.

She kicked open the doors and gasped as she saw the scene inside. The evil sorceress Circe was sitting on the throne and laying at her feet was her mother, tied up and with a cloth tied between her lips. Circe was using her like a footstool, resting her feet on the queen of all the Amazons as she smirked at Diana's shocked expression. Diana immediately lay Kara and Lena down on the floor as she glared at Circe and said "How dare you! Take your feet off of her!"

She went to charge at her but bursts of green flame suddenly exploded all around the room and from the flames Circe's demonic minions swarmed around Wonder Woman. They grabbed her and forced her down to her knees in front of Circe, holding her there as she furious groans and tossed her head side to side. "Just one last little Amazon to take care of" Circe said as she lifted her feet from Hippolyta and rose up out of the throne. She stepped over the bound form of Hippolyta and took the few steps toward Wonder Woman. She held a white cloth in her hand, ready to knock out the last conscious Amazon on the island.

"Stop! Keep that away from... mmpppphhhh!!" Diana's words were cut off as Circe pressed the cloth to her mouth. She tried turning her head away but the demons grabbed the back of her hair and held her head in place. There was nothing she could except remain on her knees and continue inhaling the chloroform. The tension in her body slowly began to slip away, the demons holding her no longer having to try very hard at all to keep her in place. "I've finally defeated you, Wonder Woman" Circe said gleefully as she watched the Amazon's eyes begin to droop

"You all belong to me now" the words were the last thing Diana heard before everything went black, she sunk down into unconscious just like her mother had, succumbing to the cloth Circe held firmly over her mouth. She passed out and the demons released her, letting her slump to the floor right at Circes feet. The villainess stood over her in a dominate pose, looking down at the defeated Amazon princess who had bested her so many times before. In one smooth motion she raised her foot and placed it on top of Wonder Woman, just so she could feel like she had truly defeated her.

She took a satisfied breath as she felt Wonder Woman beneath her foot, then said to her minions "Tie her up" She turned and walked back to the throne, resuming her position as she watched Wonder Woman being bound and gagged before her. Her smile grew wider and she tilted her head back as she let out a villainous laugh. In just one-night she had defeated the Amazons, every woman on this island was now her slave.

CHAPTER 04

Circe's Reign

Chapter Summary: With Circe now in control of Themyscira and Lena and herself back to being pleasure slaves, Kara finds herself forced into humiliating contests and acts of service. But - worst of all - she also finds herself once again kept from her beloved Lena. Can Kara find a way to turn the tables and outsmart her captors, or will she and Lena be doomed to be kept apart?

Months had passed since that night Kara had been returned to the island; since Circe had taken over in Wonder Woman's absence. But while Themyscira had a new leader, Kara's experience on the island felt very much the same. She was back to being a slave and, worst of all, Lena had been taken from her and was once again being used to keep Kara under control. Circe did have some differences from the Amazons who had previously enslaved her, however. She was experiencing such a difference right now. She stood in her skimpy modified outfit, the one with the shorter skirt and plunging top that only barely covered her sensual form. The W had been removed and in it's place a magical symbol that represented Circe's dominance. The symbol prevented Kara from using any of her powers, ensuring she would never be able to challenge Circe's reign.

In front of Kara was a metal gate and it slowly began to rumble upward, allowing her entry into the gladiatorial arena. The arena was once used for the Amazons to compete against each other in non- lethal combat; to display their skills in battle. But that was no longer its purpose. As Kara walked out, she could see Circe sitting on her throne as always, looking out over her arena with a pleased smile on her face. By her feet knelt the Amazon queen, Hippolyta, completely naked and wearing a collar with a leash that Circe loosely gripped in her hand. But on her lap was where Kara's eyes immediately darted, for sitting there in a silky white nightdress was Lena, bound and gagged and being casually groped by Circe.

She blushed as Circe's hand calmly fondled her, Lena's big wide eyes looking down to Kara as if pleading to her for help. But there was nothing Kara could do. Not only was she vulnerable to Circe's magic, but filling the arena seats were her demonic minions. They were like the prison guards of the island now: always patrolling and watching. Ready to tie up and knock out any woman that stepped out of line. Sitting amongst the minions were the Amazons and the new recruits who had submitted to Circe's power, allowed to join her ranks and freed from their bondage. Then, sitting on their laps, were the ones who refused, either Amazons or the recruits who had been so thoroughly tamed by the Amazons that they still were loyal to them.

The ones who refused Circe had all been designated pleasure slaves, to be used and dominated as Circe wished. There had been a huge shift of power, and every woman had come to their own decision on who to serve. Some of the recruits who had previously been pleasure slaves now served Circe, and their previous owners were now handed to them as slaves. Circe could see the women all bound and gagged on their new owners laps, being fondled and groped and kissed as Kara walked out into the arena. Circe made a mocking round of applause at Kara's entry, then the gate opposite Kara began to rumble upward as her opponent was revealed.

She was wearing a modified outfit too, pulled tighter at her hips to reveal more of her firm backside, cut lower so her considerable bosom bulged outward. Her boots had been removed making her toned legs seem even longer. On the stomach of her outfit was that same magical symbol and her bracelets and tiara had been removed. But even with all these modifications there was no denying the statuesque and sensual figure of Wonder Woman as the gate rose. Her hands on her hips, still standing proudly as she stared down Kara at the other end of the arena.

In the centre of the arena sat the same tools they were given each time they faced each other, rope, chloroform and a white cloth to gag their opponent. As Kara walked forward she eyed the items cautiously. She had been on the losing end of every single one of these battles, always ending up bound with the ropes that sat before her. When Circe had first started this tradition she had said she wanted Kara to win; to humiliate the Amazon princess and put her in her place. But Kara had never been able to come out on top.

Both she and Diana had been stripped of their powers, reduced to the normal level of strength they would have as women. It was technically a fair fight, but realistically Wonder Woman was far more skilled in hand to hand combat. She had grown up on an island of warrior women, she had fought and wrestled almost every day of her adult life. This experience gave her a clear advantage, and, as Kara stared down her opponent, she could see the same confident smile on her face, a knowing look that said to Kara she had no fear.

With a raise of her hand, Circe declared "Begin!" to cheers from the crowd. Kara took off at a fast run, her bare feet slapping into the ground, her skirt fluttering around her supple thighs. She ran right toward the rope, trying to stop Wonder Woman from using it on her. The Amazon took off toward the items as well, but she had no need of grabbing them yet. She timed her run to let Kara scoop up the rope first, then she lowered her shoulders and simply tackled her to the ground. The air rushed out of Kara's lungs with a wheezing moan, Wonder Woman slamming her down then immediately grabbing her.

Kara tried wriggling around under but Wonder Woman was in the more dominant position. Using her position on top of her to keep her pinned as she grabbed her and forced over onto her stomach "I'll take that thank you" she said as she snatched the rope from Kara's hands, sliding up to more comfortably sit on her lower back. Kara kicked her legs and let out a frustrated moan as she felt her wrists being tied again. Wonder Woman always managed to surprise her in every fight, she never knew what to expect but it always ended this way. Sometimes it was fast like today, other times Wonder Woman would roll around with her, wrestling for a little while then wearing her down, their bodies tangling as the practised wrestler bent Kara into some uncomfortable position.

Today had been particularly quick, it seemed Wonder Woman wasn't in the mood to toy with the helpless blonde. She quickly tied her wrists then swivelled round to bind her ankles as well, adding more ropes above and below her knees as she made her thighs squash together. There was laughter and cheers amongst the crowd as they watched Kara being dominated once again. On the throne where Circe sat, the sorceress squeezed Lena's breasts, making the innocent damsel moan as she whispered into her ear "Do you like watching your girlfriend being tied up so easily?" teasing poor Lena as her hands continued exploring her pleasure slave's delicious body.

Wonder Woman finished the final knot, trapping Kara in the tight bondage. Then she walked over to the pile of items, leaving Kara wriggling around on the floor for a few minutes. She scooped up the chloroform, the rag and the cloth, bringing them over to Kara and setting them down by her head. Kara saw them and let out a scared moan, shaking her head as she said "No! Let me go!" But Wonder Woman just ignored her, grabbing the cloth and pulling it between her lips. She tied it behind her head, settling the knot in Kara's golden blonde hair, turning her cries of defiance into muffled moans. Then she picked up the rag and made it damp with chloroform, letting Kara watch the process with her wide helpless eyes.

Once the rag was ready she set down the bottle and brought it closer to Kara's mouth. Kara tried to turn her head away but Wonder Woman wouldn't allow it. She firmly held the back of her head, turning her to face the cloth as she brought it gliding toward her mouth and nose. She clamped it firmly down, giving the blonde heroine no other choice but to inhale the chemical scent. Kara's eyes began to droop closed with every breath, her body softening as she went limp in the ropes. A glassy eyed stare settled over her dazed expression, her eyes now only the smallest sliver of white. The last thing she heard was more laughter and cheers from the crowd, watching her being utterly humiliated. Then with a soft sigh through the cloth her eyelids finally came to a close, passing out completely as Wonder Woman brought their fight to a definitive end.

Wonder Woman made a satisfied sigh as she saw Kara fall into a deep sleep. Peeling the cloth away from her gagged lips she observed her peaceful feminine features for a few moments. Then she took her shoulders and lifted her up from the floor. Wonder Woman heaved Kara up to a standing position, then let her flop down over her shoulder, hoisting her up into the air and wrapping an arm around her thighs to keep her in place. She walked closer to where Circe was watching from, looking up at the stadium and to Circe's throne as she presented Kara to her.

Wonder Woman's hand slid up Kara's legs and she gave her exposed behind a firm pat. Circe smiled and nodded, then declared loudly "It seems we have a winner!" There was more cheering from the crowd as Circe called down to Wonder Woman "And now you may have your prize!"

Kara woke to the familiar sounds of Lena's erotic moans, and as always she wasn't the one pleasuring her. Whoever won the game that Circe demanded they play got to have Lena as their slave for the night. It was maddening for Kara to watch Wonder Woman ravish her beloved, night after night. When Kara had been alone with Lena, after successfully kidnapping her best friend-turned-lover away from their shared enslavement on Paradise Island, she had thought no-one else would ever be with the beautiful damsel again, but now she was constantly forced to watch Wonder Woman make Lena helplessly shudder with pleasure.

As Kara's eyes opened she found she was bound the same way she normally was after losing. There was a white marble column in the lavish bedroom, standing at the side of the room and opposite the bed in the centre. Kara was bound to the column with white rope, forcing her arms above her head. The rope wrapped around her legs, her waist, her chest, keeping her trapped there as she faced the sensual scene on the bed. She couldn't even call out to the woman she loved, the cloth between her lips keeping her gagged as a silent observer.

Meanwhile Lena was lying naked on her back, ropes still bound her torso but her legs had been released so that Wonder Woman could spread them apart. Kara watched as the Amazon first kissed and nibbled on Lena's neck, wanting to taste every inch of her. Then she moved to Lena's gagged lips, kissing them passionately as she looked into her eyes with a dominant expression. She began kissing lower, tracing along her collarbone and making her porcelain skin tingle with small shudders. Her mouth found Lena's magnificent breasts and she began kissing and licking them, pressing into their soft shape with her tongue.

She took one of Lena's nipples into her mouth and applied a gentle pressure with her teeth, making Lena moan through her gag as her cheeks began to redden. Her body just naturally responded to Wonder Woman's mastery of the feminine form, unable to control the forced pleasure she was feeling. She writhed and bucked her hips slightly from the bed, the heat growing between her thighs as Wonder Woman worked her way down there. Then she buried her head between her legs, making Lena explode with pleasure, tilting her head back and moaning toward the ceiling as the mighty Amazon princess brought her to orgasm.

Kara let out a weak defeated moan through her gag as she watched all of this. Distressed but also unable to turn away from Lena, she watched her be forcibly brought to orgasm over and over, and she watched as Wonder

Woman removed Lena's gag, then - ignoring Lena's protests - forced her head down between her legs to return the favor. Their lovemaking went on for hours as the sun set outside, until both women collapsed from exhaustion. Before passing out, Wonder Woman found just enough strength to tie Lena's legs again, and to gag her. Then she wrapped her arms around her bound and gagged pleasure slave and closed her eyes. She wasn't pleased that Circe controlled the island now, but at least she got to fall asleep after ravishing Lena, once again feeling the warmth of the gorgeous pleasure slave's body as she held her and drifted off.

In the morning the doors flew open and Circe entered as she declared "Your time with Lena is over! She has work to do, as do the two of you!" She had brought with her three of the women that swore loyalty to her and at her command they entered the room. Smiling and giggling they pounced on Wonder Woman first, holding her down and forcing a cloth over her mouth. Her night as the champion of the arena was over and she was back to being a pleasure slave. She moaned under the cloth, wriggling as the three girls held her down and groped her. Squeezing her breasts and stroking her long legs as they forced her to pass out. Once she was out, they rolled her onto her front and tied her wrists behind her back. Two of them left Wonder Woman to be tied and went over to Kara. "Look! It's the loser." one of them giggled "Yes, but she does look so cute while she does it" the other replied as began feeling her up, their hands groping her so firmly that her back was pressed tight to the column behind her.

After a few moments of fondling the helpless blonde, they pressed a cloth to her mouth as well, sending her off into a drowsy sleep. Once she was out, they untied Kara from the column and gently guided her down to the ground. They began tying her wrists behind her back, giving her behind firm squeezes and enjoying the soft mewling moans she would make in her sleep. While the two former heroines were being restrained Circe walked over to Lena. She was still bound and gagged and lying on the bed, watching Circe approach with a wide-eyed helpless expression. "And you, my dear, have work to do" she said as she reached for her, gently groping Lena before pulling her off the bed.

Circe lifted Lena up from the bed, settling the captive beauty atop her shoulder and giving her pleasantly plump rump a firm spank. Then she turned to the three girls who had just finished tying up the heroines. "Bring them to my throne room and use the smelling salts to wake them up.

Sleeping is too easy for them. I want them to worship me like good slaves" With that she carried Lena toward the door. Two of the girls took a heroine each, slumping them over their shoulders and following behind Circe. The bedroom was one of many in the palace.

As they walked through the grand gleaming white hallways they passed multiple doors, and behind each one the sounds of muffled feminine moaning could be heard. Those that had pledged their loyalty to Circe were ravishing the others, enjoying the rewards that came with their submission to the sorceress. Circe smiled as she heard the chorus of sounds, it was like music to her ears. It also made her feel amorous and she couldn't help but squeeze Lena's shapely ass again, it's soft, plump, and juicy shape so tempting where it was sitting perfectly perched on her shoulder.

She had been expecting to capture the Amazons, but Lena had been the best kind of surprise. Not just stunningly sexy, but also one of the greatest minds in the world. Circe had set the sweet, innocent, and utterly helpless Lena to work soon after conquering the island, and now she was taking the captive genius to continue her work, as she did every day. Circe's reign hadn't stopped the war against Mans World; in fact, the war had become far worse. Circe now used the Amazons and her minions like a personal army. Themyscira was just one stepping stone to her conquering the world. Unlike the Amazons war, Circe had no concern for casualties. She was a ruthless war general and crushed anyone who dared oppose her.

The evil sorceress carried Lena into her throne room and over to the long table that sat along the side of the room. The table was almost the length of the entire wall and it was full of magical items and pieces of technology that Lena was expected to work on throughout the day. Circe slowly slid her off of her shoulder, their bodies pressing together as Circe handled her. Then she set Lena down on her soft and dainty bare feet. With a flourish of her hands, a green flame made the ropes binding Lena suddenly disappear. She was left in just her silky white nightdress, along with the gag bound tightly over her lips; Circe had no need to hear her speak while she was working.

"Get to work my dear" Circe said as she turned Lena to face the table. She then gave her butt a firm smack, making the small and shapely damsel squeal into her gag and hurry over to a chair to sit down. Lena already had an incredible mind for technology, and after studying the magical items on Themyscira, she had become adept at manipulating them as well, learning their mystical secrets remarkably quickly. Through a combination of technology, the magical items here, and Circe's own dark magic, Lena was creating weapons that were decimating Circe's opponents on the battlefield. She didn't want to help the evil sorceress, but she had no choice; not only was she a captive here but so was Kara, and she didn't want to risk either of their lives.

Of all the bound, gagged, and ravished captives, Lena was the most hopelessly helpless due to her lack of any combat training or superpowers. She was a peerlessly brilliant mind, but remarkably easy for almost anyone to overpower, kidnap, and have their way with. Lena hadn't appreciated how much Kara had protected her back in her previous life as a free woman, but now, as she found herself constantly subject to the whims of her various captors, Lena knew that her future would depend on either Kara finding a way to escape and recapture her, or giving herself over to Stockholm Syndrome and surrendering herself completely to her newest captor and her wicked subjects. Either way, Lena knew her future would be one of bondage, enslavement, and ravishing. Her time in Kara's possession had made it clear to her that her friend would not be content to return to the previous "status quo" of their old lives. Kara wanted to own Lena just as much as any of her other captors. The difference was that Lena herself was quite amenable to being kidnapped, enslaved, and kept in bondage by Kara.

Circe left Lena to work there while she went over to her throne. The girls had set Kara and Wonder Woman down at the feet of her throne and they were retying them in the way that Circe liked.

They tied them so that a length of rope ran between each ankle, giving them just enough room to make small shuffling steps. Then they tied their hands in front of them the same way, giving them enough room to reach for things. They also tied their upper arms to their torsos, so they could only lift their arms beneath the elbow. It allowed them to serve Circe while remaining bound, a constant reminder of their enslavement.

Kara awoke by Circe's feet, moaning softly as she looked up at her mistress. Wonder Woman had been awoken a few minutes earlier, and she was already serving Circe by feeding her grapes. "Good morning my little super slave" Circe said with a cruel smirk as Kara's head rose, her blonde hair falling down against her shoulders "Why don't we start today with some light worshipping.

Massage my feet. Now" Kara sighed and nodded as she shuffled into a kneeling pose by Circe's feet, reluctantly lifting one foot onto her bent knees then slowly massaging the sole with her thumbs.

Circe opened her mouth and Wonder Woman fed her another grape, once she had swallowed it she patted Wonder Woman on the behind and said "Good girl" then she looked down to Kara "Kiss my feet as you massage them slave, and tell me how much you love worshipping your mistress" Kara made another small nod and sighed. She slowly lowered her head down to Circe's foot and began planting soft kisses on it. Circe had made her do this many times and she knew what the sorceress wanted to hear "Thank you for letting me worship your feet mistress" she said in a defeated tone as she lowered her head again, the soft wet sound from her lips delighting Circe.

After a short while, she instructed Kara to bring her some wine, and Wonder Woman took her place at Circe's feet.

Kara had to move slowly in her bondage, the ropes limiting her to gradual movements as went to retrieve a golden goblet for Circe. When she returned, there were two Amazons standing on either side of Lena. As the innocent and beautiful genius tried to work, they were groping her and kissing her neck, treating her like a plaything even as she displayed her incredible intelligence. Kara's brow furrowed and she stopped in place for a moment. She wanted to go over there and throw the wine in their faces, to tell them to remove their hands from Lena. But with Circe's magic still in control of every woman on this island there was nothing she could do. Any outburst would only result in further punishment.

With a frustrated sigh, she brought the wine to Circe who took a long sip and said "Very good, super slave. Now kneel down right here, I want to put my feet up" Kara blushed with embarrassment as she sunk down to her knees. Wonder Woman moved out of the way and Kara slowly crawled in front of Circe's throne. She felt the sorceress's feet settling down on her back, using her like a footstool. Wonder Woman continued massaging and worshipping Circes feet in the propped up position, both heroines completely humiliating themselves at the feet of the sorceress. From her position, Kara could turn her head and see Lena continue to be groped, the two women becoming more forceful with their roaming hands.

Then, one called over "Mistress can we take Lena to play with for a while? Please?" This was a common occurrence, whether Lena was working or not, her body was always in high demand on the island. She was highly coveted for her beauty and submissiveness, how she would so easily be tamed by the hands and tongue of a skilled and stern lover. The Amazons had never found someone who took to bondage and domination as well as Lena did, her body seemingly made for rope, her mind so easily conquered by any woman who wanted her. Circe was always willing to allow Lena to be taken, especially when Kara was in the room. The sorceress was well aware of their relationship, and she loved seeing Kara squirm whenever Lena was taken advantage of right in front of her.

"I think she could use a break. Enjoy yourselves" Circe replied to her slaves, as she said this she glanced down at Kara, seeing a slight tightness in her jaw as the blonde gritted her teeth. "It's a shame you can't join them, super slave. But your work being my footstool is far too important" she said teasingly as Kara watched the two women begin to subdue Lena. They had brought chloroform in preparation of Circe's approval and, as soon as they were given permission, they began using it. They clamped a cloth down over Lena's mouth and nose, pulling her out of her chair and into their arms. Bringing her to the ground, one remained at her head keeping the cloth in place, while the other began caressing and kissing her long smooth legs.

As she began to grow more drowsy the one at her legs began tying them up, squeezing her thighs together as she restrained her. The one with the chloroform groped her breasts with a fiery passion, kissing her neck as she did this. Lena was overwhelmed by their hands all over her, and yet at the same time she felt her senses being dulled, this barrage of pleasure the last thing she felt before sinking into a deep sleep. She moaned weakly beneath the cloth as her eyelids fluttered closed. As soon as she was out they continued binding her, rolling her limp form over and pulling her hands behind her back. They would wake her in bed, bound and gagged and ready to be ravished. For now they just focused on the ropes, making them so tight they squeezed into the softness of Lena's skin.

SEX AND CHAOS

From across the room Kara watched all of this, silently seething as her beloved was bound then hoisted up over one of the womens shoulders. She saw them spanking Lena's rump as they carried her away, treating her like the pleasure slave that she was. Kara's whole body was tense with anger, and it took everything she had to not to run after them. As she knelt there she realised this couldn't continue any longer. She had to have Lena back; she needed a plan. She kept losing to Wonder Woman because she was just used to relying on brute strength. But that wouldn't work here, not against a woman as cunning and devious as Circe. She needed to outthink her and as she knelt beneath her feet an idea slowly formed...

When Circe's goblet was empty she instructed Kara to fetch her another. By then Kara knew exactly what she was going to do. She went to the kitchen for the wine and, while she was alone, she found some parchment and made a note. Then as she walked back to Circe she waited until the sorceress was distracted by Wonder Woman worshipping her. She quickly scrunched up the note and tossed it over to Lena's workbench, knowing that Lena would see it when she returned. That note was only one part of her plan, though. The next would be considerably more difficult.

She had to defeat Wonder Woman in combat.

The next day Kara stood behind the gates again, waiting for them to rise as she listened to the rumbling of the crowd. She took a deep breath and steadied herself, preparing for the fight ahead of her. Then she heard that metallic sound, the gears turning as the gate begin to rise. She stepped out into the light of the arena, looking up at Circe with Lena on her lap. As Circe casually groped her, Kara's eyes scanned downward and when she saw Lena was wearing an ankle bracelet. Kara knew that meant her beautiful and brilliant lover had retrieved her note.

She kept walking forward, focusing on Wonder Woman as she emerged on the other side of the arena. They had done this dozens of times and the Amazon looked utterly assured of another victory. She had a steady confident stride as she waited to see what Kara would do, knowing that whatever it was she would be able to stop her. This time Kara didn't run, she just kept steadily walking until they were within speaking distance. "Ready to lose Kara? You could just lay down and make this easy on yourself" Wonder Woman said mockingly, putting her hands on her hips in a confident pose.

Kara glared at her and replied "Not this time" then she lunged forward for the items that sat between them. Wonder Woman assumed Kara was going for the rope and she grabbed at it, but Kara snatched up the bottle of chloroform instead. She quickly unscrewed it and managed to pour some out on both her hands, just before Wonder Woman tackled her to the ground. They began wrestling on the floor, Wonder Woman trying to pin Kara down and get her to turn over. But as they struggled against each other Kara began pressing her hands over Wonder Womans mouth and nose, forcing her to inhale the chloroform she had poured onto them.

Wonder Woman tried to keep a hold of Kara, but that chemical scent forced her to lean back, not allowing her to use her strength. "Stop... get off...." Wonder Woman groaned angrily as Kara suddenly managed to roll her over, pinning her down and sitting on her chest. She clamped her hand down over Wonder Woman's mouth and nose, and this time, the Amazon couldn't pry her free. She gripped her wrist and tried twisting it away, but Kara used her free hand to grab Wonder Woman's arm and slam it down to the ground. She let out a series of frustrated groans beneath Kara's palm, her legs kicking and wriggling around on the floor. But slowly she began to succumb, that constant scent of chloroform wearing her down with every breath she took.

There was a hushed air of silence as Kara knocked her out, the crowd all stunned by her trick with the chloroform. Then, finally, Wonder Woman's eyes closed, her writhing legs going still as she made a weak sigh then passed out. Kara let out a deep sigh of relief and finally lifted her hands.

Then she picked up the ropes and began tying up Wonder Woman. The crowd began cheering as the Amazon was finally defeated. Kara tied her arms behind her back then tied her ankles together. Then she looped a length of rope between her ankles and tied them to her wrists, pulling it tight so her feet lifted from the floor, securing her into a hogtie.

With the hogtie in place she grabbed the final piece needed to secure her victory. Taking the white cloth she tied it firmly between Wonder Womans lips. Kara could feel a surge of adrenaline rushing through her, she couldn't help giving Wonder Womans behind a firm smack as she said "I've been waiting a long time for this" then she stood and put her foot on Wonder Womans back, showing off her dominance as the crowd continued to cheer.

SEX AND CHAOS

With the Amazon defeated, Kara walked toward the throne which sat amongst the higher level of the stadium. She put her hands on her hips and glared at Circe as she called up "I want my prize! Now!"

Circe sighed and rolled her eyes at the blonde as she replied "Fine." It didn't matter either way to her. She would let Kara have her fun tonight and humiliate her all over again tomorrow. Using her magic, she made Lena float in the air, then slowly glide down to rest on Kara's shoulder. "You got my note. Does it work?" Kara whispered to Lena as she slipped the gorgeous brunette's ankle bracelet off, disguising her movement by giving the soft and pale soles of Lena's bare feet a quick tickle. She heard Lena make a muffled moan of approval (and a small, gagged giggle from the tickling of her sensitive bare feet) and she smiled, knowing her plan had worked perfectly. She secured the bracelet onto her wrist and felt a huge surge of energy.

Her powers had returned.

Kara's note had told Lena to create this device, something that would be capable of giving her powers back and blocking out Circe's magic. Kara felt so good she couldn't help but give Lena's gorgeous and shapely asscheeks a triumphant and possessive little spank. She knew Lena now belonged to her again, but that wasn't enough. She was tired of being dominated, she wanted to be the one in charge now. She flew straight up in the air, to a series of gasps from the crowd. Then she made her eyes glow red and with a burst of her eyebeams made a section of the throne beside Circe's head explode.

Circe cowered from the explosion as chunks of the throne rained down on her. Then she looked up in fear at Kara's glowing red eyes. "Leave now or I'll turn you to ash" Kara growled as she stared at Circe with her red eyes ready to destroy her "You... You..." Circe muttered in disbelief. Then, unable to find the proper words, she just let out an angry screeching yell and, with a flourish of her hands, she disappeared in a burst of green flames, as did her demonic minions amongst the crowd.

Everyone was silent now, watching as Kara floated higher and addressed them all, her voice bellowing loudly across the stadium as she hung in the air with Lena still slung over her shoulder "All of you belong to me now!" she declared as she looked down at their worried faces "On your knees! All of you!" The Amazons, the new recruits, and the pleasure slaves all looked amongst each other, seeing if anyone would dare defy the powerful

Kryptonian. Then, slowly, they all began to sink down to their knees, the entire stadium submitting to the newly dominant Kara. She smiled as she watched them all kneel. Then she gave Lena's rump another firm spank as she said "That's more like it"

CHAPTER 05

The Kryptonian Queen

Chapter Summary: Kara's rule brings changes to Paradise Island and a challenge from Man's World...

Kara sat on the golden throne of Themyscira. She had discarded her modified slave outfit and was back in her regular superheroine attire. Since overthrowing Circe she taken her place as the new queen of Paradise Island, a role she found suited her quite well. The biggest benefit to her new status was sitting on her lap: her beloved Lena Luthor. The beautiful genius was currently bound and gagged, curled up on the blonde heroine's lap as she was stroked, fondled, and lovingly squeezed. There was nothing Kara liked more than feeling the supple skin of Lena's feminine form, running her hand along the sensual curves. She stroked up her leg as she kissed her neck, sending small shivers of pleasure through Lena.

As her hand glided up to Lena's breasts she heard her make a muffled moan of pleasure, the sound blocked by the thick white cloth tied tightly over her lips. She nibbled gently on the porcelain skin of her neck, her hands slowly yet firmly squeezing her breasts. A redness shaded Lena's body as a heat built within her, the sensations of Kara's hands and lips making her shudder as she sat on her lap.

Their embrace was intimate but not unobserved, for beside the throne knelt Wonder Woman, bound with her own lasso and just as tightly gagged as Lena. The golden lasso ran round her neck like a collar and leash, the end resting on the arm of the throne should Kara have need of it. Kara kept Wonder Woman in the same modified skimpy outfit that Circe had her in, only now the house of El crest was emblazoned in gold in the centre of the chest. Her gauntlets had a thin metal chain connecting them, turning them into handcuffs which Wonder Woman let rest in her lap as she knelt.

Her head was bowed and she stayed quiet, knowing that submission was her only option. Using Lena's knowledge of technology and now magic, Kara was far too powerful for any Amazon on the island to challenge her. The days where Wonder Woman could bind and gag the blonde heroine were long since past, she now willingly submitted to her reign. As she knelt there the sound of bare feet pressing against the polished marble floors approached. The golden doors to the throne room opened and the former queen of Paradise Island entered. Hippolyta no longer wore her flowing white regal robes, instead she now wore little more than a nightdress, a thin piece of white fabric that only barely contained her voluptuous figure.

As she walked in, the skimpy garment rode up with every stride, showing off a tantalising glimpse of her white panties. Above the bulging cleavage within the silky white fabric sat a thin choker necklace with a golden pendant. The circular pendant had the house of El crest on it just as her daughters clothing. Whether it be clothing or jewellery, every single inhabitant of the island now wore the House of El crest, whether they were a warrior or a pleasure slave, it was a symbol that they now all served Kara.

Kara lifted her head from Lena's neck but continued casually groping her as Hippolyta entered the room. Kara had been the queen for long enough now that Hippolyta knew to approach the throne then kneel before speaking "My queen, the representatives from Man's World are ready to accept your terms. As you commanded, they have gathered to speak with you" Kara nodded with a satisfied smile, her hand sliding down from Lena's breasts to give her leg a small pat as she said softly "I have work to do my love, perhaps you should spend some time out of the palace"

Kara called out to her personal slaves, a handful of Amazons she had chosen to wait on her at all times. They were just outside the door but came in immediately at her call. At her command they went and retrieved an uncovered palanquin that Kara liked to sit Lena in sometimes. Carried by four Amazons, one at each corner, the palanquin would be taken around Themyscira, displaying Lena's beauty to the other women on the island. Kara wanted everyone to see her beautiful prize, the one gorgeous pleasure slave that was off limits to everyone except for her.

She cradled Lena in her arms and floated gently toward the palanquin, sitting her beloved carefully in it. Then, with a loving kiss on sweet Lena's gagged lips and a playful spank to her lusciously plump rump, Kara sent her off to be displayed. As soon as Lena was out of the room a more serious expression crossed Kara's face, she retrieved Diana's leash and led her out

SEX AND CHAOS

of the room with Hippolyta following closely behind them. Kara walked into a room that had once been for war council meetings, it had mostly the same purpose as before except now it was fitted with holographic technology designed by Lena.

"On your knees, both of you" Kara said sternly before the hologram device was turned on. Hippolyta knelt on one side of her and Diana on the other. It was important for the representatives of Man's World to see that both the queen and princess of Themyscira now submitted to her. After a few seconds the holograms came to life, displaying military generals from the armies of various nations across the globe. Since taking over, Kara had been negotiating a cease fire for the ongoing war, and today her terms were finally going to be agreed upon.

As they submitted to the beautiful blonde heroine there was a tense atmosphere in the room. Many were not happy about agreeing to the kryptonian's terms, but there was no other choice. The world was losing to the overwhelming might of Themyscira; it was either surrender or be destroyed. The call didn't last long, they made a final request for the captured pleasure slaves to be released and it was quickly denied. After that, they made the agreement official, the war would end and Kara would keep the beautiful enslaved women she had on the island.

As the hologram shut off a snide voice spoke from behind the war generals "Well that was pathetic. Did you invite me here to be an audience for your humiliation?" They turned to the man who had been sitting in the shadows, one of the generals replying "No Mr Luthor, we invited so you could see what we're dealing with. A Kryptonian ruling over a magical island with enough power to destroy the world. There's nothing we can do to stop her, and we want your help"

Luthor smiled, basking in having his superior intelligence acknowledged. On either side of him stood Mercy Graves and Eve Teschmacher, his beautiful and deadly associates that protected him at all times. With a simple commanded the trained women could take out everyone in this room within minutes. He rose up from his seated position and calmly replied "I'll see what I can do" then, escorted by the two women, he walked out of the room.

The next day Kara was in an exceptionally good mood. She could see her future laid out before her now. The war was over, the island - and, more importantly, Lena - now belonged to her. It was a future she had wanted for a long time and now it was clearer than ever. For a while now she had been planning to marry Lena, the traditional Kryptonian marriage ceremony would bind Lena to her forever. But before that, Kara had another surprise for her beloved Lena.

It was one of the rare times she was allowing Lena to walk freely around the estate of the royal palace. There was a lavish garden at the back which she found Lena in. Her beloved was wearing a thin silky nightdress, showing off her longs legs and bare feet as she walked on the grass. Kara came up behind her, wrapping her arms around her in a loving embrace as she kissed her neck.

Lena let out a small moan of pleasure as soon as she felt Kara's lips on her neck. Her body melted willingly into Kara's strong yet gentle embrace, her shapely behind pushing back at Kara's hips in a small grinding motion.

"I have a surprise for you my love" Kara whispered into her ear as she gently fondled Lena's breasts, her fingers pressing into their soft shape. "But first..." Kara reached back for the cloth she had tucked into her skirt. It was already damp with chloroform in preparation, the chemical enhanced by magic to make it even more powerful. She smoothly brought it round in front of Lena's face and calmly pressed it over her mouth and nose. Lena let out a muffled sigh against the cloth as she felt her senses begin to fade, a glassy eyed stare settling over her expression. Kara continued groping and kissing her as she weakened her, Lena's body becoming limp in her tight grip.

Just before she passed out, Kara peeled the cloth away, leaving Lena in a subdued, barely conscious state. She spun her around and held her tightly, kissing her on the lips and pushing her tongue into the confines of her mouth. Lena was too weak to raise her arms, hanging listlessly in Kara' grip as she made a mewling moan of pleasure. Then, Kara moved her mouth away and hoisted Lena up over her shoulder. She gave her beloved a firm pat on the backside, her perfectly plump rump perched neatly on her shoulder. Then she carried Lena away from the gardens and to their room.

In their room, Kara had prepared a small pot of magical paste, made with the magic of Paradise Island. She sat down on the edge of the bed and slid Lena off of her shoulder. She then lowered Lena down so she was lying across her knees, in a pose in which Lena had been spanked many times when Wonder Woman was her mistress. Kara had no need to punish her, however.

SEX AND CHAOS

She gave Lena's backside a firm squeeze then slid her nightdress up so the small of her back was visible, as well as her gorgeous ass in her white silky panties. Then, using the paste, Kara drew the House of El crest on the small of Lena's back, just above her right rumpcheek.

The paste glowed for a moment, then became a thick, black marking like a tattoo, painless yet permanent, marking Lena for all time as her property. Lena made a small moan as she felt the magic tingle through her, too weak to fully understand but a part of her accepting what this marking meant. Keeping her in this position for a moment Kara leaned down and kissed the marking, smiling at how permanent it was, how no-one would ever take Lena from her again.

It was too beautiful to not be shared, and she wanted to show off her beloved slave to the other Amazons who had once ravished Lena so freely. She lifted her up off of her lap and laid Lena down on the bed. Then, taking some ropes which were always on hand in their bedroom, she lovingly began to tie Lena up. She first pulled the shapely brunette's arms behind her back and bound her soft, dainty wrists. Next, Kara wrapped ropes around Lena's body, above and below her beautiful breasts and around her bare upper arms, as well as around her forearms and soft tummy, further pinning Lena's arms immovably to her body. Kara was now quite skilled with rope and quickly finished the knots. She then tied Lena's legs at the ankles, knees and thighs, making a special point to squeeze Lena's soft, supple thighs together with the tight lengths of rope.

She finished Lena's bondage with a gag, pulling a white cloth tightly over Lena's lips and tying it behind her head. With the gag in place she groped and fondled Lena for a little while longer, laying atop her on the bed as she played with her helpless pleasure slave. Then, Kara pushed the chloroform cloth over her beloved's mouth and nose again. Lena's already dazed eyes became even more hazy, her eyelids slowly fluttering closed as Kara loomed over her on the bed. She was too weak to even smile, but as she passed out Lena's last thoughts were of how much she loved being Kara's concubine.

Kara watched Lena's eyes close then she lifted the cloth and kissed her again. She hoisted her beautiful damsel up from the bed and settled her bound and gagged form atop her shoulder. With Lena in place, Kara reached up and slid up her nightdress, making sure that House of El crest could be seen tattooed on the small of her back. Then she carried Lena out of the palace and through the streets of Pardise Island, displaying Lena to her subjects. Every Amazon and pleasure slave she passed bowed their heads in a show of submission. But behind their submissive poses many of them were burning with jealously. Lena had once been free for any of them to dominate and ravish, and now this beautiful prize was kept all for Kara. They weren't the only ones observing this tantalising scene of utter dominance, for high above in the sky an invisible drone silently monitored Kara's proud walk through the streets.

"Fascinating" Luthor muttered aloud as he watched the video from the drone, it's high tech camera able to get a read of Kara's biology just by scanning her "It seems she's found a way to eliminate her weakness to kryptonite." He knew this was due to Lena; with her brilliant mind on the island along with the magic it was making his task nigh impossible. He was in his private research facility monitoring the large screen, surrounded by his high tech experiments. Mercy and Eve were there as well, their eyes intently watching the screen as it followed Kara carrying Lena.

Since his meeting with the war generals, Lex had been thinking of any possibility of defeating Kara and still none had presented itself. His scan of her now made it clear that she had become almost invulnerable, except for one thing. Her love for Lena was her only weakness, one which wouldn't be easy to get to. "I need to get on that island" he muttered angrily, his fists clenching as his superior intelligence hit a brick wall.

From behind them they heard a strange sound, like a flame growing larger. The two women spun round instantly, drawing pistols and staring at a circle of green flame that was growing on the ground. Neither one of them looked afraid as a figure began to emerge, their fingers beginning to squeeze down on the trigger of their weapons "Wait" Lex said calmly, easing the eagerness of his personal guard.

The figure stepped through and Circe brushed a strand of hair to the side with a playful smirk "Lex Luthor I presume?" she said non-chalantly, placing her hands on her hips in a confident pose. Lex had an extensive list of enemies and Circe wasn't on it so he had no reason to be alarmed. He eyed her curiously as he replied "And you're.... Circe isn't it? I don't believe we've met" Circe began walking toward him with a devilish glint in her eyes as she replied "It's been long overdue. We have a shared interest Lex, a certain blonde Kryptonian. I'm going to help you take Lena from her"

Lena tilted her head back and let out a loud shuddering moan, her cheeks reddened from all her gasping and writhing on the bed. Kara lifted her head from between her thighs and kissed slowly up her stomach, taking her time to lovingly press her lips to Lena's skin. She kissed up to her breasts then licked her nipples, sending more shivers of pleasure through Lena even as she recovered from her explosive orgasm. After tasting her breasts, Kara kissed up Lena's neck and found her concubine's luscious lips, her mouth pressing against Lena's as she kissed her passionately.

Both women were completely naked and their bodies writhed sensually against each other on the bed. Their skin had a subtle glow form the perspiration of their lovemaking, small beads of sweat giving them a glossy sheen. Lena could barely catch her breath after being brought to orgasm, Kara's mouth against hers so overwhelming she had to breathe through her nose. The kiss went on for a long while then Kara lifted her mouth ever so slightly to say "I love you Lena, I'm never going to let anyone have you ever again. I would burn the world to ashes to keep you safe"

She had almost told her about the wedding plans right there and then, the words had been on the edge of her lips. But she controlled herself, wanting to wait for the perfect moment to surprise her beloved. Lena could see the love in Kara's eyes and in a soft submissive tone she replied "I love you too" That was all Kara needed to hear and she kissed Lena again, another long and passionate embrace with both women moaning deeply.

Kara could feel just how worn out Lena was from the ravishing of her sensual form, and, as they kissed, she decided it was time to give the beautiful brunette some rest. In the morning she would be ready to be taken again. Her hand slid over to the nightstand where she had laid out a white cloth, and as she lifted her mouth from Lena's she replaced it with the cloth. Still lying on top of her she pressed the cloth firmly over her mouth and nose, watching as Lena's beautiful eyes became tired and weak. "Sleep, my beloved" Kara whispered softly as she kept the cloth firmly in place, letting Lena sink down into sleep in the warm afterglow of their lovemaking.

Lena was already so relaxed and loose from her orgasm that the sleep came even faster than normal, her muscles went limp as her brain became foggy and unclear. With a soft sigh beneath the cloth, Lena's eyes fluttered closed, her body becoming listless beneath Kara. The loving kryptonian kept the cloth in place for a few more moments, ensuring Lena's sleep would be long lasting, then she slowly peeled it away. Lena's lips hung ever so slightly apart, taking slow peaceful breaths.

Kara kissed them gently then put the cloth away and slid off of her.

Once Kara had lovingly bathed Lena in their lavish, pool-sized bathtub and redressed her precious soon-to-be-wife (Lena had remained sleeping peacefully throughout), she returned them both to bed and began to lay her head down beside Lena when she suddenly heard a massive boom far on the other side of the island. It sounded like some kind of explosion, the kind only something from Man's World could create. Her calm loving expression became more stern and serious as she quickly got dressed, then she flew out from the open balcony and shot across the island, flying to investigate the sound.

The Amazon guards on the steps of the palace watched Kara shooting off into the night. Then, in front of them, a green flaming portal began to appear. None of them showed any surprise or concern about the portal; this was all part of the plan. There were still many Amazons that were not truly loyal to Kara, mostly due to their jealousy at not being able to ravish Lena. Circe had found these willing conspirators and had convinced them to assist her. It wasn't long ago that Circe had been the ruler of this island, and it didn't take much work for her to find her way back to it.

Through the portal stepped the sorceress, flanked by Mercy Graves and Eve Teschmacher. The palace itself had too many magical protections for her to open a portal directly into it, but the steps she could just about manage. "Is she alone?" Circe asked the guards and they nodded, stepping aside to let her pass. Two of the guards approached the doors and opened them for the three women. Circe sauntered through with a pleased smile on her face, leading Mercy and Eve through the palace.

She took them straight to the royal bedchambers, where Lena lay scantily clad in the usual nightie Kara loved to dress her in and barely covered by the white silk sheets of their bed. "As promised, one helpless and gorgeous damsel in distress" Circe laughed as she motioned to the sleeping beauty. She had done all of the work in getting them here but now Mercy and Eve took over. They approached the bed then moved onto it as they began taking hold of Lena. They each had brought lengths of rope with them as well as a cloth soaked in some of Themyscira's magical chloroform which Circe had provided, and they worked together to drug and bind Lena so she would be ready to be taken.

They first pressed the cloth over Lena's mouth and nose as she began to groggily stir in response to their intrusion. The unsuspecting damsel opened her eyes weakly for a brief moment, let out a soft "mmmph!" of surprise and fear at seeing the intruders, but then quickly was ushered against her will back to a gentle slumber. The two minions then turned Lena over onto her front then moved her arms behind her back. They handled Lena in an efficient and precise manner, with none of the love that Kara would always show her. They simply moved her body where they required it and tied her limbs tightly. Lena barely made a sound, only a few small sighs which were quickly silenced as they mercilessly gagged her as well, stuffing her mouth with a small wad of cloth and then binding a strip of silk tightly over her lips. With the gag in place, Mercy lifted Lena off of the bed and hoisted the soon-to-be-kidnapped concubine up onto her shoulder, holding Lena's soft thighs to keep her in place.

The three kidnappers knew they didn't have much time. They had bound and gagged Lena in only a few minutes and now they quickly made their way back out. Circe led them back through the halls of the palace, Lena resting neatly on Mercy's shoulder, completely unaware that she was being captured. The operation had been a complete success, they reached the portal and stepped through, whisking Lena away from the island and from Kara.

Kara slowly floated down to the smoking crater on the beach, the explosion had left a huge hole

with sand scattered everywhere. In the centre of the hole she could see a shape and she lowered toward it with her fists clenched. As she got closer she saw it was some kind of device, and her presence made it glow green with a rippling magical flame. That flame suddenly exploded, the force sending Kara flying back and tumbling across the sand.

She instantly got up, unhurt but angry as she seethed "Circe." she spun around as she awaited another attack, calling out "Show yourself! You're not welcome on my island!!" but after the second explosion the beach had gone completely silent. Kara slowly unclenched her fists as a look of confusion crossed her face, then she realised that this was just a distraction "No" she gasped softly before shooting up into the air and heading like a rocket back to the palace.

She knew something was wrong immediately when she saw her guards weren't at their stations, the steps were abandoned and the doors to her palace were slightly ajar. She kept flying at a tremendous speed, breaking the doors apart as she shot through the halls of the palace. She came to a sudden halt in the bedroom, her massive rush of speed making the sheets on the bed flutter and fly off. She looked left and right, taking panicked breaths as she saw Lena was gone.

Slowly she lowered down to the floor, her heavy breathing becoming more enraged. She knew exactly why Lena was taken. They were going to try and use her as leverage. Kara's eyes became watery then those tears evaporated as her eyes glowed red. Letting out an enraged roar she turned her head upward and let out two huge laser beams from her eyes. The beams broke through the ceiling and shot up into the night sky as Kara's angry cry echoed throughout the island. If they thought taking Lena would make her submit to them, they couldn't have been more wrong. The whole world was about to experience the wrath of an enraged Kryptonian.

CHAPTER 06

The Hunt for Lena

Chapter Summary: Kara relentlessly pursues her beloved, Lex grows impatient with Lena's resistance, and new characters are drawn into the conflict...

Kara smashed through the final floor of the underground facility, letting out an angry yell as the concrete and metal broke into pieces all around her. Just as she slammed down to the ground a green fiery portal began to close. "CIRCE!!" she yelled angrily at seeing the portal diminish to a tiny green circle. She flew straight at it but couldn't make it in time, once again they had escaped.

On the other side of the portal Lex Luthor angrily brushed a bit off dust from the shoulder of his expensive suit. They had all heard that angry yell before the portal closed, and they all knew who it had come from. For the past few weeks they had been playing this cat and mouse game, staying constantly on the move in order to keep Lena away from Kara.

They were now in another of Lex's underground lairs, one of many he had all around the world, always prepared for any eventuality. But, even with all his resources, he couldn't keep this up forever. Kara would seemingly never stop hunting him as long as he had Lena in his possession, and so far the acquisition hadn't even been worth it. Lena refused to co-operate, he needed her to design weapons to fight Kara's Amazon army. With the time Lena had spent there she could easily design an arsenal that would be devastating to the Amazons. But she was being annoyingly stubborn.

In this new facility with him was Circe, who had helped them escape at the last second, and his henchwomen, Mercy Graves and Eve Tessmacher. Lena was there as well, scantily clad in a skimpy silk nightdress, bound, gagged and slung over Mercy's shoulder. He turned to face Mercy and sternly said "This cannot continue. Are you certain you can make her talk?"

Mercy smiled and stroked her hand up Lena's soft and supple legs as she replied in a sultry tone "Absolutely, Mr. Luthor. She just needs... a little more softening up first" she accentuated her point by giving Lena's plump rump a firm pat, her hand make a slight stinging slap against the soft flesh. Lena moaned and wriggled her hips slightly, but she was too tightly bound to do much more than that. Her legs squeezed together with rope, her wrists bound behind her back, and rope wrapped around her upper body to keep her from being able to move her arms at all.

With an unconvinced sigh Luthor replied "Fine. Take her away. I want her to co-operate as soon as possible. Do you understand?" This time it was Eve who replied "Yes sir" then the two women walked off to continue their 'interrogation' session. Lex watched them go with an angry glare. He was starting to doubt that they were interested in getting Lena to work with them at all. They seemed much more concerned with just getting her alone so they could have their way with her. Lena seemed to have that effect on any woman she was around, and now his two loyal henchwomen were constantly in bed with her, drugging her and ravishing her at every opportunity.

"Was this part of the plan?" Lex said to Circe who had been watching this all with a bemused smile. With a small shrug the sorceress replied "I told you I could get you Lena. Not that I could make her play along. Don't forget I have as much invested in this as you, I want the Amazons destroyed just as much as you do. But we must be patient" Lex let out an angry grumbling noise then turned and walked off, calling over his shoulder "My patience is wearing thin!"

Eve and Mercy quickly found a bedroom in the underground facility, dumping Lena on the bed and pouncing on her. It had been far too long since she had been chloroformed for their liking. Those wide, beautiful eyes of hers needing to be brought back down to a sleepy stare. Eve stripped down to her white bra and panties and lay on top of Lena, grinding into her and kissing her, Lena moaning and writhing in defiance, her struggles only exciting Eve more.

Meanwhile Mercy prepared the chloroform, laying out a white cloth and drizzling some of the chemical concoction onto it. They had to at least pretend like they were trying to get the information out of her, even if secretly they didn't want her to tell them anything. If she did co-operate it would mean the end of these sessions, and the end of getting to use her irresistible body however they desired. Eve squeezed Lena's ample breasts firmly, then her hands slid up behind the captive damsel's neck and undid the white cloth tied tightly over her lips.

Eve gently slid the gag out of Lena's mouth, then, before asking her a single question, began to roughly and possessively kiss the helpless beauty, replacing the gag with her soft lips and pushing her tongue into the confines of Lena's mouth. As they kissed, Mercy undressed as well, stripping down to her underwear. Eve let out a sensual moan against Lena's mouth, then slowly peeled her lips away as she said "Now... are you going to tell us how to defeat the Amazons?"

Lena let out an angry groan as she wriggled under the weight of Eve's half naked form, her body writhing as she replied "Never! Let me go!" Eve giggled and glanced over her shoulder to Mercy as she said "She's still resisting. I think she needs to be weakened a little more" Holding the cloth, Mercy slid onto the bed, crawling over to Lena like a predator stalking her prey. Eve rolled off of Lena to give Mercy some room, letting Mercy lay on top of Lena to keep her pinned down to the bed.

"You really should just do what we want..." Mercy said in a soft seductive manner, her hand gently pressing the cloth down over Lena's mouth and nose "...Lex wont keep you around forever if you don't co-operate" Lena tried to fight it, but with every breath she took her body began to feel numb, a weak drowsy sensation settled over her mind as her eyes glazed over. Mercy's hand was firmly in place, forcing the chloroform into Lena's lungs. The wicked henchwoman could hear Lena's soft whimpers and moans from beneath the cloth, and she could feel the tension melting out of Lena's body as she lay atop her.

As Lena was put into a sleepy subdued state, Eve quickly untied her legs, sliding her hands under them and finding the knots. Mercy rolled slightly to the side to give Eve more access to Lena's supple thighs, but she kept the damp cloth constantly in place, not wanting a single breath to go by without weakening Lena more. With the ropes out of the way, Eve began to sensually kiss up Lena's legs, each soft touch of her lips sending pleasurable tingles through Lena's body. Even in her weakened state, the kidnapped damsel couldn't help but moan in response, feeling Eve's lips kiss higher and higher until they were right on the edge of her silky white panties.

Just before Lena passed out, Mercy peeled the cloth away and began kissing her, letting out a pleased moan against Lena's lips. The beautiful captive was far too weak to do anything but lay there and be ravished, her sleepy stare showing absolutely no resistance. As Mercy continued kissing her, Eve slowly wriggled Lena's panties off of her hips and down her long legs, the two women now using her as a pleasure slave just as she had been used on Themyscira.

At the same time, Kara was ravishing her own pleasure slaves, although she was getting less enjoyment out of it. She had returned to Themyscira; to the island which she now reigned over. In the past few weeks she had been capturing dozens of beautiful women with the aid of her Amazon army. In an attempt to comfort her after Lena's kidnapping, the new pleasure slaves were now brought to her chambers every night. Each time she would wear them out with her insatiable appetite, and each time they would be utterly unable to compare to her beloved.

She now lay naked on the bed in her royal chambers, three of her new pleasure slaves sleeping soundly beside her - all of them having been thoroughly ravished - their bodies glowing with perspiration, having practically passed out from the passionate lovemaking of their mistress. Kara wasn't satisfied, though, and she stared angrily at the ceiling as she thought of her precious Lena. All of her leads regarding the location of the woman who Kara's heart belonged to had gone cold. Even with her army conquering the world and capturing women in every country, no-one knew where Lex was hiding her.

Kara was about to command a new batch of pleasure slaves to be brought in when she heard a knock at the door. "My queen. We... have visitors." With an angry sigh Kara slid off the bed and got dressed in her red pleated skirt and tight fitting blue top, marching to the door as she left the three beautiful women to sleep. Now that she was done with them, they would be handed down to one of her trusted generals.

She walked into her throne room to see two women she hadn't been expecting. Pausing with a look of confusion she asked "What are you doing here?" then she flew over to her throne and sat down, awaiting their response. In front of her were Lois Lane and Vicki Vale, two reporters she'd had encounters with in the past. Lois was wearing a black pencil skirt and a light blue blouse. Vicki had similar attire, although her grey pencil skirt was a little shorter and her white blouse a little tighter.

Lois stepped forward and spoke first "The world's leaders didn't know what else to do, so they requested we come and speak with you. All the women you've been kidnapping, Kara... this has to stop!" Kara gave her a hard stare as she sat on her throne, the beautiful blonde looking much more intimidating than the last time Lois had seen her "This is their fault!" she cried out, angrily, "They conspired with Lex and Circe to steal my beloved Lena from me!

Vicki tried next by saying "Well they're not going to give her back if you keep acting like this! Maybe you should try letting some of the women you've enslaved go free? Show them you're willing to co-operate?" Kara's fists clenched as she contained her anger, her eyes narrowing as she seethed "Co-operate? I am the queen of Themyscira! I will enslave every single woman in the world until I get my Lena back!!! Guards!!! Restrain them!!!"

The doors of the throne room burst open and Amazonian guards rushed up behind the two beautiful reporters. They grabbed the women and pulled their arms behind their back, holding them in place as Kara rose up and began calmly walking toward them "Hey!" "Let go!" Vicki and Lois shrieked as they wriggled about, their feet shuffling on the floor as they tried to pull themselves free from the Amazons tight grip.

Another Amazon walked over to Kara and knelt down, presenting her with a cloth that had been dampened with the magical chloform mixture made on Themyscira, the concoction far more powerful than the regular chemical. Kara took it from the kneeling Amazon, holding it flat in her palm as she slowly approached the two struggling reporters.

"No! Don't!" Vicki moaned as she saw Kara approaching her first, the cloth raising then pressing firmly over her mouth and nose. Kara pushed her body against Vicki as she chloroformed her, letting her know just how completely outmatched she was. Her head slowly drooped down as the chloroform knocked her out, her wide trembling eyes coming to a close as she let out a soft sigh from beneath the cloth.

Lois let out a scared gasp at seeing how quickly Vicki had succumbed to the cloth. She continued her struggling motions but the Amazon holding her was far too strong. No matter what she did, Lois' arms remained firmly pulled behind her back and her body was easily held in place for Kara. "Take her to my chambers and tie her up" Kara commanded once Vicki was fully unconscious. The Amazon holding Vicki instantly turned her around and hoisted her up onto her shoulder, carrying her away.

"You... you can't do this!" Lois moaned in disbelief, she had come here as a negotiator, and now realised she was going to be a pleasure slave instead. Kara walked in front of her, assessing Lois' beauty for a moment. She was stunningly gorgeous, even as she wriggled and moaned in fear, but still nothing compared to Lena. Kara raised the cloth and clamped it down over Lois' mouth and nose, silencing the reporter's helpless moans as she drugged her.

Lois let out another defiant moan against the cloth, her eyes widening as she tried to keep them open. But, with only a few more breaths, that fierce nature quickly simmered down, her eyelids fluttering as her shoulders sagged. The Amazon behind her was keeping her on her feet now, Lois' long legs wobbling as her body went limp. Kara kept the cloth in place as Lois' eyes closed, ensuring she was fully unconscious before peeling it away. "Give her to me" she said to the Amazon then hoisted Lois up on her shoulder. Vicki would be in her bedchambers by now and Kara could take Lois there herself to join her. She was still angry about not having Lena back, and breaking these two in would be a welcome distraction.

It only took a few days for Vicki to submit to the constant drugging, bondage and passionate lovemaking, as well as being sternly spanked if she ever resisted. Lois was proving a little more difficult, but her will was starting to break. Kara was confident she would have her as a willing pleasure slave soon. She had Vicki dressed up in a silky white nightdress that only barely covered her shapely behind, and she had her bound and gagged on her bed. Lois had been stripped down to her black bra and panties. She would only be dressed in silk once she submitted. Kara liked to do that part herself.

Lois lay bound across Kara's knees, sitting on the edge of the bed with the now submissive Vicki laying on the sheets. Kara raised her hand and brought it slamming down on Lois' backside, her palm making a stinging slap against the soft flesh. Lois let out a loud feminine gasp, her hips wriggling slightly as she moaned in pain. Kara's hand rose again and Lois winced in anticipation, then once again it came down with another hard spank.

SEX AND CHAOS

"Are you ready to submit? You can't resist me forever" Kara said calmly as she spanked Lois again, easily keeping the bound and wriggling woman across her knees. Kara had Lois tied up, but not gagged so she could hear her response. She heard Lois make a pained struggling moan, as if she was coming close to the verge of submitting. But then she just replied "No! I wont!" in a defiant tone, going back to her writhing as she tried to free herself from the white ropes.

Kara sighed and picked up the cloth she had laid next to her on the bed. She took the back of Lois's head and tilted her up, then pressed the cloth over her mouth and nose, getting her to calm down with the forced scent of chloroform. Lois let out a little muffled gasp, then a sleepy sigh from beneath the cloth as her eyelids drooped half closed. Kara brought Lois down into a subdued hazy state, then she peeled the cloth away and let her rest across her knees again.

She brought her hand up and continued spanking her, leaving little red marks on the soft shape of Lois' backside. Now that she was all sleepy, her moans became more girlish and submissive, each spank slowly wearing her down until she would be ready to serve Kara willingly. As Kara was spanking her, the blonde suddenly heard a knock at the door and the voice of Hippolyta calling to her. "My queen. We have caught someone trying to sneak onto the island. Diana has her in the throne room."

Kara gave Lois another firm spank, grumbled "I'll be back for you later," then hoisted the reporter off of her knees and laid her down next to Vicki on the bed. Kara pulled a cloth between Lois' lips to gag her, then slid off the bed and left her two captive reporters laying helplessly for her to return. She opened the door to see Hippolyta, her most trusted advisor. Hippolyta was now fully submitted to Kara's reign; it was natural for any Amazon to yield to a more powerful woman, and Kara had fully proven that she was the most powerful woman on this island.

Kara walked to her throne room with Hippolyta by her side "She flew a stealth plane onto the beach and we caught her trying to sneak in here" the former queen said as Kara pushed open the doors. Inside the throne room Wonder Woman had the intruder bound, gagged, and slung over her shoulder, waiting for Kara's arrival. Like her mother, Diana now completely submitted to Kara, sliding the intruder off of her shoulder as she said "Would you like to speak with her my queen?"

"Alex?" Kara said with a confused expression as she saw her adoptive human sister being turned to face her. Then, her confusion hardened as she looked from Alex to Diana and said "Ungag her" Diana loosened the cloth tied between the brunette's lips and pulled the gag free. Alex was wearing her tight fitting black tactical gear, the fabric fitting the shape of her feminine form nicely. As was common practice for the Amazons, she had been stripped of her footwear upon her capture and Alex looked up anxiously at her captors, who all towered over the barefoot agent. Ropes were tied around her legs and her wrists were crossed and secured behind her back. More rope encircled her torso, above and below her breasts and around her abdomen; the common Amazon method of binding captives proving more than sufficient to contain the special agent. Alex made a moan of distress as the gag was pulled free, wriggling in Diana's grip, who continued to hold her tightly, keeping her faced toward Kara.

"Explain yourself" Kara said coldly as she assessed Alex with a distrusting stare. Alex look over her shoulder at Diana still holding her, then, with an angry groan she faced Kara and said "I just came here to talk, Kara! You can untie me." Kara took a moment to think, but even with her sister standing in front of her, the blonde couldn't let go of her anger and she replied "No. Diana captured you, so you belong to her now. Those are the rules."

Alex felt Diana's hands squeezing her a little tighter, showing a clear excitement that she now belonged to her. "What?! Kara you can't... mmmppphhhh!!" before she could finish Diana pulled the gag between her lips and silenced her. Diana's hands ran up Alex's chest then she spun her around and lifted her up onto her shoulder "Thank you, my queen" Diana said with a pleased smile as she stroked Alex's long legs and gave her shapely ass a firm squeeze.

"I'm certain you will soon have Lena back in your posession. Under your rule, Man's World will soon be conquered. They cannot hide her from you forever" Diana said as she saw the longing look in Kara's eyes. She began to carry Alex away but before she could, Kara stopped her. "Wait! She's a government agent She might have information on Lex's whereabouts. Get your lasso of truth." With a submissive nod, Diana replied "Yes, my queen" both women ignoring Alex's muffled moans.

"What seems to be troubling you, Lex?" Circe said in a soothing tone of voice that rolled off of her tongue so naturally. He was sitting at a large computer console, running through a digital display that showed a map of the world. On the map was a list of his secret facilities, and the majority of them had a large red X going through them, indicating that they had been destroyed.

"Isn't it obvious?" he said angrily without looking back at her, his mind calculating how much longer it would likely take for Kara to find him. Circe came up behind him and rested her hands on the back of his chair as she said "Lena will give us what we want eventually. Then the Amazons will fall, and Kara will be defeated. You just need to have..." before she could finish Lex interrupted "Patience. I know. If advice is all you have to offer I'd rather be alone"

Circe shrugged and with a small sigh conjured a portal to take her to her own magical dimension, she stepped through the circle of green fire, then it disappeared. Lex sat there for a few moments in silence, then he began typing at the computer. In seconds, there was a ringing noise and the digital display of the map disappeared and in its place popped up a video call. A woman wearing a figure hugging red dress appeared on the screen. She smiled as she saw Lex and said "Mr Luthor. It's been too long. What can I do for you today?" He smiled back at her and replied "Roulette. I have someone I think you might be interested in purchasing"

He was tired of Lena's defiance, and tired of being constantly hunted by that blonde Kryptonian. In only a few minutes he arranged a deal to sell Lena off. He didn't even care about the money, he just wanted to get rid of her as quickly as possible. With the deal arranged he switched off the display and went to find Lena, she was no doubt being toyed with by Mercy and Eve, since arriving here he had barely seen them they were so taken with her.

He found them in one of the common rooms of the facility. They were sitting next to each other on a couch, Lena was on Eve's lap and her legs were stretched out across Mercy. As Mercy stroked her supple legs, Eve was kissing Lena as she groped her breasts. Lena was bound and made small wriggles against the groping motions of the two women, but it was clear she would never be able to get away.

They were so focused on her that the two henchwomen didn't even notice Lex's arrival in the room, at first. Then, with a loud clearing of his throat, their eyes finally snapped up to him standing by the door. "Mr. Luthor! She.... She still isn't talking" Eve said nervously with a slight embarrassment, it was quite clear they hadn't been asking her any questions in quite some time.

"Let me g...mmppphhh!!" Lena tried to cry out as Eve finally stopped kissing her, but the blonde henchwoman just clamped her hand firmly over Lena's mouth to silence her. "Knock her out and gag her. We're leaving. Now." Lex said sternly before turning and leaving the room. Eve let out a said sigh and kissed Lena on the cheek as she said "Looks like our fun's over, cutie"

"Pass me the cloth" she said to Mercy who also looked disappointed at having to give Lena up. But she still complied, taking the cloth which sat beside her on the couch and handing it to Eve. "No! Mmmmpphhh!!" Lena let out one last defiant word as Eve lifted her hand from her mouth. The cloth quickly took its place, silencing Lena and forcing her once more to inhale the chemical scent of chloroform.

As Lena slowly succumbed to the chloroform, the two women groped her passionately, knowing this would likely be the last time. They stroked and caressed her long legs, squeezed the supple shape of her breasts. Their hands were all over Lena as her eyelids began to flutter closed, her weak moans becoming softer and softer until they stopped altogether. With a final soft sigh, Lena passed out, the tension leaving her body as she went completely limp. Eve pulled the cloth away and planted a final kiss on her plump lips. Then she tied a cloth over her mouth and lifted Lena's limp form up from the couch. She hoisted Lena up and settled her shapely bound figure atop her shoulder, carrying her away to be sold.

They had left the facility in Lex's private helicopter hours before Circe returned. The green fiery portal grew and she stepped out to find the place deserted. As she was walking around to make sure Lex had truly betrayed her she heard a rumbling from somewhere above the facility. That familiar sound let her know that Kara had discovered this facility as well, and that she was most likely smashing her way underground.

With angry sigh she began to conjure another portal to take her away from here. But just as the portal began to grow Kara arrived. She smashed through the ceiling, landing right between Circe and her portal. The sorceress could see her path was blocked, her normal calm demeanour flickering with fear. Kara saw her immediately, her eyes glaring at her with an enraged stare.

Before Circe could react Kara shot across the room. She grabbed Circe and slammed her into a nearby wall, knocking the air out of her.

Circe groaned as Kara held her up against the wall, then she felt a collar being slipped around her neck and locked into place. As soon as the collar was on she felt her magic leaving her, a weak sensation washing over her as the portal disappeared. "What... what did you do to me..." Circe moaned as her body trembled, her eyes fluttering as the lack of magic made a hazy stare settle over her expression.

"This collar was designed by Lena before you took her from me! Now where is she?!!" Kara yelled angrily as she slammed Circe into the wall again, making the sorceress moan from the heavy impact. "I... I don't know... I swear..." Circe sighed softly before passing out, the second slam into the wall having forced her into unconsciousness. Kara sighed, unsure if she should believe her or not. Either way she was coming back with her to Themyscira, another addition to her collection.

She lifted her up and settled her on her shoulder, hugging the woman's legs to keep them in line.

As she turned to fly away with Circe she noticed the computer monitor that Lex had been sitting at earlier. She walked over to it and tapped a few buttons, bringing the screen to life. On the display she saw an electronic readout, detailing Lena's sale to a woman named Roulette. It was some kind of online receipt, her beloved had been sold off like a common slave. Kara trembled with rage, her eyes narrowing as she stared at the name of the woman who now owned Lena. Her eyes burned red and her heat beams made the console explode in a fiery burst. Then, through the hole she had made in the ceiling she flew back up, capturing Circe and continuing her rampage across the world.

CHAPTER 07

Enslaved by Roulette

Chapter Summary: Roulette and Diana both begin to tame their new slaves - with starkly different methods - and Alex has a surprising request for Wonder Woman. Meanwhile, Kara's quest to rescue her beloved takes an unexpected turn.

"Mmmpphhh!! Mmmmpphhh!!" Lena moaned desperately with every firm spank. She was bent over Roulette's knees as the cruel villainess spanked her mercilessly. Lena had been in Veronica's clutches for weeks now, and the spankings were a common occurrence, yet the pain still felt fresh each time. Her backside was so juicy and soft, each time Roulette's hand came slamming down the pale skin grew slightly redder and more tender. Lena couldn't help herself, moaning through her gag as her hips wriggled side to side.

Lena was dressed in just a skimpy matched set of white bra and thong panties, the rest of her sensual figure completely bare. Her wrists were bound behind her back with a thin length of rope, as were ankles, keeping her neatly restrained as Roulette spanked her. Other than keeping her in captivity and routinely punishing her, Roulette had been taking care of her prisoner. She was washed and fed, kept in fresh skimpy underwear, even her hair had been styled and makeup applied. Roulette wanted her slave to be as beautiful as possible.

Roulette was wearing her usual tight fitting red dress, the long slit at one side showing off her long legs, the hole at the stomach displaying her toned midsection. She was a villain who had a lot of practise in capturing and enslaving women, it was her profession after all. She normally ran an underground fighting tournament, featuring men and women with superpowers, all enslaved and forced to combat for her guests amusement. That wasn't why she had captured Lena however.

Every now and then a beautiful woman would catch her attention, and Roulette would use her considerable resources to enslave them. But for her pleasure alone. Lena was one of those women. Except, much to Roulette's frustration, she had so far refused to submit.

Roulette delivered another few hard spanks to Lena's soft behind, letting her hand sink into the soft shape with a series of loud smacks. She smirked at the moans each spank elicited. She wasn't as caring or as gentle as Lena's previous owners, she simply wanted to break the woman's will; make her an obedient and submissive pleasure slave. They were deep in one of Roulette's underground facilities. The bedroom looked completely normal, a large double bed, soft sheets, a white carpet.

But outside were only steel hallways and prison cells, where Roulette kept her other acquisitions.

The final spank rang through the room, then Roulette's hand went still, resting on Lena's reddened backside for a moment, taking slow yet firm gropes as she let Lena catch her breath. Then she took her hips and rolled her over, sitting Lena up so she was in her lap. Roulette could see the look of distress on the gorgeous brunette's face, her eyes had become watery, her chest heaving up and down with her tired breaths. Roulette smiled, hoping that maybe this long spanking session had finally broken her.

One hand began calmly fondling Lena's breasts, first only squeezing outside the bra, but then slipping beneath the white fabric to feel her bosom in her palm. Lena made soft whimpers as Roulette pinched her nipples, her hand cupping each of Lena's breasts and squeezing them firmly. The other hand stroked up Lena's back, brushing her hair aside and finding the knot of the gag tied between Lena's plump lips. Roulette's fingers swiftly untied the knot then she pulled it away, the white cloth slipping from between Lena's lips.

Lena let out a small sigh as the gag was removed, her lips no longer stretched open. However the gag was quickly replaced by Roulette's mouth, forcing a long passionate kiss on Lena. Roulette pushed her tongue inside of Lena's mouth, letting out a pleasurable moan at the taste of the gorgeous woman. Then she pulled her mouth away and said "Mmmm so sweet." She quickly gave her another peck on the lips, then she looked deep into Lena's eyes "Are you ready to submit to me Lena? It really makes no difference either way, I'll never let you go. So you might as well just enjoy it. Give yourself to me. Surrender." Lena swallowed and looked away from Roulette's piercing gaze. It was difficult to resist the dominant woman but her thoughts of Kara gave her strength. She was still hanging onto the hope that she would be rescued by her beloved, and with that thought in her mind she looked back to Roulette with a defiant glare and replied "No! I'll never submit to you" Roulette let out a disappointed sigh and shook her head. She went back to firmly groping Lena as she said "Such a silly decision. I'm going to ravish you anyway, Lena, there's nothing you can do to stop me. Sooner or later you will submit. I waited patiently to have you as my prisoner, I can wait for as long as I need to for you to accept your place." Saying this, Roulette scooped Lena up from her lap, showing off her impressive strength as she cradled the helpless woman in her arms and tossed her onto the bed.

"I was planning on capturing and enslaving you long before you were a slave on that island, Lena." Roulette said calmly as she peeled off her red dress, leaving her just in a set of skimpy red lingerie "You see, this was always your fate. Wonder Woman struck first. But you were always supposed to belong to me." Lena made a frightened moan of fear as Roulette slowly moved onto the bed, closing in on her helpless prey.

Without the dress Lena could see just firm Roulette's body was, how much stronger and more powerful she was. It made Lena feel even more vulnerable. She could see how obsessed Roulette was with her, the woman's firm gaze getting closer until Roulette pounced. She quickly untied Lena's legs then pushed them apart as she began kissing and grinding on top of her, ravishing her for the hundredth time as she stripped off the white bra and panties.

"Tell me. Tell me you belong to me" Diana said as she lay atop her slave, their naked bodies entwined after a long session of passionate lovemaking. Their was a soft glow to their skin, the perspiration making them warm and hot. Alex had an exhausted yet satisfied smile on her face, her eyes half closed. Diana had worn her out; the Amazon princess having such an insatiable appetite that Alex felt on the verge of passing out. In the weeks , that Roulette had tried and failed to tame Lena, Diana had been far more successful with her slave.

Alex didn't hesitate at all, her lips parted as she replied softly "I belong to you" Diana smiled, stroking and squeezing Alex as she claimed her as her own. Then she kissed her deeply, grinding against her as she pushed her firmly into the soft sheets. After the long kiss Diana whispered into Alex's ear "Don't worry, I'm going to let you sleep now, my slave. Take a long deep breath for me" as she said this her hand slid over to a bedside table, smoothly picking up a cloth that was damp with chloroform.

Just before Diana could press it over Alex's mouth and nose her slave timidly asked "Mistress... before you put me to sleep.... Can I ask you something?" Diana paused with a curious expression. She wasn't a cruel mistress, she was willing to listen to her slaves as long as they were properly respectful in their requests. Keeping the cloth near she looked down into her slave's submissive gaze and replied "Very well. Go ahead" Alex smiled with a small flutter of eyelashes then said "I was hoping you could kidnap and enslave my girlfriend, Kelly Olsen. I love being your slave but I... I miss her. I know she'd be a good slave for you mistress.... We both would be..."

Diana smiled at the request, stroking her hand along Alex's head. She truly had tamed this once strong government agent. She was politely asking for her girlfriend to be captured as well, a request Diana was only too happy to oblige. A deep part of her mind still yearned for the days when she used to own and ravish Kara and Lena, but that was a long time ago, and neither of them had been as obedient and respectful as Alex (though Lena had always been soft and submissive, it was more due to how utterly helpless she was against Diana and her sisters, unlike Alex's clear and growing admiration for her mistress). The gorgeous brunette had taken so well to her training, and Diana was happy with spending her days here ravishing her. Adding her girlfriend would be even sweeter. But she'd have to get Kara's permission first.

"Very well, my slave. I will bring her here, and you will both serve me" Diana said as she gave Alex another long kiss. "Thank you mmmmpphhh...." Before Alex could even finish thanking her mistress, Diana pushed the cloth against her mouth and noise, enjoying the muffled moan she made as she silenced her words. It only took a few seconds for Alex's eyes to glaze over, her eyelids fluttering as her body went limp. Diana watched her gradual descent into unconsciousness with a pleased smile, watching as Alex's eyes drooped lower and lower until they closed completely.

Once Alex was unconscious, Diana tied her up and tied a white cloth between her mouth to gag her. She enjoyed putting her slaves into bondage whenever she had to leave for a while. If they weren't being used to pleasure her, then they would wait on the bed until she untied them. She tied Alex into a hogtie, making sure her nude form was nicely restrained. She also put a cloth with fresh chloroform under her nose, the scent would keep her out for hours. Then she got dressed in her red and blue superheroine attire, the modified version which had Kara's insignia on the front, never letting her forget who she served.

Slipping on her boots, she completed the outfit, then headed to the throne room, closing the doors and leaving Alex unconscious, naked, and bound on the bed. She walked through the palace and to the large golden doors of the throne room, pushing them open and heading inside. Kara was inside as she usually was, passing the time with her two new slaves. The leads for Roulette's whereabouts had run dry, so between waging her war on Man's World, Kara could normally be found here. She had recently broken in Lois Lane and Vicki Vale, and the two women were with her now, dressed only in white silk lingerie.

Vicki was kneeling at Kara's feet, kissing and worshipping them, pressing her lips softly into her mistress's feet as her backside stuck up in the air. Lois was sat on Kara's lap, tilted back slightly as Kara kissed her, groping and fondling her breasts at the same time. Kara had become the most dominant woman on this island, and both Lois and Vicki had been helpless to resist her commanding presence. Neither one resisted her anymore, not after a few initial weeks of training, their wills bending to the powerful kryptonian.

Diana walked up to the throne then lowered down to one knee, bowing her head to show her submission to Kara. The blonde Kryptonian peeled her lips away from Lois and looked down at Diana before saying "Speak." Losing Lena still haunted Kara, and her stony expression showed the anguish deep within her. Diana lifted her head as she said "My queen, with your permission, I would like to go to National City and kidnap a new slave: Kelly Olsen. She's my current pleasure slave's girlfriend, and I want to reunite them in servitude to me"

Kara took a moment to think about it, her hand casually stroking up and down Lois's bare thigh. Then she nodded and said "Very well" Diana thanked her and quickly left the throne room, going to prepare for her mission to National City. As Kara watched her go she let out a sad sigh, her mind as always still on Lena. Vicki was kissing her feet and Lois nuzzling her head against her neck, both her slaves just waiting to be played with. She reached down and pulled Vicki onto her lap again, letting them pleasure her as she tried to forget her longing thoughts.

She let them kiss her for a little while then hoisted them up onto her shoulders, using her impressive strength to carry them to her bedchambers. But, just as she tossed them down onto the bed, one of her Amazonian guards entered the room, running breathlessly to announce "My queen! One of our spies in Man's World has finally found it! We know where Roulette is hiding!" Kara instantly spun round, her fists clenching tightly as she said a single word "Where?!"

Lena's eyes fluttered open, a sleepy look going from confusion to fear as she made sense of her surroundings. After Roulette had ravished her she had swiftly knocked her out with chloroform. Usually Lena would normally awake bound and gagged on Roulette's bed, but this time she was strapped down to a medical table in an empty room. A ballgag was stuffed between her lips and she made muffled moans through it. Her wrists and ankles were secured with leather straps, keeping her flat on her back and facing the ceiling. She was still only in a pair of white bra and panties, her half naked body wriggling on the table to no avail.

She moaned and writhed on the table for a few minutes, her head tossing side to side, when finally the door opened. Roulette came strolling in, smiling at her helpless captive. As she walked alongside the table, she ran her hand along Lena's leg, stroking up to her thigh, then along her toned stomach, and finally squeezing her breasts firmly. She paused as she reached her head, stroking her hand along her cheek as she looked down at Lena and said "Your defiance has gone on far too long, my dear. So I've decided to speed things up." Roulette looked toward the door and spoke in a commanding tone as she said "Slaves! Come in here."

Lena's eyes widened as she saw two familiar women enter the room, one had jet black hair and was dressed in black lingerie as well as a pair of fishnet tights. The other was a redhead in green lingerie. Lena recognised them immediately, the first was the superheroine known as Zatanna, the other was a villainess called Poison Ivy. Roulette smiled at them then looked back to Lena and said "They've both been my brainwashed slaves for a little while now, and you're about to join them" seeing the two powerful women enslaved terrified Lena, they both had slightly mindless looks in their eyes, standing perfectly still as they waited for Roulette to tell them what to do.

Roulette walked up behind and gave them both a firm smack on their rounded behinds as she said "Help my new slave here, she's having trouble submitting to me like she should" in unison both brainwashed women replied "Yes mistress" then they began to advance on Lena. Zatanna began speaking in her backwards language, and Ivy walked right up to Lena and blew a cloud of pheromone dust right in her face, filling her lungs with the sweet smelling substance.

Lena could feel the combination of magic and pheromones turning her mind to jelly. It felt like a warm pulsing sensation slowly erasing all of her thoughts, destroying her will to resist. Her moans began to soften as she gave in to this feeling, her eyes glazing over as Roulette's slaves thoroughly brainwashed her. Roulette watched as she saw the submission grow in Lena's defeated gaze, a wide smile spreading across her face as she used her slaves to brainwash yet another helpless woman.

Lena belonged to her now and nothing was ever going to change that.

As Lena was being brainwashed, Roulette walked up beside her table, looming over as she looked down at her slave. Her hand ran back behind her head and she undid the ballgag, slipping it from between her lips "Now. Tell me you belong to me" she said as she looked straight into Lena's eyes.

Lena had nothing left to fight with, her mind was completely blank, conditioned to submit, and in a whimpering tone she replied "I... I belong to you..." Roulette smiled and replied "That's right"

She spent the next couple of hours continuing Lena's brainwashing, slowly breaking down her mind and installing a series of instructions that would keep Lena enslaved forever. Zatanna and Ivy continued affecting Lena's mind as Roulette spoke to her, each woman using their unique methods to keep Lena completely under Roulette's control. The therapy was still continuing when suddenly the whole facility shook. Something was breaking into the underground hideout, and it was approaching the room quickly.

Roulette smirked as she stroked Lena's soft cheek and said "Let's see just how brainwashed you are" Just as she said this the door flew open, an enraged blonde kryptonian stood there shaking with anger. "Lena!" she called out as her eyes widened with delight. She rushed over, pushing Roulette aside and instantly breaking the straps of the table as she freed her beloved. Lena blinked rapidly as her mindless stare focused on Kara. Then as Kara tried to pull her off of the table and into her arms Lena screamed in fear.

"Stay away from me!" Lena shrieked as she wriggled out of Kara's grip and scurried over to Roulette, hiding behind her as she whimpered "She's trying to take me away from you, mistress!" Kara's mouth hung open in shock, her eyes becoming watery as she realised Lena had been completely brainwashed, her beloved didn't even seem to recognise her. Roulette smirked at Kara as she hugged Lena close and said "Don't worry my slave. I won't let her have you"

Kara gritted her teeth in anger, trembling as she prepared to attack Roulette for what she had done. But then suddenly vines broke through the floor, wrapping around her legs, magical glowing chains suddenly appeared around her arms pulling them behind her back. She hadn't noticed the other two women in the room were Poison Ivy and Zatanna, she had thought they were just more of Roulette's slaves. She groaned furiously as she was restrained, forced to watch as Roulette began groping Lena right in front of her.

Roulette reached into her dress and pulled out a white cloth as she said soothingly to Lena "I'm going to knock you out now my slave. That's what you want isn't it? To be made helpless by your mistress?" Kara moaned angrily as she tried to break free of the vines and chains wrapping around her, but she went silent as she saw Lena look fearfully at her then lovingly at Roulette "Yes mistress. That's all I want. Please kidnap and ravish me." Lena said in a soft tone, making Kara go back to her furious moaning.

Roulette made Kara watch as she held Lena close and pushed a white cloth over her mouth and nose, forcing her to inhale the fumes of chloroform as she calmly squeezed her backside. Lena's eyes slowly drooped closed and she went limp in Roulette's grip. Roulette lowered her down to the floor and turned her over, pulling her wrists behind her back as she quickly tied her up. Once Lena's limbs were bound, Roulette gagged her sleeping captive as well, then she lifted the drugged and brainwashed damsel up and hoisted Lena over her shoulder.

SEX AND CHAOS

"She belongs to me now" Roulette said mockingly as she displayed Lena's bound and gagged form over her shoulder, giving Lena's shapely rump a possessive spank and squeeze. Kara tried to jerk forward but her restraints wouldn't allow it. Lena was so close yet she still couldn't have her, and the blonde kryptonian tensed her muscles as hard as she could. Roulette looked to Zatanna as she said "Open a portal then take care of blondie here" Zatanna nodded and replied "Yes mistress" then with a few magical words a shimmering portal opened and Roulette stepped through with Lena.

"NO!!" Kara screamed as the portal closed, taking Lena away from her once again. Feeling a sudden burst of rage she broke free of the chains and the vines, sending them scattering around the room. She then flew at Zatanna and Ivy, slamming them into a wall and instantly knocking them out. She looked at and took heavy breaths as she held them up against the wall, then she lifted them and placed them over her shoulders. Lena had been taken again, but these two would help her get her back. With an unconscious woman on either shoulder, Kara flew out of the room, heading back to Paradise Island.

Diana's boots touched down on the balcony of Kelly Olsen, making a quiet landing as she closed in on her prey. The door was open and on the other side of the curtains Diana could hear two female voices. It seemed Kelly wasn't alone. Diana peered through, seeing that another gorgeous woman was with her, she didn't know it but the woman's name was Samantha Arias and she was a close friend of Kara, Lena, and Alex. All Diana saw was another woman to be captured and enslaved, and she stayed on the balcony while she prepared two cloths to subdue them both.

Kelly and Samantha were both sitting on the couch discussing Kara's, Lena's, and now Alex's disappearances with grave concern as Diana suddenly walked in from the balcony. They were both well aware that the Amazon princess had been capturing women lately, and they both tried to run for the door as she advanced on them. She was far too quick though, she rushed forward and grabbed them, pulling them back against her and pressing the cloths over their mouths at the same time. They both moaned and struggled, but the Amazon was far too strong, she easily kept them in her tight grip as she felt them going limp in her arms.

Kelly was just as beautiful as Alex, and Diana was already looking forward to taming her, having two women who were once girlfriends now serving her. Samantha was just a welcome addition to the slaves on Paradise island, it would be up to Kara to decide what was done with her. Diana held them until they both passed out, slumping against her as she kept them on their feet. Then she slowly slid the cloths away, revealing their now resting features. She spun them around and crouched down, letting them slump over her shoulders as she hoisted them into the air. She gave each of their backsides a firm squeeze then she carried them to the balcony, easily capturing the two beautiful women.

By the time Diana walked off of her private jet, Kelly and Samantha had been stripped down to their bra and panties, and they were both bound and gagged. Diana had taken the time to prepare the new slaves properly to Kara, but as she walked into throne room Kara was busy with two more new arrivals to the island. She had Ivy and Zatanna wrapped in the lasso of truth, the magical item now belonging to the kryptonian queen. Diana walked in and paused, not wanting to interrupt.

Kara looked to her and Diana slid the two women off of her shoulders, lowering them to their knees as she said "My queen. I captured Kelly Olsen with your permission. But there was another woman... what would you have me do with her?" Kara looked Samantha up and down, she was still sleepy from the chloroform, kneeling with her eyes half closed, barely conscious. She might not be Lena, but she still looked utterly alluring in just her bra and panties. Kara nodded in approval and replied "Take her to my bedchambers and leave her there for me. You may keep Kelly for yourself."

Diana smiled and the lifted the two women back up, putting them back over her shoulders as she replied "Thank you, my queen" she was looking forward to reuniting Alex with her girlfriend, and to breaking in this new beautiful slave. As she left she could still hear Kara interrogating the two woman she had tied up, but she knew not to get involved unless her queen commanded it.

With the lasso of truth Kara got all the information she needed out of Ivy and Zatanna, learning everything about Lena's deep brainwashing. There was apparently no straightforward way to break the powerful combination of pheromones and magic that had broken her mind. Kara would need to capture Lena and retrain her like any other slave on this island. She would effectively have to enslave this new version of Lena, and force her to love her again. It wasn't what Kara wanted, she wanted Lena to willingly give herself over, as she had done before. But she had no other choice.

Kara prepared some ropes and a dampened a cloth with chloroform. She then knocked out and tied Ivy up, handing her over to her most trusted Amazons to be trained. She kept Zatanna, forcing her to open a portal to wherever Roulette was hiding. The portal opened and Kara gagged Zatanna so she couldn't speak another word, tying a thick white cloth between her plump lips. She then chloroformed her just to be safe, leaving her on the floor of the throne room and Kara shot through the portal.

She emerged in a bedroom, in another one of Roulette's underground facilities. Roulette was on top of Lena and they were kissing passionately. Lena was smiling between deep moans, happily submitting to Roulette "Get off of her!" Kara yelled angrily rushing over and tossing Roulette across the room. Lena screamed and tried to scramble off the bed but Kara grabbed her and held her down. She was so focused on Lena that she didn't notice Roulette grabbing her red dress and hurrying away, escaping the kryptonian's wrath for now.

"No! Let me go!" Lena squealed as she tried wriggling away. But Kara simply held her to the bed, looking down at Lena with a firm expression as she replied "No! You're coming home with me" Lena tried to fight her, to turn her head to the side. But Kara wouldn't allow it, she took the cloth tucked into her skirt and pushed it against Lena's mouth and nose, forcing her to inhale the scent of chloroform. Lena used to look lovingly into Kara's eyes whenever she did this to her. But now Kara could only see fear as her beloved's eyes slowly fluttered closed.

With a muffled sigh Lena sank down into unconsciousness, her struggles dying down until she went completely still. Kara lay on top of her, keeping the cloth in place just to be sure. Then she slowly peeled it away from Lena's lips, looking at how beautiful Lena was as she slept. She leaned down and kissed her gently on the lips, then she rolled her over and tied her wrists together.

She moved down to her legs and tied those as well, restraining Lena like she would any other slave. Zatanna's portal was still open, and Kara wanted to get Lena back home as soon as possible. Roulette could be dealt with later. She hoisted Lena up onto her shoulder, stroking her long legs with a small smile at finally having Lena back. Then she stepped through the portal and it disappeared.

Roulette sighed a breath of relief as she watched Kara leaving on a monitor. She had fled to a safe room that displayed CCTV footage of this entire facility, hiding from the kryptonian in fear. But now she saw that Kara was letting her get away, and she let out a small laugh at how foolish the decision was. Behind her in the shadows was an unseen accomplice who Roulette had been working with, and the villainess glanced over her shoulder as she remarked "She's taken her.

Everything is going perfectly according to plan…"

CHAPTER 08

Lena's Mental Manipulation

Chapter Summary: *Kara grows increasingly frustrated with Lena's brainwashed state of mind while Diana seeks to tame a surprisingly defiant Kelly. Just as Kara's frustration reaches a tipping point, she makes a promising discovery...*

"Let me go!" Lena moaned as she wriggled beneath Kara, her limbs flailing as she tried to get free. They were lying on the bed in Kara's private chambers, the silk sheets now all ruffled from Lena's squirming. She was wearing only a pair of white bra and panties, her sensual figure practically nude from how revealing her underwear was. Kara was dressed in her red pleated skirt and blue top with her house crest emblazoned on the chest, the only thing missing were her boots which she had removed to get on the bed with Lena.

Kara had hoped being gentle with her, caressing and kissing her, as she untied her would ease Lena back to her old self. But as soon as the ropes were off she had begun struggling and trying to get away. "Stop... you love me... I know you do..." Kara said in a frustrated tone as she pinned Lena's wrists to the bed, looming over her as Lena continued wriggling her legs up and down "No I don't! Let me go!" moaned Lena in reply, her hips trying to buck up from the bed as her head tossed angrily side to side.

"Fine! But you will submit to me!" Kara finally snapped, her frustration growing to a boiling point. She had been trying to patiently bring Lena's memories back, but it was too much for her to withstand, having the woman she loved constantly trying to escape her. She pulled her over to the side of the bed, her super strength easily overpowering Lena. She then sat down and forced Lena over her lap, holding her across her knees as she rose her hand into the air.

SMACK! Kara's palm came down on Lena's soft rump with a loud sound, her hand slamming into the tender flesh and making it jiggle. She then rose her hand again and settled into a steady rhythm, spanking Lena over and over again as she said "You might not remember our love but you will submit to me Lena! I am your queen!!" She continued spanking her at that same pace, her hand rising and falling as Lena moaned in pain.

Lena made small wriggles of her hips as she was spanked, the pain pulsing through her as her bottom turned a light shade of red. Then finally, with a girlish whimper, she cried out "Please! Please stop!" her eyes became watery as she begged for her punishment to end, and with a final extra hard smack, Kara let her hand rest on Lena's backside. "Tell me you submit" Kara said sternly, ready to continue the spanking if needed. "I submit. I submit." Lena moaned weakly, trying to hold back tears.

Kara let out a satisfied sigh and pulled Lena off of her lap, then back over to the bed. She lay on top of her again, and this time Lena didn't resist. But as Kara started kissing her she didn't see that

loving look in Lena's eyes that she cherished. She saw fear and submission, but it wasn't what Kara wanted. She continued kissing her gently, grinding her body into Lena's on the bed as she whispered "You love me Lena... I know you do..."

"Let me go this instant!" at the exact same time that Kara was struggling to bring back the old Lena, Diana was also having a problem with one of her slaves. She had been trying to train Kelly for the past few days, but no matter how many times she spanked her, or left her in tight bondage, the attractive young woman just wouldn't submit. She had Kelly sitting on her lap, tied up in just her underwear, the ropes pressing into her supple light brown skin.

Diana had left her in a rigid hogtie overnight, then she had woken her with a long spanking session, then finally she had forced her to inhale a little chloroform while she kissed and groped her on the bed. All of that combined normally began to break Diana's slaves, easing them into their new roles as her submissive playthings. She had expected to remove the gag and hear whimpering pleas, but instead Kelly just went right back to squirming around on her lap, moaning angrily about not wanting to be in captivity.

Diana sighed and clamped her hand down over Kelly's mouth. Diana was in a silky white nightdress, it showed of her powerful figure nicely, the white silk resting against the svelte curves of her feminine frame. Despite Kelly's protestations she easily kept her hand in place as she looked at her said "Wouldn't you be so much happier just submitting to me? Look at how much your girlfriend is enjoying accepting her place as my slave."

SEX AND CHAOS

As she said this she glanced down at the floor where Alex was currently on her knees, kissing and worshipping Diana's feet. She was completely naked, bent down to plant soft kisses on her mistresses feet, going from one foot then the other. Kelly looked down at her and moaned angrily through Diana's palm. She was well aware that Alex was now the Amazon's submissive slave, but the anger still hadn't faded, and every time she saw her girlfriend submitting to this woman, it made her livid. Diana smirked at how angry Kelly was, and she leaned in to kiss her gently on the neck in a soothing manner.

"Relax, my pet..." she whispered as she planted another soft kiss on Kelly's smooth skin, her tone becoming sultry and soft "I brought you here so you could be together. So you could both submit to me... In fact, it was your girlfriend who begged me to bring you here. She wants you to submit just as much as I do." It was the first time Kelly had heard this and her eyes snapped open wide in shock. Then she began squirming even more furiously in Diana's lap, her muffled moans becoming louder beneath Diana's palm.

"Hmmm I don't think your girlfriend is enjoying herself..." Diana said teasingly as she began calmly groping Kelly, squeezing her breasts as she writhed around. "Why don't you tell her how much you love being my slave, Alex" At Diana's command Alex instantly rose up so she was kneeling with her behind resting on the heels of her feet. She made her back straight and lay her hands on her thighs, her perky breasts hanging weightlessly on her chest. Once she had settled into the submissive pose at Diana's feet she said "I love being your slave mistress. I live to serve you"

Alex's tone was timid and soft, her lips curled into a dreamy smile as she happily spoke of her submission. "You see? Don't you want to be just like her? You could be kneeling right next to her, submitting to me" Diana said as she kissed Kelly on the neck again and gave her breasts a firm squeeze. But still, Kelly just moaned angrily through Diana's palm, her bound body wriggling side to side.

Diana pulled her lips away and looked calmly into Kelly's eyes as she assessed her. She might've been wrong about this one; there were some women who needed to be given an amount of power. "It seems you have something to say. If you behave yourself I'll remove my hand." Diana said as she looked firmly into Kelly's eyes, making it clear if she didn't obey she would be gagged and put back in the hogtie. Kelly let out a small sigh and nodded to show she understood, then Diana slowly peeled her hand away from her mouth.

Kelly took a slow breath then looked down at Alex, she couldn't believe how submissive her girlfriend was now, nothing like the strong government agent she had known. But still she loved her and as she looked down at her she said "Alex... what are you doing? I thought you were infiltrating this island to rescue Kara and Lena and all the other women who have been enslaved here. And now you're just another slave yourself? Snap out of it!"

Alex just sighed and shook her head as if Kelly was saying something completely absurd, then she replied in that same timid tone "Don't be silly, Kelly. No one can escape Diana or queen Kara, they're just too strong. Against women like them, submission is the only option. I love being Diana's slave, I'm happy here and you will be too" Kelly could see that Alex had been completely enslaved, there was no reasoning with her. Diana had truly tamed her mind and body. She let out a sad sigh and as she did Diana began gently groping her again, leaning in to whisper at her ear "See? Happy and submissive. I take good care of my slaves. But I can see that you're something special, so I'll make you a different offer..."

Kelly's brow furrowed and she looked at Diana curiously to see what she meant. Diana smiled as she saw she had Kelly's attention and continued "On this island there are soldiers and slaves. I will train you to be an Amazon soldier. You will still belong to me, but Alex will be below you. When I permit it, she will be yours to do with as you please" Kelly remained silent for a moment, looking from Diana down to Alex who was still kneeling, obediently waiting to be told what to do. She couldn't deny there was something alluring about seeing her girlfriend nude and on her knees; she was so submissive that Kelly could already imagine dominating her in bed.

"It's either this or bondage and a prison cell, and you'll never see her again..." Diana said softly as she made another playful squeeze of Kelly's bosom. Kelly looked to her and nodded as she let out a defeated sigh "Okay... you win... I'll let you train me..." Diana smiled happily, every woman was a unique puzzle to figure out in their enslavement, and this one had just been been broken. "And that means you'll be my willing slave, Kelly. I want you to say it" Kelly nodded and sighed softly "I... I'll be your willing slave"

SEX AND CHAOS

"Good girl" Diana said as she planted a soft kiss on Kelly's lips. The two of them reminded her of Kara and Lena when she had first brought them here and began their training. Kara had been so headstrong and defiant, while Lena was a natural submissive, becoming obedient almost immediately. Kelly and Alex were the exact same way, one easily tamed while the other was unable to be fully controlled.

It made Diana crave for the days when she had Kara and Lena in her possession, the two types of personalities were so much fun to enslave at the same time, especially when they both had feelings for each other. Diana had felt these feelings before, but she was unwilling to betray her queen. Kara had taken over the island completely, and for now Diana would still submit to her authority.

"I have to get approval for you're training from our queen" Diana said as she kissed Kelly again, letting her know that she would now be kissing her whenever she desired "But as a reward for your submission, I will allow you some time alone with your girlfriend. However, you must follow the rules of this island. Alex is a pleasure slave, and you must treat her as such. Do you understand, Kelly?" Diana watched as Kelly looked down at Alex, then nodded and replied "Yes. I understand"

Just like with Lena and Kara, using the submissive girlfriend was an effective way of getting the more resilient girl to comply, and Diana could see this was already working with Kelly, she had a small hint of lust in her eyes, and the more she ravished the submissive Alex, the more she would come to enjoy being here. Diana lifted her up from her lap and set her down on the bed, then she began to untie her, loosening the ropes on her arms and legs.

She freed Kelly but left the ropes lying on the bed, laying a cloth that could be used as a gag beside them. Diana then slid off of the bed and stood beside it as she said "Onto the bed, Alex. Kelly is one of my soldiers now and she has my permission to use you as she desires; you're to let her tie you and gag you" Alex nodded with a happy smile as she said "Thank you mistress" quickly getting to her feet and sliding onto the bed. Alex shuffled up onto the bed then lay down on her back, waiting for Kelly to take her.

Diana crossed her arms and looked to Kelly who was still a little hesitant "Tie her and gag her.

Show me you deserve to be a soldier here. Once you have her properly restrained, only then may you ravish her" Kelly could feel herself being pulled into Diana's control, but when she looked at Alex she just couldn't resist. Her girlfriend was lying there so submissively on the bed, her nude form right next to a pile of ropes just waiting for her. "Yes... mistress..." Kelly said before turning her attention on Alex, snatching up the ropes and looming over her.

Diana stood there and watched as Kelly began binding Alex. Every now and then she would instruct her to make the ropes a little tighter, but mostly she remained silent as she enjoyed the sight of one of her slaves tying up another. She could see Kelly was enjoying herself, stroking and squeezing Alex's supple skin as she tied ropes around it. She tied her wrists tightly behind her back, confidently handling Alex's body into the position she required it. She then tied more ropes around her torso, above and below her breasts so that they squeezed into the two soft shapes.

"Very good..." Diana said in a sultry tone as Kelly finished with a final few ropes around Alex's legs "...now the gag" at Dianas instruction Kelly picked up the white cloth, stretching it out between her hands. She leaned down and kissed Alex on the mouth, then she pushed the cloth between her lips and tied it behind her head. With the gag in place Alex's bondage was complete. Kelly could feel her heart pounding in her chest as she looked down at her bound and gagged girlfriend. She had just tied Alex up like a slave, and she had found it utterly thrilling.

Diana could see the excited look in Kelly's eyes and she smiled as she said "I'm going to ask permission from our queen. While I'm gone you have my permission to ravish her. You may untie her legs if you wish but the other ropes remain on. This reward is to celebrate your submission to me Kelly. But after today you will have to earn your time with Alex by serving me faithfully. Do you understand?"

Kelly could barely take her eyes off of Alex's naked body, she was practically trembling in anticipation of using her for her own pleasure. She turned her head and nodded eagerly as she said "Yes mistress. Thank you!" Diana smiled and went to the door as she replied "You're welcome, my slave. Have fun" she then slipped out of the room and closed it behind her. She waited by the door for a second, and almost immediately she began to hear both women moaning in pleasure as Kelly ravished the helpless Alex.

Diana felt an immense sense of satisfaction in taming both women, it made her feel strong and in control. But as she walked down the hallways of the palace she knew she was going to a woman who held even more power. The queen's chambers were only a little way from hers, and she soon made her way to the door, knocking on it and waiting for an answer. Inside, Kara was still lying ontop of Lena, kissing and groping her as she tried to remind her of how much she enjoyed this.

Kara heard the knock and tilted her head up from Lena with an annoyed expression. She then looked down at Lena and said firmly "Don't move. I don't want to have to punish you again" Lena nodded and Kara slid off of her, getting to her feet and calling out "Enter" The door pushed open and she saw Diana walking in then bowing her head in the appropriate pose of submission to her queen.

"What is it, Diana?" Kara asked impatiently, her failure with Lena still making her feel angry. Diana raised her head and replied "My queen, Kelly has proven that she would be better served as a soldier. I request your permission to train her. I intend to keep both her and Alex as my slaves, rewarding Kelly with Alex at appropriate times" Kara was well aware this was exactly what Diana had done with her and Lena, but neither woman spoke of this. At least back then, Lena had loved Kara back.

Kara looked over to Lena on the bed as a thought came to her and she said "Very well... But while you're training her, I want you to train another of our recent captives: Samantha Arias is still being kept in the prison cells. Take her and train her as a soldier as well. She will be acting as Lena's personal bodyguard when I'm not around. No one is ever going to kidnap my Lena and take her from me again. Do you understand?"

Diana was about to reply when she was suddenly interrupted. From the bed Lena gasped "You have Sam, Alex, and Kelly all here as your slaves? Let them go, you monster!" she began trying to slide off of the bed and run for the door, but Kara grabbed her and tossed her back on the bed. The kryptonian then angrily looked at Diana and said "Follow my orders. And close the door behind you!"

"Yes, my queen" Diana said as she left Kara to wrestle Lena down to the bed. She quickly slipped out and closed the door then walked through the halls of the palace and out of the main doors. The walk to the prison cells took her through the city streets, past Amazons and their slaves being led around by ropes tied to their wrists or their necks like a leash. The prison cells were quite comfortable, they had soft beds for when the Amazons would come in and ravish their captives. All the women being kept here were yet to be claimed, neither soldier or pleasure slave, this was a type of waiting area where they were kept in constant bondage until a decision was made.

Diana made her way along a row of steel doors. At the end of the row was a much thicker door that led down into a dungeon, but she had no need to go there, that was only for the worst of Themyscira's enemies. She stopped at a door about halfway down the row, unlocking it to reveal Samantha bound and gagged on a bed, her body wrapped up so tightly with so many ropes she could barely move. Like Kelly, she had proven to be resilient, but Diana was just looking forward to another challenge and she stepped into the room and beheld the wide-eyed and whimpering captive with an excited smile.

"You remember their names, but not mine!" Kara seethed angrily as she kept Lena pinned down to the bed, holding her wrists and looming over her. "Let my friends go!" Lena moaned in reply, going back to her struggles to escape. It killed Kara to see Lena remembering everyone else except her, the one person who Lena had once loved the most. Her eyes trembled with rage and she let out an angry yell as she looked for the nearest rope she could restrain Lena with.

It happened to be the Lasso of Truth, which now belonged to her, neatly coiled on the nightstand by the bed. Kara snatched it up without thinking, then she began wrapping it around Lena's midsection, pinning her arms down by her sides. As she tied her tightly with the golden rope she spoke in angry heaving breaths, trying to hold back tears "You love me Lena! Some part of you has to remember that! Please just tell me..."

Before Kara could finish Lena suddenly spoke in a calm voice, lying still on the bed as her struggles stopped "I love you" Kara paused in shock, still holding the rope but staring down in disbelief at Lena "What... what did you say?" she asked nervously, hoping she hadn't just imagined the words coming out of Lena's mouth. Lena let a small sigh then smiled as she repeated "I love you, Kara."

Kara couldn't control herself, she smiled giddily then instantly lay down on top of Lena and began to kiss her. They kissed for a long while, smiling and letting out small moans of pleasure, until finally Kara said "I don't understand. Has the spell been broken?" Lena's happy smile turned to sadness as she shook her head and replied "No, my love. Roulette's brainwashing is still holding me captive within my own mind. I'm aware of everything - able to hear you pleading with me - but on the outside I can only respond as if I have no idea who you are. I'm... sorry..." Kara leaned down and kissed her again then said softly "Don't be sorry. I'm going to find a way to keep you like this. Are you sure it isn't permanent?" Lena shook her head again and said "No, it's just the lasso. I can feel it fighting against Roulette's influence but it won't work forever"

Knowing their time was short, they continued kissing for a little while, the soft shape of their lips pressing together over and over. Kara's hands ran over Lena's body, stroking and groping her. With the lasso against her, Lena now moaned in pleasure, smiling and kissing Kara happily as her body was gently caressed. It was exactly what Kara wanted, but she couldn't keep Lena tied up in the lasso of truth forever, she needed a way to make this permanent.

They made out on the bed for so long that the sun set outside, the two women lost in their passionate embrace. While they had been kissing, a thought had come to Kara, and she now knew what she had to do to try and save Lena from her brainwashing. She leaned over to the nightstand by the bed, sliding open the drawer and retrieving a small brown bottle along with a white cloth. She then drizzled some of the chloroform from the bottle onto the cloth, making the fabric damp.

Lena could see what she was about to do, and she knew it was necessary; as soon as the lasso was removed she would go back to struggling to escape. Kara was hesitant to remove the lasso, but she had to be sure that Lena's mind would revert back to its previous state without it. She sadly took one end of the magical rope and said "I promise I'm going to find a way to reverse this" then she leaned down and kissed Lena one more time before untying her.

As soon as the rope wasn't touching her skin Lena made a few confused blinks, as if she didn't know where she was. Then a scared expression came across her face, that loving look disappearing completely "Get away from me!" she shrieked as she tried to scramble off the bed. But Kara was prepared for this reaction, and she quickly pinned her down and grabbed the cloth with the chloroform.

She lay down on top of her, keeping her body against the bed with her own, her weight able to control Lena's writhing motions. Then she simply pressed the cloth over Lena's mouth and nose, holding it there and forcing her to inhale the chloroform. Kara had a sad expression as she watched Lena fading away, those brief moments of having her back now gone. Lena kept trying to fight even as her body went limp, her hands pushing weakly at Kara until they flopped down to the bed.

Lena let out a small muffled sigh as her eyes drooped half closed, becoming soft and listless as she looked up at Kara's unhappy expression. Then with a small flutter they sank closed, Lena fading into unconsciousness and going limp beneath Kara. She lay atop Lena for a few moments longer, keeping the cloth in place to ensure she was deeply asleep. Then she peeled it away and kissed Lena softly on the lips.

Kara was more determined now than ever to reverse the magical influence on Lena's mind, and her sad expression hardened into a steely stare. After securely binding and gagging her beloved captive, Kara left Lena sleeping peacefully on the bed as she flew out of her bedchambers, shooting through the night toward the Themyscira prison cells. Her feet touched down on the floor in front of the prison building and she walked right in with angry strides.

Her fists were clenched and swung by her sides as she walked past the rows of steel doors, her firm gaze focused only on the door at the end, the one that led down into the dungeons. She pushed open the door to the dungeons, making a loud clang that echoed down the staircase that led beneath the island. That clanging sound bounced against the stone walls, travelling all the way to the woman who was locked inside the most high security cell.

In that dark dungeon, behind a thick metal door, knelt Circe. A steel collar was around her neck, a chain attaching it to the ground. Her wrists were shackled and bolted down to the ground as well, keeping her stuck on her knees. On the collar and shackles magical symbols were inscribed, dampening Circe's magic. On the floor around her a much larger symbol was drawn, cutting her off from her magic completely as long as she remained in the centre.

She had been stripped down to just her underwear, a skimpy pair of black bra and panties. Around her mouth was a thick leather gag, buckled tightly, the straps pressing into her cheeks. But despite the gag and the heavy bondage, a small smile began to form under the thick leather, her head tilting up toward that loud clanging noise of the door high above her opening. The sorceress knew Kara was coming for her help, and in the darkness of her cell her eyes sparkled with delight.

CHAPTER 09

Circe's Bargain

Chapter Summary: *Circe can help Kara get Lena's memories back... for a price. While considering Circe's proposal, Kara diplomatically reaches an agreement with her disgruntled subjects.*

Deep in the dungeon of Paradise Island, Kara had wrapped the Lasso of Truth around Circe's neck. The villainess was still chained on her knees, trapped with the restraints that cut her off from her mystical powers. But, while she seemed helpless, her expression was smug and confident. She looked up at the blonde kryptonian with a sly smile and said "Oh you don't need that. I wouldn't lie to you... my queen" her voice was light and teasing, for even though she was on her knees, she knew she had the power over Kara.

Kara finished looping the rope over her neck, and stood up straight, holding one end while her other hand rested on her hip. The lasso began to faintly glow with a golden sheen and Kara took a slow breath before saying "You obviously know why I'm here. The spell on Lena's mind... can you lift it?" Circe smiled as she looked up into Kara's nervous eyes and replied "I can. But I won't..." Kara's eyes widened in shock and she opened her mouth to angrily say something. But Circe cut her off, smoothly continuing "...Unless.

You agree to three requests. No negotiations.

You will agree or you will never have your beloved back"

There was a tense silence as Kara sighed angrily, looking down at Circe as she went over her options. She had none, Circe was her last chance and the wicked sorceress knew it. Kara's jaw clenched, knowing she wouldn't like the answer to this question but saying it anyway "Fine. What do you want?" Circe smirked at how difficult this was for the little impudent queen, and she took a moment before replying, to leave her in suspense "My first request is the restoration of all my powers." Kara nodded, as this was the most obvious. "Second, my unquestioned freedom. You will release me and never attempt to restrain me again"

Kara took a second to think then replied "Only on the condition that you never set foot upon Paradise Island again. I won't allow you to mount another attack against me once you have your freedom" Circe was happy to comply and quickly replied "Agreed. As long as you're in charge, I will never return. And for my third request..." Kara knew something bad was coming, she could see the devious glint in Circe's eyes. The first two requests were an easy trade to have Lena's mind restored, but now she was holding her breath with a worried anticipation.

"I want Hippolyta. The original queen of this island is coming with me to be my personal pleasure slave" Kara eye's widened and she furiously replied "Absolutely not! The Amazons follow me because they know their loyalty will be rewarded. I can't sell off their former queen! There has to be something else..." Before she could finish, Circe raised her voice and spoke over her "You will give me Hippolyta or you will never have Lena back. I told you there would be no negotiations, Kryptonian. So either leave my cell, or agree to my terms"

Kara went silent for a moment, glaring angrily at Circe before replying "Okay. You will have what you desire" She was blinded by her love for Lena, willing to do anything to get her back. But to capture and subdue Hippolyta was a great betrayal of the Amazons who served her. Kara had a lot on her mind and she didn't want to spend a second longer in Circe's presence. She turned and stormed out of the cell, slamming the door shut as she tried to figure out what she should do.

Lena was back in Kara's bedchambers, laying on her bed in just a silky white nightdress that failed to cover the curve of her pleasantly plump, heart-shaped bottom. She lay there bound and gagged, thin ropes tied tightly to her body, and a white cloth tied equally tightly over her pouty lips, holding in her mouth a wad of cloth that muffled her thoroughly. This was a necessity now, for if she wasn't restrained and gagged at all times, she would immediately try to get as far away from Kara as possible and cry out in protest at her captivity. She lay there making muffled moans through her gag, her sensual figure writhing around on the soft sheets.

As she moaned, Lena heard footsteps approaching the door, her wide eyes looking across the room and expecting to see Kara bursting in. But when the doors opened it wasn't Kara, it was three Amazons sneaking in with cautious expressions. They were unarmed and wore simple white dresses that stopped at their thighs, their sandals making a soft tapping on the marble floor of the royal bedchamber. "There she is" one whispered and they made their way toward the bed.

The three of them were quite beautiful, they had the toned figures of Amazons; the chiselled features and flowing hair. But, despite the abundance of beauty on the island, they only had eyes for Lena. Before Kara had conquered the island, Lena had been passed around to all the Amazons, given to them like a present to be used as they wished. These three Amazons weren't able to forget the memories of ravishing the helpless beauty, and they were here now to once again kidnap and have their way with her.

Lena watched them approaching and shook her head, making a frustrated moan as she tried to wriggle away from them. "Are you sure about this?" one of them asked, nervously looking around the bedchambers. One of the Amazons was clearly leading this operation, and she opened a bedside drawer to reveal a white cloth and a small brown bottle "Yes I'm sure." She said as she took the items out and set them on the bed "This is the most desirable pleasure slave on the whole island..." As she said this she reached for Lena, stroking a hand along her leg and rump, as if to display just why this was worth the risk.

"Our queen can't just keep her locked up for herself. It isn't right!" The other two still seemed

nervous about incurring Kara's wrath, but as they looked at Lena lying on the bed in her skimpy nightwear, they decided to stay. Their eyes took in her soft and smooth legs, her creamy skin yearning to be stroked. Her breasts pushed out at the white fabric on her torso, the silk rippling against the two bulging, soft mounds. While they looked at her in awe, their leader prepared the chloroform, drizzling out some of the chemical onto the white cloth.

"Mmmppphhh!!!" Lena moaned as she saw the cloth become damp, knowing exactly what was about to happen. She made a wriggling motion as the lead Amazon crawled toward her on the bed. Then the Amazon lunged forward, pressing the cloth down over Lena's mouth and nose in one smooth motion. The other two watched with a pounding in their chests, eager to get their own time to make Lena helpless. After a valiant but pitifully useless struggle, Lena's legs and the toes of her bare feet made a slight twitch, then went still, her eyes drooping with a faraway stare. But the Amazon wasn't ready to knock Lena out fully just yet; not when they had the whole night to ravish her.

She brought Lena down into a drowsy state, then peeled the cloth away from her plump lips. She leaned down and kissed Lena, then began sliding her off of the bed "Let's go" she said firmly as she pulled Lena up and over her shoulder, handling the innocent and helpless damsel's body with ease. It was still late at night and there was no-one on the streets as they stole her away, the three of them hurrying out of the palace, then through the city. Lena was so dazed she didn't make a sound, staring sleepily at the ground from where she was perched atop her captor's shoulder.

The other two made constant nervous glances side to side as they took Lena to a hidden shelter far from the city, a small stone building that sat alone in the forest. However, none of them looked up; if they had, they might have seen a dark shape hovering in the sky...

They got Lena into their modest hiding place, closing the doors quietly and laying her on the bed. The three of them began to undress as they moved onto the bed with Lena. They kissed and stroked her sensual form, carefully untying her knees to give them better access to her supple thighs.

They had just started having their way with Lena when the doors burst open, flying off their hinges with a loud bang. Kara hovered slowly into the room, then her red boots touched the floor with a demonstrative stomp, her eyes glowing with red with rage as her fists clenched. Two of the Amazons shrieked and threw themselves down to the floor on their knees, begging Kara to forgive them. But their leader remained on the bed, she had a defiant look and was ready to accept any punishment, be it exile or something worse.

The red glow in Kara's eyes faded as she looked at the defiant Amazon, her fury slowly subsiding as she realized keeping Lena to herself wasn't working. She had already been betrayed once when a group of her own subjects had helped Circe, Eve and Mercy kidnap Lena. It was that betrayal which had led to the difficult situation she was in now. If she was going to continue her rule here, Kara knew she was going to have to ease her possessive nature regarding her beloved Lena.

The two Amazons on their knees were still begging pitifully as Kara uttered a single word "Quiet" They fell silent, looking at her with trembling eyes as they awaited her judgement. She unclenched her fists, her body losing that angry tension as she stepped toward them and said "Stand up. I'm not going to punish you" They looked to each other with surprise and slowly stood. Their leader slid of the bed with an intrigued look, coming over to stand next to them.

"I know it's been difficult having Lena paraded around in front of you and not being able to have her for yourself. Clearly, I need to be more generous in sharing her. I appreciate your loyalty and I want it to be rewarded. So, from now on, you will be allowed to play with Lena when I deem it suitable. As long as you always ask for my permission and that you understand Lena ultimately belongs to me alone"

Kara looked at their stunned faces awaiting a reply. This was better than they could've imagined, not only were they not being punished but they were being given Lena willingly. They all spoke over each other with a frenzy of excitement, thanking her and telling her what a great ruler she was. Lena was still making sleepy muffled moans from the bed and Kara glanced over at her, then she looked back at them and continued.

"When you're done with her, I expect Lena to be bathed and redressed in her prettiest slave dress. She will be bound and gagged thoroughly, ropes secured around her arms, torso, wrists, thighs, knees, calves, and ankles - the same way she was bound and gagged when you abducted her from our bedchamber this evening. She will then be chloroformed and left on my bed to wait for me.

This will be done after every time I allow you to play with her. Do you understand?" They all nodded and quickly agreed. Kara could tell they were eager to get back on the bed with Lena, but she could also tell they were taking her instructions seriously.

With the agreement made, Kara nodded and said "Good. After tonight you may spread the word to others who also wish to spend time with Lena." She made a final glance at Lena on the bed, feeling that warmth in her heart every time she looked at how beautiful she was. Then, with a small sigh, Kara turned toward the doorway. Lena had been too dazed to understand much of what was said, but she had assumed Kara was here to rescue her. She now made a confused expression as she watched Kara leave, tilting her head up from the bed as she moaned softly through her gag.

The Amazons all continued profusely thanking Kara, showering her with praise for being such a wonderful queen. Then, as soon as she flew off, they all turned on Lena. The risk of getting caught was now gone; they were free to do with her as they pleased. There wasn't a moment of hesitation, in unison they slid onto the bed and resumed caressing her soft skin, squeezing and groping her as they covered her in kisses. Lena writhed helplessly beneath the warm bodies sensually assaulting her from every angle, her body shuddering as she was untied and undressed, every inch of her laid bare to their ravenous desires.

Kara had resolved one problem tonight, but she now had a much larger one to contend with. She returned to her bedchambers and paced up and down for a little while as she tried to think of what to do. The cloth with the chloroform still lay on her bed and she looked at it for a long while before picking it up and tucking it into the back of her skirt. She then left her bedchambers and walked through the palace, her eyes full of worry and guilt as she moved down the gleaming hallways. It was silent and her boots made a soft tapping noise, her cape swishing behind her. She walked through the halls until she found Hippolyta's room; the former queen of Paradise Island.

While Hippolyta was no longer the queen, she was still showed respect by everyone on the island, and rather than just walking in, Kara politely knocked then waited. "Who is it?" she heard after a moment of waiting and she called back "Kara..." her voice soft and unsure as she glanced around to make sure no-one else was awake. "Come in, my queen" she heard Hippolyta call back, and she pushed open the large golden door, shyly stepping into Hippolyta's bedchambers.

She had clearly woken her. Hippolyta was in a thin white nightdress, the fabric almost see through. Even in the delicate feminine attire, Hippolyta still looked formidable. She was statuesque and curvy, her perfectly proportioned figure suiting the first queen of the Amazons. She smiled as Kara entered, brushing a few strands of her blonde hair behind her shoulders. She had the warmth of a mother, her eyes taking in Kara as she asked "Is there something wrong, my queen?"

Kara closed the door and nodded as she walked into the room. She hesitated as she thought of what to say, then replied "Yes... I have a decision to make. You're aware that Lena's brainwashing has made her forget our love. That she's terrified of me now and can't break free from that horrid spell." Hippolyta's smile faded with a sympathetic look as she replied "Yes, my queen."

"Well... I went to Circe to see if there's anything she could do..." Kara replied "And she thinks she can break the spell... but... she has certain demands..." Hippolyta was intrigued, her tiredness fading as she listened intently "...But I don't know if I can do what she asks. I need your advice. Do you think I should choose love or loyalty?" Kara still looked unsure and Hippolyta could see how heavily this decision was weighing on her.

She took a long moment as she thought of how to help her new queen, then, with a warm smile she said "My queen, you should follow your heart" Kara sighed and nodded, a part of her had known that would be the response, but she wasn't looking forward to what came next. "I think the same thing" she said guiltily, then she began walking straight toward Hippolyta.

Hippolyta was standing close to her bed and as Kara approached she reached back and took the cloth tucked into the waistband of her skirt. She then pushed it over Hippolyta's mouth and nose, using that force to push her down onto the bed behind her. "Mmmmpppphhhh!!" Hippolyta hadn't been expecting the betrayal at all, and her eyes went wide as she began squirming under Kara.

While Kara wasn't as tall or curvy as Hippolyta, she was a kryptonian and was able to easily hold down the more mature woman, keeping her pinned to the bed as she overpowered her.

Hippolyta's eyes went from shock to anger, then to a sleepy wet glaze as they lost any emotion at all. Kara could feel her going limp and she kept the cloth firmly in place, waiting until Hippolyta's eyes finally began to flutter closed. She made a small, weak sigh through the cloth, her legs shuffling on the bed, then lying flat. Each breath she took made the darkness seep in more and more, until finally it consumed her.

Her eyes snapped shut and she lay motionless beneath Kara, having succumbed in only a few minutes. To fell the former queen of the Amazons had once seemed like an impossible task, but Kara was in control of this island now, and Hippolyta was as helpless as any other of the island's inhabitants. Kara swallowed as she felt a surge of guilt running through her, but she focused on Lena and pushed those emotions deep down.

She pulled Hippolyta up off the bed, hoisting her in the air and gently resting her atop her shoulder. Her curvy rump was almost too big to fit on Kara's shoulder, but she wrapped an arm around her thick thighs, squeezing her legs together as they dangled down her chest, keeping a firm hold on this curvaceous package. With Hippolyta unconscious and over her shoulder, Kara quickly stole her away, heading to the balcony then flying out into the night, going high up so no-one would see.

She flew over to the dungeons and landed quietly, opening the heavy metal door and slipping inside. She then hurried through the dark stone hallway, heading deep into the dungeon, to an unused cell near where Circe was being kept. Within this cell Kara had left some ropes and cloths to bind and gag her captive. They were sitting on the floor by the simple prison bed in the corner, and Kara carried Hippolyta over toward them.

She laid Hippolyta down gently on her back, arranging her in a neat position in the centre of the bed. Then she pushed her ankles a little closer and took the first length of rope. She tied her ankles together first, then she moved higher, sliding Hippolyta's nightdress up to give her better access to her legs. She tied more rope above and below her knees, pressing her legs firmly together. Then she rolled her over and crossed her wrists at the small of her back. She quickly tied her wrists then rolled her back over, handling her limp form gently. She then sat her up and slid behind her, wrapping rope all the way round her torso, going above and below her breasts, pinning her bound arms against her back.

With Hippolyta tightly bound Kara moved on to the cloths, balling one up in her hand and stuffing it between her lips. It was crucial that Hippolyta not be able to call out so she made the gag extra tight, padding the confines of her mouth first then tying one cloth between her lips and another one over her mouth. She then took a final cloth and tied it over Hippolyta's eyes as a blindfold, not wanting her to know where she was being kept in case she woke up.

She laid her back down on the bed and made a few checks of the knots she had tied, running her hands along Hippolyta's body to make sure it was secure and tightly restrained. Then she stood up and sadly sighed "I'm sorry..." before turning and heading to the door, unable to look back at the bound, gagged and blindfolded blonde she had betrayed.

Kara had spent quite a while coming to her decision, then capturing Hippolyta. By the time she returned to her bedchambers, Lena had been returned to her, prepared exactly to her specifications. She was laying on the bed bound and gagged and smelling like roses, her porcelain skin gleaming from her bath. They had left her with her legs slightly curled up on the bed, making the hem of her nightdress slide up to reveal her silky white panties. Kara smiled as she saw her, feeling more confident in the decision she had made.

She walked across the room and sat down next to Lena. She was completely unconscious, not only was she likely exhausted after being ravished by the three Amazons, but they had also used chloroform on her just as Kara had instructed. She looked so perfect lying there in her bondage that Kara couldn't help but stroke her gently, running her hands along her legs then giving her breasts a small squeeze. As she felt her bosom she noticed there was a card tucked between her cleavage, and she stroked along the top of Lena's breasts before plucking it out.

The card had a small note of thanks from the Amazons, telling Kara that they would be loyal to her forever, that they would never go behind her back again. Kara smiled and set the card down on her nightstand. Then, she leaned down and kissed Lena on her gagged lips. She was pleased she had regained control of her subjects, and she enjoyed seeing how beautiful Lena looked after being bathed and dressed up for her. She could get used to coming to her bedchambers to find her beloved looking so fresh and soft, tightly tied, and waiting to be released. She was enjoying thinking of this future, but then her mood darkened as she remembered what she had to do to get there. Hippolyta was still in that cell, and Circe was waiting...

With another small caress of Lena's bound form, Kara slid her hands under her, sliding beneath her and the sheets and lifting Lena from the bed. She cradled Lena in her arms, one hand resting under her legs the other under her back. She held her tightly against her chest, letting Lena sleep in the loving pose like a bride being carried across the threshold. Then she gently flew out of the window on the balcony, rising up and heading toward the dungeons.

Lena had been so heavily drugged she didn't stir at all during the brief flight, and soon Kara was carrying her through the dark halls of the dungeons. She passed by the cell holding Hippolyta, glancing toward it with a guilty look. Then she reached Circe's cell, opening the door and taking Lena inside. "Welcome back my queen" Circe said teasingly as she smiled at the troubled expression on Kara's face.

Kara ignored her and set Lena down gently on the floor. Then her eyes glowed red and she shot out her heat beams. They broke apart every chain keeping Circe knelt on the hard stone floor, then she cut a path across the magical symbol surrounding Circe, singeing the symbols so that they would no longer be effective. The symbol glowed purple around Circe on the floor then died down as the magic keeping her prisoner faded away.

Circe let out a relieved sigh as she stood up, smoothly rising to her feet and once more resembling her old self. With a wave of her hand to Kara she said "Leave us. I have work to do on your beloved, and you'll just be a distraction" Kara wasn't happy about leaving Lena with the sorceress, but she had come too far to turn back now. She took one last glimpse at Lena, then with a heavy heart she left the room.

Kara paced up and down outside for over an hour. She could see a faint green glow under the door, no doubt Circe's magic being used to fix Lena's mind. To pass the time, she quickly flew back to her bedchambers and prepared another cloth with chloroform, then she came back to the dungeons. Kara went into Hippolyta's cell to check on her. She was still asleep but Kara pressed the cloth over her mouth and nose to ensure she stayed out, wanting to keep Hippolyta unconscious until this deal was done.

She tucked the cloth into her skirt, then left Hippolya and went back to pacing outside Circe's cell. Then, after an unbearably long amount of time, she heard from inside "You may enter. She's ready for you" Kara cautiously opened the door to see Lena lying on a soft bed in the corner. Circe must have conjured it as it hadn't been there before. She had also used her magic to fix her appearance, her hair and her dark dress were, once again, immaculate.

Kara paid her little attention though, moving toward the bed and looking down at Lena with a hopeful expression. "You may wake her" Circe said and, with a flourish of her hand, a small bottle of smelling salts appeared beside the bed. Kara went over to it and sat down on the edge of the bed, scooping up the bottle and unscrewing the top. She drifted the salts under Lena's nose, watching as her face twitched.

Kara carefully slipped the gag out of Lena's lips, setting it down around her neck as Lena's eyes fluttered open. There was a tense moment of silence as Kara looked down at her and asked "Do you recognise me?" Lena's eyelids made a small, sleepy flutter as her vision focused on Kara leaning over her. Then she smiled and tilted up from the bed, kissing her passionately. After a brief moment of surprise, Kara eagerly wrapped her arms around Lena, pulling her beloved in even closer as she moaned with pleasure. Lena let out a soft moan as well, the shuddering noise mixing with the soft wet sounds of their lips.

Kara kept Lena in that tight embrace for a long time, kissing her deeply as she finally felt Lena willingly kiss her back. They only separated briefly for Lena to moan breathlessly "I knew you would rescue me" then they went right back to making out, unable to control their passion for each other. The world seemed to fade away as they kissed, nothing else mattering as they closed their eyes and relished in the taste of the other.

They would've continued like that for much longer, were it not for Circe loudly clearing her throat. With one last long kiss, Kara tilted her mouth away and looked at the sorceress. "My fee?" Circe said with a raised eyebrow, waiting to be handed her captive Amazon. Kara sighed and nodded, then she turned to Lena and lay her back down on the bed. "What fee?" Lena asked with a confused expression. But Kara just pulled the gag around her neck up and fastened it back firmly over her pillow-soft lips to silence her.

"Shhhhh. Everything's going to be alright" Kara said soothingly as she reached for the cloth still damp with chloroform tucked into her skirt. Lena still didn't understand, but she loved and trusted Kara. She offered no resistance as Kara gently pushed the cloth over her mouth and nose, taking deep breaths in order to pass out, as Kara wanted. "Just go to sleep, my love," Kara said in that same soft tone, leaning down to kiss Lena on the cheek as her eyelids began to flutter closed.

Lena obediently inhaled the chloroform until her mind drifted away, her eyes looking lovingly at Kara until they finally snapped shut. Kara carefully peeled the cloth away and sighed as she looked at Lena's angelic, resting features. Circe was still waiting and Kara just wanted to get this over with.

She stood up silently and walked out of the cell, heading straight into the room that held Hippolyta.

The former queen still laid there on the bed, sleeping peacefully in the ropes. Kara couldn't help but be aware of how much had changed for Hippolyta. Once the unquestioned queen of this entire island, now a slave in a dungeon about to be sold. She walked toward her and lifted her from the bed, tossing her over her shoulder then carrying her out of the room.

Circe's eyes widened with delight as she saw Hippolyta's backside perched atop Kara's shoulder. She smiled and held out her arms expectantly as Kara came toward her. Kara slid Hippolyta down off of her shoulder and passed her to Circe, completing their transaction. "Pleasure doing business with you" Circe purred as she gripped Hippolyta tightly, already beginning to feel her up in front of Kara. Then, with a wave of her hand, a green fiery portal appeared, bathing the dark cell in its soft glow.

"Remember our deal" Kara said sternly as Circe carried Hippolyta toward the portal. With a sly smile the sorceress paused and replied "Oh, I will. I will never set foot on this island again, as long as it's under your rule" then she disappeared into the flames, taking Hippolyta with her. The portal vanished and Kara was left alone with Lena. She looked down at the ground with an upset expression, then she heard a soft whimpering from the bed, Lena making a light mewling sound in her sleep.

Kara looked over to her and smiled, putting her guilt to the back of her mind. She walked over and scooped Lena up from the bed, kissing her on the cheek and carrying her away. She wanted to leave her dark feelings in this dungeon; to let go of the past and finally start her life with the woman she loved.

CHAPTER 10

Pleasure Games

Chapter Summary: While Kara attends to some unfinished business in Man's World, Diana has some fun with some particular slaves...

Months had passed since Kara's bargain in the dungeons of Themyscira. The former queen Hippolyta had not been seen again since that night, and still only Kara knew her true whereabouts: that the statuesque Amazon was in the clutches of the sorceress Circe. Kara had felt guilty at first, but that emotion had quickly given way to a much stronger one: her love and utter infatuation with Lena. She had come to realise there was nothing she wouldn't do for her beloved Lena, and that she had no regrets about the deal she had made. She would ravish Lena at every possible moment, falling deeper into her desire and erasing any doubt she had about trading away Hippolyta.

It had been a long time since she had Lena willingly submit to her. Since Lena's kidnapping and brainwashing, Kara had started to forget just how wonderful it was to have Lena's sensual and submissive form writhing beneath her. Their naked bodies would remain wrapped around each other as Kara dominated her, constantly making Lena explode with pleasure at the touch of her hands and her tongue. She would then always chloroform Lena and bind her, keeping her captive prize squeezed tightly to her beneath the sheets. Kara never wanted to leave this island, she never wanted to leave the bed, she had everything she would ever need right here. But it wasn't enough just to have Lena, she had to ensure no-one would ever take Lena from her again.

To ensure this, Kara had to put an end to the war in Man's World. They had broken the peace treaty and she was going back there to find out why. Before leaving, she wanted to ensure that her prized slaves were taken care of, so she gathered them up. It was the morning, so she went by the soliders' sleeping quarters, finding each of them lying next to an Amazon who had ravished them the night before. These Amazons didn't own her prized slaves, but Kara had learned to loan out her slaves to keep the Amazons happy, even giving Lena away at times. She woke up Sam first, gently guiding her out of the bed, then gagging her with a white cloth and tying her wrists behind her back. She then looped a rope around her neck like a collar, leaving a long line to hold as a leash.

She led Sam away from the sleeping Amazon who had dominated her, taking her to the next room where Lois was sleeping. Each woman was wearing a similar skimpy white nightdress, the preferred outfit of the pleasure slaves on the island. It clung to their bodies in such a sensual manner, the silk hanging off the shape of their breasts and rippling along their womanly hips.

When a slave was "captured" and placed atop a shoulder, the short hem of the dress would slide up to reveal their soft rumps, the attire was perfectly suited for them to be ravished at any opportunity.

Lois was woken up next, then bound and gagged in an identical manner to Sam. Then, with a gentle tug of the two leashes, Kara led them to the room Vicki was sleeping in. A few minutes later, and Kara was leading her three bound and gagged slaves out from the military barracks and back to her royal chambers. They all made soft whimpers and moans as their bare feet padded softly behind the kryptonian queen, each woman not daring to do anything other than follow the dominant blonde.

Kara led them to the room Lena worked in, then she tied their leashes to the door handle to keep them there while she went inside. Lena was wearing a silky white nightdress too and she was sitting at a marble table with a number of her experiments laid out on it. Her work to combine technology with the Amazons' magic still continued, making Themyscira unstoppable weaponry that would crush any who opposed them. Lena was sitting on a marble stool with her ankles bound. She had gotten so used to being tied up that she no longer felt comfortable without some part of her body being restrained. Even when she was allowed to walk around in her lab she would be gagged or have her wrists tied if she could still work that way.

At hearing the footsteps behind her, Lena glanced over her shoulder and smiled, her eyes full of love and warmth as she saw Kara approaching. She could see Kara was holding a white cloth in her hand, and she felt a flutter of excitement at the prospect of once again being made helpless by her beloved mistress.

"Hello, darling." Lena said with a happy sigh. "Your timing is perfect! I've just finished my latest project. Are you going to ravish me again?"

"Not quite, my love," Kara said with a pleased sigh, "though, I suspect you will most definitely be getting ravished by the one I leave you in the custody of while I'm away on business." Lena slightly crinkled her brow in confusion at Kara's words, but the gorgeous pleasure slave knew from the stern furrow set in Kara's own brow that she would not be allowed to question her mistress further about what Kara intended for her. Kara walked up to her and leaned in close, kissing along Lena's neck as her hands slid round to grope her breasts through her silky white nightdress. She kissed and fondled her for a few seconds before taking the cloth and gently clamping it down onto Lena's mouth and nose.

Lena eyes fluttered and she let out a soft sigh as she smelled that familiar scent, the chloroform filling her lungs. "Mmm... mmmph..." She leaned back a little, easing into Kara' grip as she accepted her helplessness with a small smile beneath the cloth. Kara continued squeezing her breasts in a slow, sensual motion, her fingers pressing down on one then the other. Finally, she felt Lena going limp and she let her slump forward against the table she had been working on. Kara then pulled Lena's hands behind her back and quickly tied her wrists, making a tight knot that would keep Lena's slender arms in place. After looping cords several times around the shapely beauty's torso and upper arms - paying special attention to the lengths bound above and below Lena's breasts - Kara smiled with satisfaction when she pulled Lena's chair out from her workstation and saw the way her gorgeous bare legs were already bound at the thighs, above and below her knees, and around her ankles.

Kara finished her beloved's bondage with a gag, tying a white cloth tightly over Lena'a plump, pouty lips. Once Kara was done, she gave Lena a gentle kiss on the cheek and hoisted her up onto her shoulder, handling her bound form with ease. She carried Lena back to the door and retrieved the leashes she had tied there. With a small tug she led her other three slaves through the palace while Lena slept atop her shoulder. She held the three leashes in one hand while the other squeezed Lena's heart-shaped rump, it's placement on her shoulder so perfectly positioned for her hand to fondle.

She took them all to Diana's chambers and knocked on the door. A moment later, Diana emerged, dressed in her modified superheroine costume with Kara's symbol on the chest. "My queen. How may I serve you?" Diana said humbly with a small submissive tilt of her head, her eyes flickering over to Lena's pleasantly plump bottom atop Kara's shoulder.

"I need you to take care of my most prized slaves while I'm away. You may do as you wish with them, but make sure they're kept safe. Especially my precious Lena" Kara replied with a small pat on Lena's luscious rump, showing off her most valued possession.

Diana was only too happy to take the most beautiful woman on the island, as well as the other three gorgeous pleasure slaves. She already had an idea of what to do with them while Kara was away.

Lena was transferred from Kara's shoulder to Diana's, the bound beauty passed between them like the helpless slave that she was. Kara then handed Diana the three leashes, Sam, Lois and Vicki moved over to Diana's side in response, accepting that whoever held their leash was now their new mistress.

"Thank you Diana, I'll be back soon" Kara said as she turned to leave, her cape making a small sway as she swivelled round. She began to walk down the hall when she heard behind her "My queen? Is there any news on the disappearance of my mother?" Kara paused, her shoulders tensing slightly as her head turned. In a slightly cold voice she replied "Nothing yet. My best people are looking into it Diana, you'll be the first to know if we find her" With that, she continued walking, heading straight to the palace doors then shooting up into the sky. Diana was left standing in the hall with a look of distrust on her face, her suspicions about her mother still eating away at her.

Inside of Diana's chambers, Kelly was currently ravishing Alex. They were in bed and Kelly was on top of her bound and gagged prize, a reward for progressing well under Diana's training. The door opened and Diana returned to the room. Kelly glanced over her shoulder to see Diana wasn't alone; she had Samantha, Vicki and Lois on leashes walking submissively behind her and Kelly could see the unmistakable form of Lena's shapely ass and bare legs and feet dangling limp from where they were slung over Diana's opposite shoulder. "It's time for more training" Diana said as she came over to the bed, instructing Kelly to slide off of Alex and put her gag back in place.

While Kelly was gagging Alex, Diana swiftly untied Sam, she then ordered her to pick up Lena while she went over to Lois and Vicki. They were standing close together, so all Diana had to do was get in close and pull them forward over her shoulder, hoisting them up and settling them into place as she stood up straight. She then instructed Kelly to carry Alex and told both her and Sam to follow her. She led them out of the palace and through the streets of Themyscira. She walked in front while her soldier slaves walked behind her, making their way through the city and to the outskirts.

Diana led them into the forests, then stopped and set Lois and Vicki down. These forests were well known as the place pleasure slaves would be chased down and captured, and all the women knew what was about to happen. After untying the four pleasure slaves, Diana instructed Lois, Vicki, Alex and Lena to run off into the woods, even giving Lena a small spank on her shapely rump to send her on her way. Then, when she was left with Kelly and Sam, Diana told them there would be a reward for whoever could capture the most girls.

"Whoever can capture the most? There's four of them... so... what happens if we both capture an even number?" Sam asked as she put her hands on her hips in a questioning manner. But while she was speaking, Kelly just took off into the woods, making long strides as she started the hunt. "Hey! That's cheating!" Sam yelled as she took off as well, darting between the trees. Diana remained there, waiting for her soldier slaves to return to her with a pleased smile on her face.

Lena could feel her heart pounding in her chest as she ran, her silky nightdress fluttering around her supple thighs with every rapid step. She knew there was no chance of actually escaping her pursuers, but still the feeling of being chased brought out this natural reaction within her. She had been hunted in these woods many times by many of the Amazons. She was the most sought-after woman on Paradise Island and dozens of times an Amazon had "kidnapped" her and set her loose here, only to chase her down and make her helpless once again.

She had quickly split up from Lois, Vicki and Alex. It would be too easy for them to be captured all at once if they stuck together. She was now alone, running amongst the trees, her wide beautiful blue-green eyes casting nervous glances over her shoulder. It was Sam who found her first, managing to maneuver around her and run up by her side. She only noticed Sam at the last second, then her momentum came to a halt as Sam grabbed her by the waist and snatched her up from her feet.

Sam hoisted her up, then gently lay her down on the ground, immediately straddling Lena and pinning her wrists down on either side of her head. Lena played her part of a helpless captive, wriggling and moaning beneath the more dominant woman, even though she knew her capture was inevitable now. Sam loomed over her for a moment, looking down at the helpless beauty. She was gripping her wrists to the floor, easily keeping Lena in place as her hips squirmed side to side.

Sam couldn't help herself. She positioned Lena's wrists one atop the other, holding them both with one hand. Then, with the other hand, she began to slowly grope and fondle Lena's ample bosom, pressing down into each breast and testing it's shape against her palm. She then leaned down and stole a quick kiss on her plump lips. Lena gasped in shock, wriggling a little more as she turned her head to the side. Sam just smiled and began kissing along her jawline and cheek, teasing her with each soft touch of her lips. Sam kept groping and kissing her, feeling the heat from Lena's body grow as her head slowly turned back so Sam could kiss her on the lips again.

Sam had always had a crush on Lena back in Man's World, and this was like a dream come true to have the gorgeous object of her affections so helpless beneath her. She kept playing with and fondling Lena for as long as she dared; she didn't want to lose the game by spending all her time on just one damsel. She quickly retrieved a white chloroform-soaked cloth she had tucked away and pressed it over Lena's mouth and nose, clamping the square of fabric firmly in place and holding it there until Lena's eyes began to flutter closed.

As Lena passed out, Sam released her wrists, leaving them resting above her head as if they were being held by an invisible rope. She then stood up straight and looked around, her eyes scanning through the trees. She could take Lena back to Diana now, but it would be faster to continue her hunt and come back for Lena, then she could bring back two women at once.

SEX AND CHAOS

She leaned down and kissed Lena on the lips again, enjoying how angelic Lena looked in her resting state, her features so soft and slack in their utter lack of tension. Then she went off to try and find another pleasure slave. It didn't take long for her to track down Vicki. She was trying to hide behind a tree and Sam managed to sneak up on her. She pounced and immediately pressed her cloth over Vicki's mouth and nose, pinning her against the tree she had thought could be a hiding place.

Sam kept her body pressed against Vicki's to keep her in place, enjoying the grinding motions as Vicki writhed and moaned helplessly, the sounds muffled from beneath the cloth. It didn't take long for Vicki to pass out, and soon Sam was pulling her forward over her shoulder. She hoisted her up and gave her bottom a light pat, then carried her back toward where she had left Lena.

Lena was still lying there in her helpless pose, as if the delicate maiden had just fainted on the grass. It took a little work to get Lena up with Vicki already on her shoulder, but both women were so soft and submissive it wasn't too hard to handle their feminine forms. After a minute or two she managed to get Lena over her spare shoulder, her bottom perched nicely for Sam to squeeze as she carried her. Both women slept peacefully as they were carried through the forest, resting in their proper place atop a more dominant woman's shoulder.

As Sam emerged from the forest, she found Kelly was returning at the same time. Kelly had Alex and Lois over her shoulders, all four women just as helpless as each other. They laid down their captives at Diana's feet, then Sam rolled her eyes and sighed. "See? This is exactly what I told you would... mmmppphhh!!!" While Sam was talking, Kelly simply walked up behind her and reached around to press a cloth over her mouth and nose. Her other arm wrapped tightly around Sam's midsection, just beneath her breasts, gripping firmly as she began to knock Sam out.

Kelly hadn't asked for permission; the rules of the game said whoever captured the most women won, and Kelly knew that meant Sam was hers for the taking. Sam wasn't quite as helpless as the pleasure slaves that lay unconscious on the ground. She tried pushing back and pulling at Kelly's hands, but Kelly had the far better position in their little struggle, being behind Sam with her arms already locked into place. Sam made frustrated moans as she tried twisting her body side to side, her muscles tensing as she tried every possible way of escaping Kelly's grip.

Soon Sam's struggles began to weaken, then her arms flopped down by her sides as her body began to go limp. She let out a soft sigh from beneath the cloth, her eyes fluttering as she felt the chloroform overwhelming her senses. A glassy stare settled over her features, then her eyelids drooped shut as she leaned back into Kelly's clutches. Kelly smiled and gently eased Sam down to the ground, letting her rest alongside the other unconscious beauties.

"So, I guess I win!" Kelly said with a confident smirk as she looked to Diana for approval. Diana clapped her hands together a single time with a wide smile as she said "Excellent work! You are truly talented, Kelly Olsen. It's like you were made to be one of my soldier slaves. While Samantha questioned me, you simply took the initiative. You have impressed me, and you will have your reward..." Diana gestured to the women at her feet as she said "Once we are done with the games these women will all be yours to do with as you please. You have come out on top and they will serve you tonight as they should"

Kelly beamed with delight, not only at Diana's praise, but also at the thought that every woman at her feet was now hers to play with. "Thank you so much mistress! but..." for a second her smile flickered with confusion as she asked "...you said once the games are done? Are they not already over?"

With a knowing smile, Diana shook her head as he replied "Oh no, not yet. You have proven yourself to be the most dominant of my solider slaves. But now..." she looked down at Lena and Alex as she continued "...now we will find out who is the most dominant of my pleasure slaves..."

While Diana was testing her slaves, Kara was arriving at a meeting between the world's leaders. She had demanded they meet with her to explain why the peace treaty had been broken. To not attend the meeting would mean the war would start again, and like before, Themyscira would decimate any country that dared oppose them.

The mood was tense in the secret underground bunker they had all gathered in. Mostly silent, they hunched around a circular table while they awaited Kara's arrival. Then the ceiling above them began to shake, and suddenly Kara crashed through into the room with a cloud of rubble and dust. A few of the world leaders began to scramble out of their chairs in fear until Kara yelled "Sit!

Down!"

She floated toward them her eyes glowing red in anger, remembering every moment with Lena they had stolen from her. "Lex Luthor stole Lena Luthor from me and I KNOW he was advising you during the war!" She growled as they all trembled in her dominant presence, but while they were afraid they had also prepared for this and in a shaking voice one of them spoke up "He... he acted alone! Without our sanction... in order to maintain the peace, he's already been taken into custody..."

At the back of the room a door slid open and Lex Luthor was led out in handcuffs, he was furious and pulled angrily at the two large men marching him out "This is absurd! Take your hands off me!" he yelled as his captivity was displayed to Kara. The red in her eyes slowly faded as one of the world leaders continued "We're about to transport him to a high security prison and transfer his assets to his sole heir... Lena Luthor"

Hearing that her beloved was about to inherit the vast Luthor fortune Kara finally calmed down, slowly lowering until her feet were touching the floor. If Lena owned the fortune then so did Kara, and it pleased her to know she was taking everything from the man who had tried to hurt her so much. Luthor glared at her as she made a satisfied smile. Then her eyes hardened again as she said "The peace treaty will continue. But I will oversee his transport. I want to ensure he will never see the light of day again."

Lena's eyes fluttered open as a small bottle of smelling salts was wafted under her nose. She made a small moan and lifted up from the floor, seeing Diana crouching beside her. Alex had been woken up as well and Diana helped them both to their feet. She explained that, as the most submissive of her pleasure slaves, they were to compete in the next game: trying to capture and dominate the other. They were each give chloroform pads, lassos, and material for gags. Then they were sent off into the woods. Kelly watched all of this and called out to Alex that she would give her a special reward if she captured Lena.

Lena had no idea what to do. She kept hold of the items she had been given, but she had never used them before. Since arriving on the island after Diana had first kidnapped her from her home, she had only ever been a pleasure slave, and it was a role she found she was well suited to. She had become so submissive in her time here that all she could think of was to just hide from Alex. She couldn't even imagine ever trying to capture another woman, her luscious form was the one always being taken and ravished.

She scurried amongst the trees, her bare feet padding softly on the grass until she found a tree that was large enough to be a suitable hiding spot. She moved behind the tree then crouched down, taking slow breaths as she tried to remain quiet, her chest scrunching up to her knees. She put down her items by her feet while she hid, her hands resting on her thighs as she leaned back against the tree, hoping to hide for long enough to please Diana.

Meanwhile, Alex was hunting for Lena, holding the chloroform pad in one hand, and the ropes and cloth in the other. She was already more submissive than when she arrived here, Kelly's control of her had made her yearn to be made helpless. But she hadn't been here as long as Lena, she still remembered her training as a government agent and she wasn't going to just hide. She wanted to please Kelly, and bringing a bound, gagged, and captive Lena back to her would do just that.

She sneaked slowly through the forest until she spotted Lena, pausing as their eyes locked. Lena gasped and quickly got to her feet as she tried to run but Alex was much faster. She grabbed her and brought her down to the ground, Lena landing on her chest in the soft grass. Alex sat down on top of Lena's backside, using it as a perch to keep her pinned to the ground. She then leaned forward,

letting their bodies press more tightly together. She reached forward with the cloth and slowly slid it against Lena's mouth and nose, keeping her squashed to the floor by laying atop her. "You're mine, now!" Alex whispered in Lena's ear, triumphantly. "Kelly will be so happy that I've captured such a helpless beauty for her! We've wanted to get you into our clutches for a long time. Kelly and I were planning on snatching you up and having our way with you even way back when we were all free and living in Man's World." Lena moaned helplessly at Alex's words, knowing she would soon be ravished by her longtime friends.

It was clear who the most submissive one of them was now, Alex could feel Lena's small wriggles and squirms, her butt wriggling against Alex's hips. Alex had been so helplessly ravished by Kelly on this island, but she could now feel the pleasure of being on the other side, feeling a beautiful woman like Lena giving in to her. She smiled as she gently kissed Lena on the neck, letting her know it was okay to just submit to that scent of chloroform. "Sleep, sweet Lena. Kelly and I will take good care of you."

Alex lay on top of her like that until Lena went still, a soft sigh emitting from beneath the cloth as her eyelids fluttered closed. Alex made a small pump of her hips against Lena's bottom to see if she would wriggle again, but Lena just lay there limply beneath her. Alex smiled and peeled the cloth away, kissing Lena on the neck again. She then lifted up so she was straddling Lena's rump, its soft shape and generous size making for the perfect cushion to use while she tied Lena up.

She took Lena's wrists and crossed them behind her back, then she scooped up the ropes she had dropped while grabbing Lena. She quickly looped the ropes around Lena's crossed wrists, making a tight knot and binding them together. She quickly swiveled round so she was still sitting on her but facing her long legs. Alex leaned down and stroked them all the way to her ankles, then she moved them a little closer together and quickly wrapped more rope around them.

Once Lena was restrained, Alex rolled her over and sat her up, she sat behind her and eased the cloth over her lips, forcing them closed as she tightly gagged her. She tied the cloth behind Lena's head, then wrapped her arms just below the captive brunette's breasts and began hoisting her up from the floor. She got her up then turned her and let her limp body slump over her shoulder, Lena falling into the familiar helpless pose.

Alex had a wide smile as she carried Lena through the forest, her hands running along Lena's legs, then spanking her pleasantly plump and heart-shaped rump. It was so soft and squeezable, and Alex was in such a good mood she couldn't help but play with it, slapping and groping it with glee. She even tickled Lena's soft and pale bare soles, playing with every inch of supple skin she had access to. At those small tickles, Alex heard a few weak whimpers, the sounds girlish, muffled, and sleepy as Lena made them through her gag.

Kelly beamed with pride as she saw Alex return with Lena over her shoulder; it showed that Alex had obediently followed her command and come out on top. Alex saw that proud smile and her heart fluttered, a slight blush colouring her cheeks as she looked back at Kelly. "Well done... my slave" Kelly said in a sultry tone as Alex brought Lena right up to her. Then Kelly gently took the side of Alex's head and kissed her, Lena still dangling over her shoulder as the two women tasted each others mouths.

"As your reward, you will be first to ravish Lena" Diana said as Kelly and Alex's mouths separated. Sam had awoken to find herself bound and gagged, and upon hearing this she stomped her bare feet on the ground, letting out a frustrated moan through her gag. Kelly and Alex went back to kissing as Diana crouched down over Sam and said softly "It's your own fault for letting your guard down..." she reached down and began stroking and squeezing Sam's bound form as she continued "The line between solider and slave is very thin... you can only be one or the other at any given time..."

Diana leaned down and kissed Sam softly on her gagged lips, smiling at the still unhappy look in Sam's eyes "Don't worry, my dear Samantha. Once Alex and Kelly are done with Lena, you may have her next." This seemed to appease Sam who made a small whimper through her gag "But for now, you will serve me" Diana said as she hoisted her up, lifting her from the floor and easily placing her atop her shoulder. While waiting for Alex to return, she had tied Lois and Vicki with leashes again, and with a small tug she began leading them back to the palace while carrying Sam.

Alex and Kelly followed behind her with Lena still atop Alex's shoulder. Diana praised Alex a final time before they separated, then they were allowed to finally take Lena to bed. Her soft form so naturally suited the soft sheets of a bed. They placed her atop it and untied the ropes around the upper part of her legs so they could kiss along her thighs. Kelly took on a naturally more dominant role in their lovemaking, while Lena was simply a slave to be pleasured and guided in how to bring them pleasure.

Their three bodies were soon naked and writhing against each other, Kelly and Alex united in ravishing Lena, every sensual curve and sensitive area so sweet to their lips. Diana, meanwhile, had taken her three slaves to bed and dominated them all at the same time. The powerful Amazon lay them down and descended upon them with her unquenchable appetites, using their bodies so ravenously that each of them came to the verge of passing out, constantly rocked by the orgasms she brought out of them.

SEX AND CHAOS

The games had concluded and Kara had ensured Lex Luthor was locked up in the high-security prison. She was certain no one would take Lena from her now, but, while Luthor had planned this whole thing, there were two women who had helped him do it. With Luthor's assets seized she had access to the location of every one of his underground bunkers, and she quickly found the women she was looking for. Before heading back to Themyscira, she went to deal with them first.

Eve and Mercy could hear her breaking through the bunkers defences, the sound of Lex Luthor's security systems being ripped apart got closer and closer until Kara burst into the room. They both immediately surrendered at the sight of Kara, not even trying to run or use some kind of weapon against her. Kara was used to people submitting to her by now so she thought nothing of it. She tied each of them up, binding them then slinging them over her shoulder.

They would be taken back to Paradise Island as her prisoners, finally giving Kara the revenge she desired after Lena's kidnapping. However, in that bunker there was a hidden camera watching her, observing as she flew off with Eve and Mercy, bound and gagged over each shoulder. That camera led to a monitor in a darkened room, and in that room the villainess known as Roulette made a sinister smile, her eyes narrowing as she watched her plan fall into place...

CHAPTER 11

The Queen's Lie

Chapter Summary: While pleasure runs rampant across the island, Kara has something special to ask of Lena. Meanwhile, Diana discovers the truth behind her missing mother's whereabouts.

Pleasure raged through Themyscira like it never had before. Gasps and moans filled every bedroom, echoing down the halls in a hedonistic chorus of orgasmic release. This new wave of ravenous desire was all due to a new invention created by Lena. This invention had come along at a time of peace, with Lex Luthor's imprisonment, the war was over and at the behest of her queen, Lena had created an item for the Amazons to fully indulge in their victory.

The item was a strap-on. Brown leather attached to a pure white appendage, the shade as if it was made from marble. It was more flexible than stone though, made from a magical clay Lena had concocted, the clay tested and adapted by her technology. When strapped to the wearer the long, thick rod would become linked to them and they would feel every thrust and every pleasurable sensation as if it was the real thing.

So too would the woman being ravished feel that realistic sensation, it would feel warm and throbbing inside of them, it would feel like a part of their lover, and the two women would become connected in their outbursts of pleasure. During these lovemaking sessions, the appendage would secrete a potent aphrodisiac, one which would significantly enhance the pleasure of both parties, quite literally driving them wild with their desire.

Kara had ordered enough of these strap-ons to be made for every woman on the island. She knew this was the way to keep them happy and loyal, and from the moment they had begun using them, Kara had never been more popular as queen. The Amazons had become obsessed with the strap-ons as soon as each of them had made her initial plunge into whichever slave she had chosen.

The hedonism was rampant, no pleasure slave was safe from being constantly captured and ravished to the point of exhaustion. Not even some of the soldier slaves could guarantee they would not be taken, for it was the Amazons who truly ruled the island, and their hunger for more pleasure could not be abated.

While the hunting and ravishing of slaves had always been an enjoyed activity on the island, now it was the only thing the Amazons could focus on; such was the intense pleasure they felt when thrusting the strap-on deep within the helplessly captured women they ravished, feeling the pleasure slaves squirm beneath them as each lustful Amazon dominated her beautiful prize with each strong pump of their hips.

This new age of unchecked debauchery was ideal for Kara. No-one questioned her reign anymore, and no-one asked any questions regarding Hippolyta's disappearance. She had finally achieved a long-lasting peace. Her enemies were seemingly vanquished, the Amazons were overjoyed with their new toys, and she had her precious Lena bound and gagged in her bed every night.

She had just finished making love to Lena a fifth time, a long passionate marathon that had left Lena all sweaty and tired, her supple skin moist and gleaming. Kara was just as taken with the strap-ons as every Amazon on the island. She loved using them on Lena, bending her over and pumping into her so hard her pleasantly plump asscheeks would make a soft clapping noise.

She drew the long appendage out of Lena, the wide strap-on now glistening with her juices. Then she unstrapped it and set it aside, letting out a satisfied sigh as Lena lay crumpled before her on the bed. Kara brushed a few strands of her blonde hair back behind her shoulders, then scooped up Lena from the bed, cradling her to her chest.

She carried her beloved through a doorway that led to a large pool-sized bath, lines of steam rising from the soapy water as Kara stepped inside. She lowered into the water and settled Lena beside her, then she remembered something and whispered in Lena's ear "Wait right here, my love." Kara then slipped out of the water and walked back to the bedroom, leaving Lena to soak in the special oils the bath had been run with.

She returned a moment later with a golden bracelet in her hand. It looked similar to the one Lena had made for her, Kara's bracelet designed to make her immune to the effects of magic and kryptonite. "I made this for you" Kara said with a loving smile as she lowered into the water beside Lena and pulled her in close.

"On Krypton, instead of rings, lovers exchanged bracelets when they wanted to propose marriage..." Kara said as she took Lena's wrist, lifting her arm up and out of the water. "...This bracelet also contains a beacon which emits a sound frequency I'll be able to hear no matter where you are. No one will ever steal you from me again..." She secured the bracelet on Lena's wrist, snapping it firmly into place.

Lena looked at it, then to Kara, leaning in to kiss her as they embraced passionately. Lena now had the bracelet as well as the small House of El tattoo on her skin, two symbols that marked her as Kara's property. She loved belonging to Kara and they kissed deeply for a long while in the soapy water, their soft wet forms pressing into each other.

After the long kiss and telling each other of their love, a guilty look flickered in Kara's eyes. She glanced away for a second then back to Lena as she explained "But... even when we are bound by marriage your role on the island can't change. You'll have to remain a pleasure slave to keep the Amazons happy..." Still looking away she let out a nervous sigh and continued "I'm sorry that I have to keep you as a captive pleasure slave... I love you, Lena, and I know you've basically been just an innocent captive since Diana kidnapped and enslaved us both all those months ago, and I don't want to feel like I'm forcing you into marriage as well..."

Before she could continue, Lena took her chin and turned her head back to face her, looking into her eyes lovingly as she said "I love you too, Kara Zor-El, and I've never been happier, or felt safer, than during my time in your possession." Lena leaned in and kissed Kara then leaned back with a wide smile as she continued "Nothing would make her happier than to be your slavewife"

Kara could feel her heart pounding with how excited and in love she was. They embraced again as they kissed, their tongues dancing against each other as their mouths locked together. She had been planning to bathe with her beloved for a little longer, but she was too taken in the moment. Kara peeled her mouth away then hoisted Lena up from the water, slinging her dripping wet naked body over her shoulder.

Lena let out a small giggle, then a feminine moan as she felt Kara stroking her legs all the way up to between her thighs, pleasuring her before they had even reached the bed. She carried her to the sheets and lay her down, grabbing the strap-on as Lena spread her legs in anticipation.

As Kara was starting another ravenous lovemaking session, Diana was asleep in her room. She lay in her bed, her naked form resting beneath white silk sheets. Kelly and Alex lay either side of her, both of them tired and spent from Diana using their bodies with a strap on, the dominant Amazon having worn out both women.

They lay resting in the dark as the door to the room began to slowly open. The two shadowy figures entering were Eve and Mercy, the only two 'labor slaves' on the entire island. Since being captured and brought to Themyscira, they had both been thoroughly punished by Kara. She was still furious at them for their role in Lena's kidnapping, and she had ensured their time on the island would be as unpleasant as possible.

They were fitted with chastity belts, designed by Lena with the combination of technology and magic that she had become so adept at using. The special devices would constantly tease them but never allow them a release. While all the other women on the island received near constant pleasure, they were denied it. As well as the chastity belts, they were forced to wear cheap, scratchy, and uncomfortable burlap sackcloth dresses, unlike the fine and lavish silks and other precious materials that the other slaves and Amazons wore.

They weren't kept in a dungeon or cell, for on the island there was nowhere they could escape to. Instead, they were made to work, performing menial tasks that Kara or Diana demanded of them, sometimes forced to serve other pleasure slaves, or being "practice dummies" for Kelly and Sam's soldier training.

The women crept into the room and moved closer to Diana's bed until they were looming over it. Eve and Mercy had been on the island for long enough now to know almost every area and, as such, it had been easy for them to steal some chloroform. They both had a small brown bottle each, holding it in one hand while the other held a white cloth. They opened their bottles and drizzled a small amount of the liquid on their cloths, then they slowly leaned forward.

SEX AND CHAOS

They subdued Kelly and Alex first, even though they were already asleep, they pressed the cloths to their mouth and nose, ensuring they were fully unconscious. Nothing would wake them now, which meant the two women could clamber onto the bed, crawling over them to ambush Diana who lay in the centre. The mighty Amazon was helpless to stop them, she took slow breaths as Eve gently drifted a cloth over her face, then she unknowingly breathed in the chloroform and began to go limp before she was even awake or conscious of the danger.

They looked at each other and smiled devilishly in the dark, the first step of their plan having gone perfectly. Then, they carefully pulled Diana up and out of the bed. Mercy lifted her sleeping form up onto her shoulder, then they carried her away and out of her bedchambers. Many Amazons were already asleep at this hour, and the ones that weren't were too occupied ravishing their slaves with their strap-ons. No-one noticed Diana being whisked away from the palace and through the city streets, her naked form hanging limply on her captor's shoulder.

Diana's nose twitched at the scent of the smelling salts wafted under her nostrils. She let out a soft sigh as her head began to rise from the stone floor. She didn't make sense of her surroundings straight away, all she knew is she wasn't in her bed anymore, and that Mercy and Eve were standing over her.

Her sleepy look cleared as her eyes flared with anger. She shot up and grabbed Mercy, gripping the front of her sack and using it to hoist her into the air. "You dare to try and capture me!" the Amazon yelled as she held the woman up like she weighed nothing at all. "No... We would never... we brought you here to show you the truth..." Mercy groaned as her legs flailed in the air.

"Look where we are" Eve added with a sly smile, watching as Diana's head turned left and right "This... this is Circe's dungeon..." Diana muttered in a confused tone. For, other than the three of them, it was empty. Circe should've been here but she wasn't. For a second, Diana thought to accuse them of freeing her, but that would be impossible for them to have done, the chains and spells holding Circe couldn't be broken by two mortal slaves.

She slowly lowered Mercy down to her feet and began looking around "Where is she? I'm not in the mood for games" She said angrily as she traced her hand along the walls, testing every inch of the cell to see if there was some kind of weakspot. She spotted a small shimmer in the corner, there was something silvery there and Diana focused in on it.

She walked toward the corner and crouched down, her hand reaching out. From behind her Eve answered her question "Only Kara has the answer you seek..." As she said this, Diana picked up what she had found, a necklace that belonged to her mother. These two couldn't have freed Circe, but Kara could have, and as she looked at the necklace her suspicions began to rise.

She stood up straight and glanced over her shoulder at the two women "I will forgive you for this transgression. Just this once. Go back to your duties. Now!" With pleased smiles they scurried off, leaving Diana to look at the necklace as an angry expression came across her face.

Diana went straight back to her bed-chamber and got dressed in her red and blue armour, then she woke up Kelly and Alex with smelling salts. She allowed them to put on the silky white dresses she liked to see them in, then told them to follow her. Diana knew what she was planning to do was dangerous, but she couldn't stop herself now. She had been ignoring her suspicions for too long about her mother's disappearance, and she demanded answers.

Both Kelly and Alex were loyal to Diana. She had treated them well and rewarded their obedience. They followed her eagerly as she led them to the Kryptonian queen's bedchambers, marching on either side of Diana, who strode ahead with a determined glare in her eyes.

Kara's most recent long lovemaking session with Lena had ended about an hour ago. During this time, she had also invited Samantha into her bed, and she had thoroughly dominated both her and Lena, thrusting her strap-on deep into them until they were both a quivering mess. After ravishing them both, she had tied and gagged them, and she now had her arms wrapped around her beloved Lena as they lay sleeping in bed, Lena's bound form hugged to Kara's chest while Sam slept on her other side.

Diana quietly entered the royal bedchambers, taking a first step to potentially betraying her queen. She stood there in the dark for a moment, then nodded toward the bed as she whispered "Take the other two. You may ravish them to your heart's content, but make sure they do not awaken. The queen will stay here with me" She didn't move, but Kelly and Alex did, quietly sneaking up to the bed while Diana watched.

SEX AND CHAOS

They had brought cloths soaked in chloroform with them, Lena and Sam were already bound and gagged, making it even easier. They just pressed the cloths to their faces until both of the already groggy beauties were lulled into an even deeper sleep, then pulled them out of the bed. Kelly slung Lena over her shoulder while Alex took Sam, their rumps sticking up on their shoulders as they carried them past Diana and out of the room.

The door quietly closed and Diana was left alone with her sleeping queen. She had a cloth in her hand too and she slowly approached. She knew this could break the peace that had settled on the island, but she wouldn't be able to rest if she didn't know for sure. If this peace was built on a lie, then Diana felt it wasn't worth having.

She came closer and knelt on the bed beside Kara. The blonde kryptonian was naked beneath the sheets, the white silk resting on her and showing the outline of her strong figure, her breasts rising and falling with her slow breaths. Diana moved the cloth toward her mouth and nose then held it there, keeping it in place until she was certain Kara was unconscious. Then she took the edge of the sheets and slid them off of her, revealing Kara's nude body.

She pulled the sheets off, then took Kara's wrists and brought them together, resting them on her midsection. Then she unclipped her golden lasso from her side and wrapped it around Kara's wrists, binding her with the magical item. Diana took a slow shaky breath, nervous about what the lasso would reveal.

"You know what happened to Hippolyta. Don't you?" she asked in a stern tone. The magical power of the lasso compelled Kara to answer, even in her unconscious state. As if she was talking in her sleep, Kara's lips began to move and she softly mumbled "Yes..."

"What happened to her? Tell me" Diana spoke breathlessly, her eyes eager and intent as she leaned closer to Kara "I gave her to Circe, in exchanged for restoring Lena..." Kara mumbled in reply.

Diana remained silent for a moment, shaking with anger "You... You're a traitor!" She declared loudly, no longer caring if anyone heard her "You're unfit to rule this island!"

The lasso compelled Kara to reply to Diana's furious outburst and before Diana could continue she said "I never wanted to rule this island. I would've been content to stay at the Fortress of Solitude with Lena. You decided to pursue us and kidnap us after we had escaped the first time. You brought us back here, Diana, leaving Paradise Island undefended. You allowed Circe to invade this island in the first place. This is all because of your obsession..."

"I've heard enough from you!" Diana angrily shot back, grabbing the lasso and quickly unwrapping it from Kara's wrists. She lay down on top of her and clamped the cloth back down, just to ensure Kara would stay asleep, her hand pressing firmly to Kara's mouth in anger at what she had said. "My obsession?" Diana seethed as she squashed Kara into the sheets of the bed, her full weight pressing into the blonde's nude body.

"You have no idea how much I've been controlling my obsession..." Diana said as she peeled the cloth away to reveal Kara's plump lips "...my queen." she added disdainfully, no longer having any respect for the word as she lowered her mouth toward Kara's. She kissed her deeply, hungrily, having waited for so long to finally taste Kara, to feel the sexy blonde lying helplessly beneath her.

She kissed her for a long while, letting her tongue explore the confines of Kara's mouth. But it wasn't enough, she squeezed and fondled her breasts, grabbing and stroking at Kara's body as she allowed every impulse she'd been resisting to burst forth. She saw the strap-on sitting beside the bed; the one Kara had used on Lena and Sam.

Sliding off of Kara, she grabbed the strap-on and quickly secured it to herself, that large rod now pushing forward from her groin. "You were never the rightful ruler of this island..." Diana said with her heaving breaths, her eyes wild with anger and desire. She positioned herself between Kara's legs, gripping her knees and pulling them up and spreading them apart, lining up Kara's opening for her entry.

"Your rightful place... yours and sweet little Lena's... are as my slaves." She said as she thrust her hips and buried the strap-on deep inside of Kara, ravishing her with that one firm pumping motion.

It felt so good to feel Kara around the strap-on, and it felt equally as good to admit that she wanted her and Lena as her slaves again, a truth she had been holding in for far too long.

She began pumping her hips back and forth, making a soft wet sound with each thrust. Even while unconscious, Kara could feel the throbbing sensations inside of her, and she began moaning with her eyes closed, her face tightening slightly as she moaned exactly the way Diana wanted her to. As a good slave should when she's being dominated by her mistress.

She made her forceful love to Kara long into the night, moaning on top of her as she thrust her hips like a piston, driving the strap-on into Kara over and over. She kept going until she exhausted herself, orgasming multiple times from the powerful aphrodisiac. Kara orgasmed as well, but every time the pleasurable sensations threatened to wake her up, Diana clamped the cloth back down, keeping it in place as she continued ravishing her.

Diana's body was glowing with perspiration when she finally pulled the strap-on out of Kara, her breaths were heavy and tired. She unstrapped it, carefully cleaned it, and placed it back beside the bed, then she gripped the sheets and pulled them back over Kara. She could still feel her skin tingling with the aftershocks of her orgasm, that warm glow still pulsing through her chest. She knew now that tonight wouldn't be enough. That she had to have Kara back in bondage as her slave.

She left for a few moments, then returned with Kelly and Alex, the two of them carrying the equally ravished forms of Lena and Samantha back into the room. They put them back in the bed with Kara, settling them in the same place so that Kara would never realize what happened tonight. They were all still sleeping peacefully from the chloroform so there was no need to slip out straight away. Diana took a moment to make Kelly and Alex swear to secrecy, then she made them lie down at the base of the bed so she could tie them up.

Diana felt the need to dominate her slaves after reigniting her passion with Kara, so she quickly tied Kelly and Alex, squeezing their legs together and wrapping rope around their wrists. She finished by tying a white cloth between their lips, pulling it tightly before finishing the knot to make sure they were properly gagged. She then picked them both up and hoisted them over her shoulders, they had served her well tonight but she no longer needed them to do anything for her, so they were better suited to being over her shoulder where she could stroke and squeeze their rounded behinds.

She gave their rumps a few firm pats then turned toward the door, carrying them away. She had to leave Kara in her bed for now, but tomorrow morning she would start plotting the necessary steps to lead a revolution on the island. Once she told the other Amazons about Kara's betrayal, she was confident she could raise a small army against her. With these thoughts in her head, she carried Kelly and Alex back to her own bedchambers, not realising that everything that had happened tonight was all part of a carefully constructed plan...

Back in their room, a small and bare place which had a single uncomfortable bed, Mercy and Eve where speaking on a communication device. It had been magically enhanced to break through Themyscira's enchanted barrier, and it worked like any other phone. "Diana has been told about her mother's fate. The revolution will begin soon…" Mercy whispered into the phone, an evil smile spreading across her face.

Their capture had been part of this same plan, this communication device smuggled to the island when Kara had brought them here. On the other end of the phone was the woman who had devised all of this: Roulette was reclined in a leather chair, her lithe form clad in her tight-fitting red dress. "Excellent work…" she said with a pleased smile "…It won't be long now…"

CHAPTER 12

Betrayal

Chapter Summary: Diana decides to take drastic action in her plot to overthrow Kara, with Lena as the target of her scheme.

Diana and Nubia were walking through the forests of Themyscira together. It was a warm day and the sun filtered through the leaves above them. Nubia was wearing the standard skimpy white dress of the Amazons, the hem fluttering around her dark creamy thighs. Diana wore her modified superheroine attire, the symbol of their kryptonian queen emblazoned on her chest.

They had been walking for a little while and now they were far from the city, far enough that no-one would hear their words. For their conversation could have dire consequences. Since learning of her mother's fate, Diana had been quietly trying to build enough followers to lead a revolution; to overthrow Kara and put Diana in her rightful place.

But that attempt so far hadn't gained enough supporters. Despite telling the Amazons what had become of their former queen, many of them were still happy with Kara's reign. It was Kara who had provided them with the strap-ons that they delighted in using to ravish their slaves, and it was Kara who shared the most prized slave of all with them: the beautiful Lena.

"There's just not enough of them, princess" Nubia said calmly as they walked side by side "Not only does Kara have the numbers, but she has one of our greatest fighters. Artemis is extremely loyal to the kryptonian, she'll never turn against her." Diana let out an angry sigh, her fists clenching then relaxing as she replied "Then they're traitors just like her! All of them will be my slaves when the time comes! If she didn't have Lena with her…"

Diana trailed off as if she was thinking of some plot against the queen. The look on her face seemed to worry Nubia who squeezed Diana's shoulder reassuringly and said "All of your supporters want to see you on the throne princess. But none of us want a civil war between the Amazons. Too much would be lost. We just want what's best for Themyscira" Diana sighed and nodded, although deep down there was still a bubbling frustration.

They continued their walk as they discussed peaceful ways to try and gather support for Diana's revolution. But by the time they returned to the city, they were no closer to finding a solution.

Nubia hugged Diana warmly and said "Have patience, princess. Trust in your sisters" They parted ways and Diana returned to her room in the royal palace.

Waiting for her in bed were Alex and Kelly. Diana had tied them up and gagged them before going on her walk, and they were just where she had left them. She felt a little better seeing them there, her frustration fading as she made a sultry smile. She had left them in silky white nightdresses, then tied them so tightly that the silky fabric was now squeezed into them.

Diana began to undress, slipping her boots off as she took her strap-on from the nightstand. However, before she could ravish her slaves, the door of her quarters swung open. Her eyes darted to it angrily, no-one was allowed to just walk into her chambers unannounced. No-one except for the woman she saw standing there.

Kara stood in the doorway in her red and blue outfit, the pleated skirt resting neatly against her plump behind. She put her hands on her hips as she made a small nod toward Diana and said "Diana, I have need of Kelly and Alex. I'll return them to you when I'm done with them" She began walking to the bed where they lay in their bindings, but suddenly Diana stood and blocked her path.

There was a tense silence, Diana had never disobeyed her queen before but her frustrations had been growing and this was too much for her to ignore "They are MY slaves. You cannot..." She started angrily but Kara spoke over her, the whites of her eyes glowing a light red as she said in a stern tone "I can do whatever I wish. I am your queen and they are MY slaves first. As is every slave on this island..." Kara moved a little closer to Diana, daring her to challenge her as she said "...So step aside"

Diana glared back at her then sighed and moved out of the way as she seethed "As you wish, my queen" Kara nodded and walked to the bed. She hoisted Kelly and Alex onto either shoulder, easily carrying their bound forms, wrapping an arm around each of their thighs to keep them in place

SEX AND CHAOS

"Like I said, I'll return them when I'm done" Kara said coldly as she strode out of the room. Diana watched her go, her body trembling with anger, her eyes narrowing. Despite what Nubia had told her, she had no patience left. Something had to change and it had to change soon.

Lena was in her lab working on another pleasure device for the Amazons. She had come to love her life here: using her intelligence to combine science and magic while inventing new technology, being with her beloved Kara, and experiencing more pleasure than she had ever thought possible. A happy smile was on her face as she worked. She sat at a marble bench in front of a table, working on a design for a new type of vibrator. Her lab had many such items on the other tables along the walls. Lena wanted for nothing here.

As she worked, the door opened behind her and she glanced over her shoulder. She saw Alex, Kelly and Sam entering the room and made a confused smile at them. "Does Kara need me for something?" Lena asked innocently, to which Kelly made a sly smile and replied "Perhaps... you'll find out soon enough..."

Kelly got a little closer then pounced, she had been keeping one hand behind her back and now showed she was holding a white cloth damp with chloroform. She pressed it over Lena's mouth and nose as the other two grabbed her as well, pulling her off of the bench and gently bringing her down to the floor. Lena was used to this kind of treatment by now, and she knew how to play her part. She made helpless muffled moans from beneath the cloth, wriggling and squirming while making no real effort to get away.

Lena was wearing a silky white nightdress like all the slaves wore and it slid up her legs showing off her white thong panties as she struggled against the women holding her down. Those luscious limbs were too tempting and they began stroking and squeezing them, their hands running up her supple thighs and rubbing against her panties. Her legs weren't enough though, they began groping her breasts, kissing her neck, overwhelming her with the sensual sensations as Kelly kept the cloth firmly pressed to her face.

Lena's eyes began to flutter, a weakened tired look settling in her gaze as she continued being felt up and fondled. Their hands were all over, exploring every inch of her body as she was forced into unconsciousness. She could feel the heat growing deep within her as her senses faded, the warm touch of their hands and lips sending her to sleep with pleasurable tingles.

Her eyes fluttered closed and they continued fondling and kissing her for a few moments. Then,

they began to tie her up. Kelly had brought the cloth while Alex and Sam had brought thin lengths of white rope. They wrapped up her legs at the ankles, above and below the knees, and around the middle of her shapely thighs, squeezing them together with tight knots. Then they rolled Lena over onto her back and tied her wrists together as well. They also looped cord around her torso, above and below her breasts, framing them enticingly. Finally, they pulled a white cloth tightly over her lips to gag her, the finishing touch to make her a captured damsel.

With the thoroughly bound and gagged beauty ready to be taken, Kelly hoisted her up onto her shoulder and carried her away. The three of them walked through the streets of Themyscira with Lena's pleasantly plump rump sticking up on Kelly's shoulder. It was perfectly normal to see Lena this way, so no-one stopped them, although many looked on with jealousy that they had the island's most desired pleasure slave all to themselves.

They weren't taking her to bed or truly kidnapping her, though. Unbeknownst to anyone on the island, they were taking Lena to a private ceremony: for her wedding to the kryptonian queen to finally commence. First, they took her to one of the buildings in Themyscira that had a private room. There, they undressed Lena, groped her delicious-looking body a little more, then dressed her up in a wedding dress. It was similar to her slave dress but had a more floral and lacy pattern.

They then tied Lena back up and carried her to a private spot on the island, near a cliffside that overlooked the oceans surrounding the island. On that spot, Kara waited for them, dressed in her own bridal gown. Lena was just starting to awaken as they carried her toward Kara. They handed their precious cargo over gently and Kara held her, helping Lena to stand on the soft and sensitive soles of her barefeet as Kara gripped her shoulders firmly.

Lena's eyes slowly lost that sleepy glaze, the blurriness clearing as she looked at Kara then down at herself. She let out a small muffled moan of shock as she realised what was happening: that today was to be her wedding day. Kara smiled lovingly, taking in the sight of her beautiful soon-to-be slavewife. She looked perfect, every bit as desirable as the moment Kara had first laid eyes upon her.

SEX AND CHAOS

"Are you ready?" Kara asked softly, to which Lena nodded and made an enthusiastic moan through her gag. Kara had wanted the ceremony to be small and intimate. Watching on, she only had her close slaves: Alex, Kelly, Sam, Lois, and Vicki. They observed as Kara began to recite the kryptonian marriage rites, sealing the bond between her and her new captive bride.

Once she was done, she kissed Lena on the lips and there was a small round of applause and some cheers. Kara then hoisted Lena up over her shoulder, gave her rump a satisfied pat, and flew to a secluded royal building away from the others. It was on an isolated and elevated area of the island and housed a bedroom in which Kara intended to spend her honeymoon with Lena. Their honeymoon suite had been prepared in advance, the silky sheets were made, there was chloroform and more ropes ready should Kara need them, and there was also a strap-on lying on the nightstand.

Kara flew in with Lena and set her down on the sheets, she was thrilled that she had finally wedded her beloved. In only a few moments, she had Lena untied and fully undressed, and she too stripped down to nothing. Their naked bodies were soon grinding together, becoming moist with perspiration as they made love to each other. Kara took the strap-on and quickly strapped it to her hips, then with one firm thrust she plunged deep between Lena's thighs, pumping up and down as they both moaned in ecstasy.

While the newlyweds were making passionate love, Diana had gone to seek guidance from a less trustworthy source. Nubia's advice to remain patient wasn't good enough so she had gone to see Mercy and Eve in their humble abodes. Nubia had told Diana not to trust them, but she was too blinded by her rage to listen to her trusted ally.

At the very moment Kara was thrusting into Lena, Diana was speaking with the two lowest slaves on the island. Mercy and Eve were filling her head with thoughts of capturing and kidnapping Lena, convincing her it was the only way to get the Amazons to turn on the Kryptonian. She listened to their advice and slowly became more convinced they were right, they had been the ones to tell her the truth about Hippolyta after all...

A few weeks after the wedding, Lena was once more back in the the lab Kara had built for her where she worked on her inventions. Her honeymoon had been blissful and even now she could feel the swell in her heart with how in love she was. Sam was standing guard over her, as Kara couldn't watch her beloved at all times. She stood close by the door as Lena worked. The calm silence was suddenly interrupted as the door burst open and Diana came striding in. Lena swivelled around on her bench, but it wasn't her Diana was coming for.

As she turned, Diana was chloroforming Sam, her arms wrapped around her with a cloth pressed over her mouth and nose. "Wh... what are you doing?" Lena asked as she got up with a worried expression and came over to them. Diana just smiled at her, using her free hand to calmly grope Sam as she replied "Samantha here is a soldier-slave like any other, is she not? And now that our queen has assigned her to guard one as precious as you, I'm just taking her for some more training. There's no need to worry your pretty little head over it, my sweet Lena."

Sam was moaning softly from behind the cloth, her legs wobbling as she melted into Diana's grip. Diana continued gently fondling her breasts as she passed out, sending her to sleep with the teasing grip on her bosom. "Oh... I see..." Lena said softly "...Well you must inform Kara so she can assign someone else to stand guard over me..."

Sam let out a final sigh as her eyes closed and Diana eased her limp form gently to the ground. She began tying her up as she replied "Don't worry Lena, I'll make sure you're in good hands" She finished tying up and gagging Sam and hoisted her up onto her shoulder. Then, as she was leaving with Sam, she suddenly turned and gave Lena a playful spank and walked out of the room.

Lena let out a small gasp at Diana's hand slapping her bottom. Then, rubbing her slightly sore rump, she watched Diana suspiciously as she left with the unconscious Sam slung over her shoulder. Lena sighed and turned back to her work, she was suspicious of Diana but she had work to do, so for now she would just have to trust her.

She went back to her work but a creeping sense of unease began to grow. She couldn't help the feeling she was being watched. She looked down at her marriage bracelet, wondering if she should use it to call Kara. But before she could, she was suddenly grabbed from behind. Two pairs of arms gripped her tightly, forcing her down to the floor.

SEX AND CHAOS

A cloth was forced over her mouth and nose, and a blindfold wrapped around her eyes before she could get a good look at her captors. She immediately knew this was happening without Kara's permission; that she was actually being kidnapped, again. But that knowledge did Lena no good, the women holding her were too strong, and her struggles soon died down. She could feel the chloroform filling her lungs and with a distressed moan, she passed out. She was then quickly bound and gagged, her captors wrapping her thoroughly in rope before stealing her away.

It took only an hour for Lena's disappearance to be noticed. Kara was never away from her beloved for long and she came to check up on her. She found no-one in the room and knew something was wrong. Her greatest fear was coming true: that Lena would be taken from her again. The mere thought of it ignited a rage within the Kryptonian queen.

She immediately alerted every Amazon on the island, there would be no ravishing of slaves, no pleasure, until Lena was found. Both the soldiers and the slaves were assembled to search every inch of the island, while Kara herself flew around, looking down with her eyes a furious glowing red.

As news of Lena's kidnapping spread around the island, Diana had Nubia bring together a group of the Amazons who had refused to swear loyalty to her. They met in the basement of one of the buildings in Themyscira, where Kara's search patrols couldn't spot them.

It was now that Diana intended to lead her revolution, when Kara was distracted by her search, and when the Amazons no longer had Lena as an incentive to stay loyal to their queen. But, despite all of this, they still would not join her. Kara had earned their loyalty and Diana found she could not sway them. Artemis was the leader of those who supported Kara's rule, and she argued - successfully - that Kara's rule had been far more prosperous for the Amazons than Hippolyta's or Diana's. Diana herself left the meeting furious, returning to the hidden location where Lena was being held captive.

The doors burst open to the small bedroom. Inside, Mercy and Eve were busy groping poor, confused Lena; Diana's co-conspirators had devilish smiles as they fondled the helpless, kidnapped damsel. She was tied and gagged, still blindfolded, and had her ears plugged by her captors while she was unconscious, having no idea where she was being kept. Even though their 'punishment' belts prevented them from orgasming, the two women were still enjoying aggressively feeling up Lena. She lay between them on the bed, squashed between their bodies as they squeezed and viciously fondled her soft, shapely form.

Diana strode in and let out an angry growl "After everything my mother did for them! Traitors!" she yelled angrily as she punched a wall, leaving a large dent in the stone. Mercy raised her eyebrows as she said slyly "So... the meeting didn't go well?" Her hand kept groping and spanking Lena's ass as she talked, ignoring the kidnapped beauty's whimpering muffled moans as she squirmed between them.

Diana turned on them with an angry glare and said "No! It did not! Even without Lena, they still wont betray Kara, and now she has the whole island out searching for her! It's only a matter of time until they find us..." Diana felt a small tingle of fear and desperation run down her spine. She had Lena now, but it hadn't made any difference, it only ensured she would be found and imprisoned.

A bottle of chloroform sat on the nightstand by the bed and Diana walked over to it. She snatched it up as she said "I'm sorry... but your plan has failed, I have no choice..." She drizzled the chemical onto two cloths then pounced onto the bed. She pressed the cloths over the faces of Eve and Mercy, easily holding them down with her superior strength.

To her surprise they barely put up a fight, they moaned softly but lay submissively beneath her as she subdued them. She brought them down just enough so they wouldn't be able to get away, stopping when their eyes had drooped to a small sliver. Then, she chloroformed Lena as well, knocking the innocent damsel out fully (while Lena continued to whimper and moan in utter confusion) and hoping she would be too dazed to remember any of this.

With Eve and Mercy subdued she began to bind them, but only their torsos. She needed to make sure the bondage was as restrictive as possible, to show to Kara that she was punishing them. She tied their arms in boxties then wrapped rope around their breasts to painfully squeeze them. Diana bound them frantically, hoping her plan would work, her eyes wobbling with a nervous worry as she began tying leashes around their necks.

In her throne room, Kara had assembled her most loyal soldiers, led by Artemis who she had started to trust more than anyone. They were preparing to start raiding each and every home in Themyscira. The island had been searched and still Lena hadn't been found, so now they would check every single room, any possible place she could be hidden away. The Amazons wouldn't like having their privacy invaded, but Artemis assured her that they knew and would understand that Kara had no other choice.

Before they could set off on their mission, however, Diana burst triumphantly into the room in with exactly who they were looking for. She had Lena securely slung over her shoulder and Mercy and Eve led on leashes behind her, walking in stumbling steps with how tightly their arms were bound behind their backs. She also had them both tightly gagged so they wouldn't be able to speak of her own role in the failed revolution.

Kara let out a relieved gasp as soon as she saw the familiar shapely rump and bare legs and feet of the figure slumped over Diana's shoulder. She rushed forward and took her beloved slavewife, sliding her off of Diana's shoulder and hugging her warmly. "I found who took her, my queen" Diana said with a sharp tug of the leashes, making Eve and Mercy stumble forward. Kara was still too focused on Lena to respond straight away; she hugged her and kissed Lena all over her face and neck as she let out long relieved breaths. Then, she hoisted Lena up onto her own shoulder and nodded at Diana as she said "Thank you."

She glared at Mercy and Eve who stood behind Diana and declared loudly "Take them to the dungeons!" They were quickly dragged away and a look of relief shone in Diana's eyes, she had seemingly gotten away with placing all the blame on them. Kara smiled at her as she began walking closer, Lena's rump still perched neatly on her shoulder.

"There's just one more thing I need to know Diana..." she said as her smile began to turn more serious. Suddenly she rushed forward using her super speed, and in a blur she grabbed Diana's wrists, pulled them in front of her and tied them up with her golden lasso. Holding the other end of the lasso Kara looked sternly into Diana's eyes as she said "Did you have anything to do with my beloved Lena's kidnapping?"

All the Amazons in the throne room looked on in tense silence. To the side, Artemis smiled smugly. It was she who had told Kara of her suspicions about Diana's revolution. Artemis wanted to be the second-in-command to

Kara and it seemed she was moments away from getting her wish. Diana's mouth hung open in shock, her bound wrists held out in front of her.

"I... I..." her eyes darted around as she looked to see if any of the Amazons would help her, but she saw she had no support. Kara had turned her own sisters against her, their loyalty was to the kryptonian queen. Diana trembled as she tried to hold in the words, beads of sweat formed on her smooth skin from the strain. The magic of the lasso pulsed through her and in a pained groan she blurted out "I helped them kidnap Lena to try and overthrow you."

Kara's eyes narrowed at the admission of guilt "I see..." she said coldly as she kept her grip on the lasso, staring into Diana's eyes with a piercing anger "You are hereby stripped of all your privileges on Themyscira! You will own no slaves and hold no power! You are a traitor and a prisoner, and nothing else!" Diana's eyes became watery as she was chastised in front of her sisters, who observed her with shame. She had brought Kara here as her slave originally and now the woman she had kidnapped and enslaved so long ago had taken everything from her.

"You... you can't! Please!" Diana moaned but Kara had heard enough. Artemis and some of the other Amazons loyal to Kara advanced on Diana and dragged her out of the throne room. She was so utterly defeated she didn't even struggle, she just allowed herself to be taken from the throne room which once had been hers. Kara watched her go angrily, then her attention turned back to Lena, who was starting to regain consciousness and writhe weakly in her bonds. Kara gave Lena's long legs a slow, loving caress, then adoringly patted her shapely bottom as Lena muffled a relieved sigh into her gag, recognizing the touch of Kara's strong arms and knowing that she was back to being safely in the possession of her powerful and protective wife. Still bound, gagged, and blindfolded, Lena could only give a weak little wiggle of her rump and another happy hum into her gag to voice her gratitude for Kara rescuing her.

"Mmmph... Thmmk ymm fmr rmmscmm mm, Kmrm mph lmmv! Wmml ymph mphtmph mph, nmmph?" ("Oooh... Thank you for rescuing me, Kara my love! Will you untie me, now?") Kara smiled and continued to gently pat Lena's rump as she carried her beautiful wife back to their chambers.

SEX AND CHAOS

"No, my love. I think I'll leave you as you are - nice and packaged up for me - for what I have planned for you tonight to celebrate your safe return." Lena gave a soft moan of arousal as Kara's caresses of her rump and legs became more intimate

It had been a long day and the sun was starting to set. Kara sent the Amazons back home to return to their slaves and she returned to bed to triumphantly ravish her beloved slavewife. She was troubled by Diana's treachery, but pleased that the other Amazons were still loyal to her. It proved what she already knew, that she was the most dominant woman on the island and that no-one would ever dare challenge her again.

As Kara was gently ravishing Lena in bed with slow passionate kisses, gentle fondling, and some pleasantly spirited cheek-clapping, Diana was being tossed in a lowly dungeon, her wrists now shackled together. "Enjoy your new home, princess" Artemis said teasingly as she slammed the door shut. It took Diana a second to realise she wasn't alone in her cell: she had been put in the same room in which Eve and Mercy were imprisoned.

Her head tilted down as she let out a sigh of shame and said "I'm sorry I betrayed you..." They both looked to each other with a knowing smile then slowly began to advance on her "We don't blame you, princess..." Eve said as she walked up to one side of Diana, giving her shoulder a small squeeze. Mercy walked up to her other side, sandwiching her between them as she continued "...We would've done the same thing..."

Diana could feel the heat of their bodies on either side of her, feel the warmth of their breath as Eve asked "Do you still wish to overthrow Themyscira?" Mercy leaned in a little closer to her ear and whispered "To make Kara, Lena, and all the women on this island your slaves, as they should be?" Diana's head turned left and right as she looked at them. She had been betrayed by her sisters and had nothing left. All she wanted was her revenge and to take her rightful place as the ruler of this island.

"Yes... I'll do anything..." she said desperately. Mercy let out a pleased sigh as she began slowly stroking Diana's body "Good..." she said in a sultry purr. Eve began doing the same, groping and squeezing her as she whispered in her ear "All you have to do is partner with our mistress... you can have everything you want if you just do exactly as Roulette says... understand?" Diana shivered from the tingles of their hands all over her body, feeling them squeezing her breasts and backside in their slow gentle caress. With a small nod she sighed and gave in as she replied "Yes. I understand"

CHAPTER 13

Desire for Submission

Chapter Summary: Lena begins to grow frustrated under the restrictions Kara has put on her in the aftermath of the most recent attempt to kidnap her. With the help of Artemis, Kara makes a shocking discovery about herself.

Lena's bare feet made a soft slap against the marble floors of the palace. She moved cautiously, making hesitant steps as her head turned left and right. She approached a corner and peered her head around it, then hurried forward, the hem of her silky nightdress swishing around where it rested at the top of her thighs. She was almost at her destination and began to slow down as she approached the doors to her laboratory, the place where she had been working on her scientific research on Paradise Island.

Just as Lena began to reach out for the handles to the doors, a pair of arms wrapped around her "You know your lab access has been revoked, little one." came a gentle yet firm voice behind her, the tone familiar to Lena, but not comforting in this moment. A cloth damp with chloroform pressed down over Lena's mouth and nose, whilst the other arm was tightly wrapped around her midsection, keeping her wriggling form in place.

Lena knew it was Artemis and she knew that against the powerful Amazon she was completely outmatched. But still she attempted to struggle, her supple legs writhing up and down, her breasts jiggling as she twisted her shoulders side to side. She made frustrated moans against the cloth, the sounds muffled as they grew fainter with every breath she took. "Mmm! Mmmph! Hmmm..."

Finally, Lena let out a soft sigh, her eyes fluttering as her arms hung loosely by her trim waist. Artemis held her up now, keeping her on her feet with her strong grip. Lena could feel herself melting into the Amazon's embrace, feel her body drooping and giving up any resistance. With a last sleepy blink her eyes closed and she faded away, the darkness taking her with that white cloth still obscuring her gorgeous features.

Artemis kept the cloth in place for a few more moments, then she slowly peeled it away, turning Lena to the side as she did. She let Lena's limp body hang back against her arm as she assessed her angelic expression, looking so beautiful in this peaceful resting state. "Now, you'll have to be punished..." she said with a pleased sigh, leaning in to plant a kiss against Lena's yielding lips.

Artemis eased Lena down to the floor then began to tie her up with the rope she had brought with her. This was not the first time Lena had tried to disobey her queen. In fact, it was becoming a worrying trend. Kara had grown paranoid since Lena's capture and kidnap by Diana and her minions a short while ago. Kara no longer trusted Lena to remain safe while she worked in the laboratory and so it was strictly off limits. After all, it was while she was working there that Diana, Eve, and Mercy had taken her.

Artemis tied Lena's wrists behind her back with the thin white rope, wrapping another length around her arms and her torso, that white line squeezing just below Lena's breasts. She then tied her legs, squashing their soft shape together with multiple lines of rope. She finished Lena's bondage with a tight gag, pushing her plump lips together as she tied a white cloth over them.

The redheaded Amazon was dressed in brown leather, thin straps rested snugly on her shoulders, the top pushing up her voluptuous breasts, the pleated skirt against her thighs. She was among the best warriors on the island, perhaps only second to Diana, and her tightly toned figure displayed this fact. She hoisted Lena up as if she weighed nothing at all, settling the shapely beauty on her shoulder. Then she carried Lena out of the palace, the helpless damsel slung over her shoulder like a sack of potatoes.

Lena remained asleep as she was carried through the streets of Themyscira. Her shapely rump drew the attention of all the Amazons she passed, many looking on with jealousy as Artemis took her to her own private bedchambers. They were becoming used to seeing Lena bound and gagged atop Artemis's shoulder, the tension between Lena and their queen was well known. Artemis ignored their glances, keeping an arm firmly wrapped around Lena's soft thighs to keep her in place; her determined gaze focused on the path ahead.

SEX AND CHAOS

Artemis reached her home, only a short distance from the palace, and carried Lena inside. She gave her captive's bottom a firm slap to rouse her as she said "Time to wake up, little one. You can't sleep through your punishment" Lena made a soft moan through her gag, her eyes fluttering as her head began to tilt up. She felt herself being eased off of Artemis's shoulder, her bound form carefully handled then settled across the Amazon's lap as Artemis sat on the edge of her bed.

Lena's eyes opened wider, her hips wriggling on Artemis's lap as she made frustrated moans through her gag. "Mmmph! Nmmph!" Artemis kept a firm hand on her lower back so she wouldn't shift about too much, then she lifted her other hand in the air and brought it swatting down on Lena's backside, leaving a small red mark on the soft, creamy flesh of her rump. Her bottom jiggled and Lena let out a yelping moan. Then, Artemis rose her hand again and started spanking Lena to a steady rhythm, her hand slapping the innocent brunette's backside over and over, each strike just as powerful as the last.

There was barely a second between each spank, Artemis never tiring as she reddened Lena's behind, making that porcelain skin throb with the rosy shade. Lena knew she had disobeyed her queen but for the first time she didn't care; even when tears started rolling down her cheeks, she still wasn't sorry. Kara's control of her had gone too far. Artemis could hear this resistance in every frustrated moan she made through her gag. She had spanked Lena many times in the recent days, and each time Lena had refused to apologize. Artemis knew this time would be no different, there was a division growing between Lena and Kara that a simple spanking couldn't fix.

With a final firm smack against Lena's behind, Artemis's hand came to rest, laying flat on her captive's bottom as she sighed "I think you've had enough pain for now, little one..." her hand then slid down from the curve of her rear as she continued "...I think it's time for some pleasure" She began untying the brunette beauty's legs, carefully loosening the knots around Lena's thighs and ankles. It was difficult to focus on anything other than the throbbing of her reddened backside, but Lena could feel her legs being freed, and she knew why.

Lena shook her head and moaned angrily into her gag as she was lifted up and placed in the centre of the soft sheets. Not only had Artemis been punishing her frequently, but she had also been ravishing her, taking advantage of her position as Kara's second in command. Kara would always tell Lena whenever she was being given to one of the other Amazons, and no such discussion had taken place so Lena felt certain that this was happening without the queen's permission.

Lena glared angrily at Artemis as she watched her peeling off the leather mini-dress, letting it crumple at her feet. She stepped out of it then picked up one of the many strap-ons built to Lena's design. She pulled the straps tight to her hips then moved purposefully onto the bed, advancing on the helpless Lena, who tried wriggling away. Artemis seized her legs, gripping them firmly as she yanked Lena back to the centre of the bed. Then she took her captive's knees and pushed them apart, spreading Lena's thighs for her entry.

Lena moaned helplessly as Artemis lowered down on top of her. Then, with that first thrust, she shuddered with pleasure. Even in her anger and indignation, Lena was unable to resist the pleasure of the device, that long thick shaft burying inside of her, throbbing with pleasurable sensations deep in her core. Artemis began pumping back and forth, kissing Lena on her gagged lips as she smiled down at the helpless damsel. With each pump Lena lost herself more and more to the pleasure, her skin tingling as she was brought to climax.

After thoroughly ravishing her, Artemis retied Lena's legs, spanked her a bit more, and carried her back to the palace. She took her to the throne room, to tell the queen of Lena's transgression. A few soldier slaves were leaving just as Artemis was arriving, and she stood aside respectfully to let them pass while Lena's reddened rump continued writhing in frustration atop her shoulder. She then entered the room, walking closer to the golden throne Kara sat upon.

Kara was visibly tense, her hands clutching the armrests of her throne, her expression hardened as she watched Artemis walking in. She had been like this since Diana's betrayal, all wound up and stiff, the stress and pressure of trying to keep Lena safe having severely affected her. Kara knew why Artemis was here yet again with Lena over her shoulder, her wife's bottom red from another spanking. She assessed the marks of Lena's spanking then looked to Artemis, her eyes narrowed as she said "What did she do this time?"

SEX AND CHAOS

"Tried to break into her lab again, my queen" Artemis replied with a small bow of her head. Kara's jaw tightened with anger, then she opened her mouth to say something. Before she could Lena moaned angrily through her gag, her hips wriggling atop Artemis's shoulder. "Set her down, I want to hear what my disobedient wife has to say for herself" Kara said with a small sigh.

Artemis eased Lena off of her shoulder, setting her down to her feet then turning her to face Kara. She then carefully untied the gag and pulled it free from Lena's lips, her hands sliding down to hold Lena's waist so she wouldn't fall from standing with her legs still bound. "So. Is your punishment finally going to be effective? Have you learned your lesson, my love?" Kara asked as she looked down at Lena from her throne.

Lena couldn't hold it in anymore, and in a frustrated breath, she blurted out "She's been doing more than just punishing me, Kara! She steals me away to her chambers and ravishes me! Without your permission!" Kara sighed and shook her head as she replied "She does have my permission, Lena. I gave it to her the moment I assigned her to keep you safe" Lena's eyes widened with shock, then wobbled with a betrayed look "But... you never discussed this with me..." She said as she pouted unhappily, her plump lips pursing together.

"I'm sick of being treated like this! All of these restrictions have gone too far!" Lena yelled as she began struggling in her bondage "I've heard enough" Kara said sternly as she gestured to Artemis who already had a cloth ready. She pressed it against Lena's mouth and nose, forcing her to inhale the scent of chloroform. Then, once Lena's eyes fluttered closed, Artemis pulled another white cloth over Lena's pouty lips to gag her.

"She'll need to be punished again, more thoroughly this time" Kara said as Artemis hoisted Lena back up on her shoulder. "Do you trust me, my queen?" Artemis asked as she looked up into Kara's eyes, her steadfast gaze giving the queen comfort in her angst. "I do" Kara replied, immediately.

Artemis nodded then continued. "Good. Then I ask you trust me with punishing Lena in a new way I have devised. I will take her to the secluded spot you had your honeymoon and ensure she learns a valuable lesson... I also request you come as well, I think this lesson could be useful for you, too..."

A short while later, Artemis was gently and reverently bathing Lena's naked body, letting her soak in a tub of white marble, filled with magical oils. The bathing room was adjacent to the bedroom that Lena and Kara had spent their honeymoon in, the thick plumes of steam drifting from the bath and filling the air. Lena still hadn't fully woken up from the chloroform and she lay in the bath limp and listless, her nude form stroked and caressed as Artemis washed every inch of her.

Artemis knelt beside the tub, dipping her hands in to bathe Lena's skin, gently squeezing her supple form as she ensured the oils in the water properly soaked in. The oils had a magical quality, not only softening Lena's skin, but also making it incredibly sensitive. As she lay in the warm water she made soft moans, her body making small writhing motions as she felt Artemis's hands on her, that increased sensitivity making every touch tingle with pleasure. Artemis continued bathing her for a little while, then she helped Lena out of the water, her naked body glistening wet as she stepped out.

Artemis dried Lena off then began rubbing a magical lotion into her skin, making it even more baby-soft. Artemis made sure to rub in the lotion on every inch of Lena's body, taking her time to stroke her long legs and ample bosom, practically worshipping each part of her with the application of the cream. The oils and the cream had another effect that Lena was now starting to realise: they were a potent aphrodisiac, and they were making a heat start to grow between her thighs.

Once the lotion was applied thoroughly, Artemis carried Lena to the bed. Kara was waiting nearby, watching as per Artemis's request. She saw her beloved now glowing with a warm sheen, her skin so smooth and soft. Lena was lain down on the bed, where ropes awaited her. Artemis began to slowly bind her, wrapping lengths of rope around her ankles, calves, above and below her knees, and finally around the middle of her sumptuous thighs.

Once she was finished with her legs Artemis rolled Lena over. She gave the soft and pale soles of Lena's feet a small tickle, making the helpless damsel wriggle with pleasure, even this small touch igniting a fire from the aphrodisiacs against her skin. Artemis sat atop Lena's shapely rump, keeping that wriggling under control as she brought the disobedient beauty's hands behind her back. She crossed Lena's wrists then tied them tightly together with the soft white rope. She then rolled Lena back over and sat her up, allowing her to loop more rope around her torso, going above and below her breasts. Each rope around her torso also went around her upper arms, pinning them tightly to Lena's back.

Artemis had prepared Lena's punishment meticulously, once she was done binding her, she took a cloth soaked in more of her magical aphrodisiac. She scrunched it into a ball then stuffed it into Lena's mouth. She then pulled another cloth over her lips, tying it so tightly the outline of their plump shape could be seen beneath the fabric. Lena could feel the aphrodisiac on her tongue, making her even hornier, her body throbbing so desperately for release that she began whimpering softly through her gag.

Even the mere touch of the ropes against her now incredibly sensitive skin was overwhelming. But Artemis still wasn't done with this maddening build of arousal. Artemis showed Lena the final touch to her bondage: dangling two lengths of cord in front of her with a knowing smile. One length was normal, a straight white line. The other had two thick knots tied along its length. Lena looked on with confusion as Artemis tied the first length around her waist, almost like a belt. She then took the second length and carefully threaded it between Lena's luscious thighs.

Lena immediately could feel the purpose of those two knots as Artemis tightened the crotchrope, driving the two bumps in the rope against her most intimate areas, one at the opening between her thighs, the other between her plump ass-cheeks. Her eyes fluttered wide and she made a pleading gasp as she felt those knots pressing into her, their very presence driving her wild with desire. She began writhing and grinding her hips into the bed, her need for release making her too horny to think straight, her body wriggling like an animal in heat.

As she squirmed she could feel the ropes on her torso squeezing at her breasts, making each soft mound throb with pleasure. Her head tilted back and she shuddered, each white line tingling as it rubbed against her soft skin. Artemis watched her for a few moments, not even needing to touch the helpless beauty as she lost herself to pleasure. "You want to orgasm don't you?" She said in a low stern tone, her voice reaching Lena's ears even in the throes of her passion.

Lena looked up at her and nodded frantically, her trembling eyes pleading with her captor. Artemis leaned down, but instead of pleasuring her she took Lena's hip and rolled her over onto her front. "Well, then you need to behave yourself." She said as she began firmly spanking Lena's writhing bottom, her hand smacking down on it as she punished her.

Kara was intrigued by how dominant Artemis was being to her slavewife. She couldn't help herself; she stood and walked a little closer to the bed to watch. With another firm spank Artemis glanced over her shoulder and said "Are you enjoying watching me punish her, my queen?" Kara kept a stoic look as she nodded, her heart beating in her chest as she replied "Yes..."

Artemis smiled and slipped off of the bed, leaving Lena to writhe helplessly as she languished in her bondage "And do you trust me to do this?" She asked as she slowly circled around Kara, moving behind her. Kara was so transfixed by Lena's sensuality in her bondage she couldn't look away, and she muttered softly "Yes..." She then heard Artemis's breath by her ear as the Amazon whispered "Good, because now it's your turn"

Kara suddenly felt a lasso loop around her torso, going just below her breasts and pinning her arms to her sides. A second later Artemis clamped a cloth over her mouth and nose, keeping it firmly in place. "Hmmmph!" Kara began to struggle, letting out a shocked moan through her suddenly handgagged mouth. But, despite her struggling, Artemis easily held her in place.

"Mmmph!" Kara made another moan as she realised her powers somehow weren't working, and without them Artemis was easily overpowering her, the tall and well built Amazon far stronger than the more lithe Kryptonian. She made a few final efforts to break free, her body squirming in Artemis's grip. "Hmmm..." Then, with a soft sigh, her eyes began to flutter closed, her last thought was that she had once again been betrayed by her second in command.

Kara awakened to find herself now tied to the bed she had been sitting on to watch Lena's punishment. She was stripped naked and bound in a 'Y' position, her arms tied at the wrists to the bedposts on either side of her with her legs bound together at the ankles and secured to the foot of the bed. She was lying face down, a thick gag tied between her lips and a strip of black silk tied over her eyes. She awoke slowly, hearing a wet slapping noise that she recognised: the sound of skin on skin. She could hear Lena begin ravished, hear her loud moans through a gag with each thrusting sound, and she knew exactly who was ravishing her.

SEX AND CHAOS

Kara tried to tilt her head higher but she was so tightly and securely bound to the bed, she couldn't manage it. Her plump yet muscular ass made a small wriggling motion, her body tensing as she tested her bonds, then going still when she realized her struggles against them were useless. She was a helpless captive, just like her wife. Lena's loud pleasurable moans continued for a while, as more of the daze cleared from Kara's head. She could hear the utter ecstasy in the sounds Lena was making, that pleasure finally being released as Artemis forced her to orgasm over and over.

Kara moaned and struggled in her bondage a bit, unsure of what Artemis's intentions were for her or her beloved wife. She could hear Artemis having her way with Lena and could only assume that she had been tricked, captured, stripped nude, bound, and gagged in this way in order for Artemis to eventually do the same to her. Kara found herself perplexed at the realization that the idea of being helpless and ready to be ravished was actually making her... incredibly aroused. She knew she should be trying to figure out how Artemis had managed to dampen her powers and capture her; knew she should be trying to struggle free and rescue herself and her precious Lena. But Kara was startled to realize that she found something about this whole situation... strangely appealing to her. Being bound, gagged, helpless... hearing her wife being ravished and knowing that she was likely next. Kara couldn't explain it, but something about being Artemis's captive felt starkly different from when she had found herself in Diana's and Circe's clutches. There was no gloating from her captor, no lording her helpless state over her. Artemis hadn't taunted Kara or been particularly cruel to her. Her capture had been sensual, but strangely respectful and Kara had some strange intuition in her mind telling her that she was in no real danger from her captor, despite the very real fact that she had been overpowered, chloroformed, and successfully kidnapped.

As the sounds of Lena's luscious cheeks being clapped continued, Kara began to grow more frustrated that she was just being ignored on the bed, and she began struggling more as her wife's moans of pleasure increased. She heard Artemis make a final few thrusts into her beloved, then she heard Lena whimpering sadly as Artemis's footsteps left her and approached the other bed, on which Kara was securely bound. Kara moaned questioningly as she heard the Amazon draw near, but Artemis ignored her for now. After hearing her captor leisurely gather some supplies from a nearby nightstand, Kara felt the pressure of Artemis joining her on the bed, then she made a shocked twitch as she felt lotion and oils being rubbed into her body.

"Your body is truly magnificent, my queen..." Artemis cooed softly as she rubbed in the warm oil, making Kara's skin sleek and smooth, with a light floral scent. She rubbed it into her arms, her shoulders, down her back, firmly into each shapely globe of her rear. She took her time, rubbing slowly, admiring the grooves of Kara's muscles, her athletic figure so well defined it deserved this loving appraisal. As she rubbed the oil she would plant small kisses on Kara's skin, the touch of her lips sending tingles through Kara's body. She could feel the oil start to work its magic, the same heat she had seen drive Lena wild was now starting to slowly pulse through her. "Mmmph... hmmm..." Kara moaned softly into her gag.

"Your Kryptonian genetics are a true blessing, your majesty..." Artemis continued in her usual respectful tone, even though she had successfully captured Kara and was now forcing this pleasurable massage upon her. "...Your gorgeous wife is lusciously soft..." she said as stroked Kara's legs, rubbing up and down her thighs and making Kara moan more desperately through her gag "...Her ample bosom... her plump rump... her beauty is akin to the prized damsels of myth such as Helen of Troy, Aphrodite or Persephone."

"But your body..." She said as she stroked down to the soles of Kara's bare feet coating them in the aphrodisiac oil, then glided all the way back up to take a firm grip of her plump yet muscular rump "...so much beauty and power, you remind me more of the goddess Athena..." Artemis continued her erotic massaging of Kara's body, slipping her hands beneath the blonde beauty's captive nude form and the sheets, rubbing in more oil to her toned stomach and soft bosom.

Kara began to breathe heavily due to the heat building within her, feeling her cheeks blush red as a wetness grew between her thighs. She could still hear Lena whimpering somewhere nearby, pleading for Artemis to continue ravishing her, and soon Kara joined her, letting out small moans as she felt the need for release. Artemis just continued the massage though, rubbing her opening gently every now and then, but only in teasing touches, not enough to release that pressure.

SEX AND CHAOS

"I see you're starting to enjoy yourself, my queen. I know you wish for me to give you the same consideration that I gave to our sweet little Lena, but first, I must educate you and explain why all of this was necessary:

"Most women have dominant and submissive urges, of varying degrees, duelling within themselves. When a woman is able to fully embrace and indulge her internal desires, she can achieve a rare peace of mind and enlightenment that few ever attain. Darling Lena however... she is a purely submissive damsel, a truly rare find, it's why she's been able to accept and embrace her fully submissive urges since coming here, instead of resisting them like so many others. This ability of hers to embrace and indulge her submissiveness gives her a clarity and wisdom that is difficult for many to achieve."

"However, my queen, you are not purely dominant as you've been trying to be. Ever since your defeat of Circe you've been satisfying your dominant side, but ignoring your submissive side, and it's damaging your judgement, stopping you from being the great ruler I know you can be..." Kara heard Artemis picking up something nearby then she continued "...so from now on, I will be helping you indulge your submissive side, which will hopefully give you a similar peace of mind and wisdom as that which our sweet little Lena here has attained..."

Artemis leaned closer and whispered into Kara's ear; the captive Kryptonian was so horny at this point that even the warm breath made her shudder as Artemis said "I know no-one has been equal enough to dominate you, without the risk of them trying to overthrow you. But I'm not like Diana, I have no desire to challenge your rule, no ambition for the throne. I simply want to help ease this tension that has settled over you..."

At that, Artemis brought a riding crop swiping down on Kara's bottom, the leather making a stinging smack on her rump. With one hand she continued gently massaging Kara's body, while the other began spanking her with the riding crop. Kara let out slow, shuddering moans, then loud gasps with each smack of the crop, alternating between the two sounds as she was brought into a frenzy of arousal.

Kara's rump made slow suggestive wriggles side to side, so desperate to be ravished she was trying to tempt Artemis, abandoning any pretense of resistance to her captivity and utter domination. She wanted to be taken, to be entered and mercilessly defiled so she could finally orgasm. She could already feel the tension easing, finally giving into these sensations, making helpless girlish moans with each spank of the crop.

Artemis smirked at the wriggling motion of her queen's behind, watching it sway as she caught its round shape with the crop over and over, the small marks of red practically glowing with the glossy sheen of oil on her skin. She spanked her a final time then tossed the crop aside and retrieved another strap-on, this one a special deluxe version (which Lena had proudly designed, back when she still had lab access) with a vibrating function. She strapped it in place and set it to vibrate, feeling it moving with a soft hum. She then lined up and positioned herself behind her prize, Kara's wet opening presented so willingly to her.

Artemis drew closer then thrust her hips forward, burying the vibrating appendage deep within her queen. Kara orgasmed instantly, finally tipping over the verge she had been kept on the edge of for so long. She moaned loudly through her gag, her naked body trembling as Artemis began to pump back and forth, building up another orgasm as her whole body exploded with pleasure.

Artemis kept going until Kara was panting exhaustedly through her gag, her body moist with perspiration. The wise redheaded Amazon had made her orgasm multiple times, quickly learning just the right rhythm to thoroughly ravish her. She was leaning down with her hands nestled beneath Kara and the sheets, groping her breasts and pinching her nipples as she made a final few gyrating motions with the strap-on. Kara was overcome with pleasure, like overdosing on a drug, her head was swimming; completely lost to her carnal desires.

Keeping her in a low state of constant arousal, Artemis reached over to the nightstand, taking a cloth damp with chloroform while the strap-on was still deep within Kara. She pressed it over Kara's face, pinning the captive blonde's trembling form down to the bed with her own powerful body. She heard Kara take a deep breath, obediently inhaling the chemical without struggling.

Hearing her meek whimpering breaths made Artemis smile, it was clear the lesson had been effective and, with a final small pump of her hips, she felt Kara going limp beneath her.

SEX AND CHAOS

When Kara woke up for the second time, she was no longer bound to the bed, but she was still lying on it. She was nestled in the embrace of Artemis's right arm, her eyes opening to see the dominant redhead smiling down at her. On the other side of Artemis, Lena was resting in a similar position with the Amazon's left arm wrapped around her bound body, her eyes also fluttering open from what was likely another dose of chloroform she had received from their mutual captor.

Kara's eyes fluttered wider, but she made no effort to move away from Artemis, she merely took in her surroundings, her body still feeling weak and tired from her ravishing. She was bound, her arms tied at the wrists behind her back, with several lengths of cord looped around her torso above and below her breasts. Just like with Lena's bondage, her legs were also tightly tied, rope ran around her ankles, calves, above and below her knees, and the centre of her thighs. As she looked at the ropes squeezing her supple form, Kara noticed they all had a faint red glow, each one imbued with some kind of magic that was making her feel so utterly powerless.

She was still gagged as well, a thick cloth tied between her lips, while Lena still had her over the mouth gag. Lena was in one of her standard pleasure slave dresses, the silky royal blue fabric clinging to her luscious form. Kara looked down at herself and saw she had been placed in a skimpy, peach-coloured dress. It hugged her figure nicely, showing off her feminine shape and hung from her left shoulder by a single, two-inch wide strap. Kara instantly understood that this was to be her own slave dress, an outfit that showed off her bare arms and legs and hugged the shape of her bosom and firm-yet-beefy rump. It was distinct from the other slave dresses, but still made it clear the wearer was being shown off by their mistress.

Kara let out a pleased sigh as she looked down at herself, she felt so relaxed and at ease in her current captivity; so vulnerable curled up against Artemis. She looked up at her captor with a wide-eyed gaze, her eyes soft and submissive as she let out a small moan through her gag. Artemis smiled down at her then carefully eased the cloth from between Kara's lips, letting it rest around her neck.

"May I ask you a question... mistress..." Kara sighed, fully embracing her submissive side. Artemis's hand around her slid lower, and she gave Kara's bottom a playful spank as she replied "You are still my queen. Of course you can speak freely... as long as I allow you to remain ungagged" Kara smiled girlishly, her gorgeous features beaming with delight at Artemis dominating her so effectively.

"How did you know what was frustrating me? Even I didn't know this was what I needed..." Kara said in awe of Artemis's ability to know her inner self. Artemis smiled knowingly as she glanced over at Lena and said "You should really be thanking your brilliant and intuitive wife. Before you banned her from her lab, she had been working on imbuing red sun energy into these ropes which you are bound with, making them capable of easily and painlessly sapping you of your powers. She had already theorised that you desired to indulge in your submissive side. It seems she knows you better than anyone..."

Artemis stroked Lena's hair as she said this, praising her for figuring out what was troubling the queen. "Her only error was not coming to me sooner. I read her notes and she wasn't sure who could be both dominant enough and trusted to take control of you. She was thinking about Sam or Kelly..." At that her hand stroked lower then she gave Lena a playful spank, making the innocent genius gasp beneath the gag, blushing slightly in embarrassment "...I felt I would be better suited to the role. So I took the ropes she made and decided to capture you with them, my queen.

"Like I said, Lena is a purely submissive, so she wasn't able to perform this service for you herself. I, however, am more than happy to serve you this way, your majesty." Kara looked over at Lena with a deep, loving gaze, but there was also a touch of embarrassment in her eyes, a yearning to apologise for having been so strict with her brilliant wife. Lena looked back with a similar romantic openness in her eyes, the two wives staring at each other warmly and lovingly.

Kara began to open her mouth to apologise, but then Artemis suddenly clamped her hand down over her mouth, silencing her with a tight handgag. "Your queen wishes to apologise to you, sweet Lena, and so do I." Artemis said as she took over for Kara, asserting her control gently, yet firmly, as she kept her hand in place over Kara's mouth while the blonde could only muffle soft moans into her handgag. "From now on, your lab privileges will be reinstated" Kara made a small nod and a moan of agreement, which Artemis punished her for with another firm spank and stern "Quiet" before clamping her hand back down and continuing.

"But, my dear Lena, you must also realise your safety is extremely important, not only to our queen, but to all the Amazons. You must obediently surrender yourself to our protection whenever we deem it necessary. Do you understand, little one?" Lena could finally feel a better balance forming, Artemis was gentle, kind and loving, but also stern when she needed to be, and with her help, Lena could already see her wife would find peace and wisdom. She nodded and whimpered approvingly through her gag, showing her complete acceptance of Artemis's order.

"Very good" Artemis said with a pleased smile while planting a gentle kiss to Lena's brow. Then she turned her attention back to Kara, her hand still firmly pressed over her lips "Now, as for our arrangement: You will never have to question my loyalty, my queen. I will dutifully serve you and respect you as my queen. But I will also be capturing and ravishing you and your darling Lena at random times, to make sure you are able to fully satisfy both your dominant and submissive desires while not having to worry about our precious Lena's whereabouts."

Kara made a small moan of worry at the thought of the other Amazons seeing her being captured, kidnapped, and carried off to be ravished like a common pleasure slave, but Artemis just leaned down and planted a soft kiss on her forehead to soothe her "They will not see this as a sign of weakness, my queen, but rather of wisdom. They know how important it is to embrace your submissive side, especially here on Paradise Island"

"Diana's refusal to accept her submissive side is the reason I never truly supported her. She's far too set in her ways to change. But you, my queen, you're still young, still teachable. I believe, with my help as your second in command, you could be the greatest ruler Themyscira has ever had." Kara nodded eagerly at Artemis's words, letting out a soft submissive moan of agreement. Artemis smiled and leaned down to kiss her forehead again, then she leaned over to Lena and did the same with her, sealing their arrangement with the loving gesture.

She heard Kara make another moan from beneath her hand and she slowly peeled it away so the captive queen could speak. In a soft and submissive tone, Kara asked "Mistress Artemis... if Lena is purely submissive... does that mean there are purely dominant women out there, as well?" Artemis looked a little troubled by her question, then quickly hid that look as she smiled and said "Perhaps... but not on this island. Now, enough questions..." She smoothly reached down and pulled the gag up between Kara's lips, gagging her once more. Then, both hands slid down to her submissive slaves and she gave them each a firm spank on their bottoms as she said "I think you two need a bath, you've become a little sweaty after I ravished you and I like my slaves to be clean."

With that she pulled them both up from the bed and over either shoulder, her Amazonian strength allowing her to handle their bound forms with ease. She settled them in place, giving their luscious rumps another few spanks, making them both moan through their gags in anticipation of being ravished again. Then she carried them back to the bathing room. She hid it well, but she was still slightly troubled by Kara's question, knowing that purely dominant women were known to be some of the most dangerous in the world...

While Kara and Lena were revelling in their newfound harmony, Diana was only sinking deeper into her misguided alliance. She sat in her dungeon cell with Mercy and Eve on either side of her. They each had a hand on her shoulder as they presented her to the holographic image of Roulette. The hidden communicator they had smuggled in here beamed the image in front of Diana, letting her see Roulette's wicked grin.

She wore her usual red dress which hugged her figure with a long slit down the leg. She looked immaculate while Diana looked unkept, her time in the dungeon giving her a slight dishevelled appearance. "So you agree to my terms?" Roulette asked with a small laugh, delighted in how the once proud Amazon was giving in to her.

It had taken a little convincing, but being locked in here with Mercy and Eve had finally worn Diana down, the two women constantly whispering in her ear about how she was the rightful ruler of this island. She was willing to do anything now, including serving Roulette. Diana sighed and hung her head as she replied softly "Y... Yes... I'll do what you want... I'll kidnap one of my Amazon sisters and deliver her to you."

CHAPTER 14

The Queen's Education

Chapter Summary : *Kara and Lena find themselves kidnapped, but Kara's naive nature might just be what saves them. Meanwhile, other plots and schemes continue to develop*

It was a golden age on Paradise Island, a time of great peace and prosperity. The war was over and the Kryptonian queen had finally embraced her submissive side. For the first time in a long while it seemed the Amazons were satisfied with their leadership, and each of them were fulfilled in their desires.

It was no secret that Kara was now submitting to Artemis frequently, she even wore her special dress at all times, the soft salmon pink fabric resting on her upper thighs, clinging to her strong hips, beefy rear, and modest but perky bosom. As a show that the times of war were truly over, Kara had even put her Supergirl outfit on display in the throne room, presenting it as an antiquity of the past. She now only wore the feminine dress, leaving her arms, legs, and feet bare.

The Amazons did not see this as a sign of weakness, submission and dominance was their way of life, and they were pleased to see their queen accepting both sides. She now ruled with wisdom and patience, any issues her subjects had were tended to, any desires they had were satiated.

It had become common to see Kara - and her precious slavewife Lena - captured and slung over Artemis's shoulders. Usually they were both bound, gagged and chloroformed, their supple legs dangling limply in front of Artemis's chest, their plump bottoms sticking up in the air to be fondled and squeezed by their captor. For when Artemis dominated them, they truly were her captives; there was no safeword or way out for Kara. When she was submitting to Artemis, the redheaded Amazon was in full control of the kryptonian queen's freedom.

At first it was only Artemis who had the pleasure of educating their queen, but soon the displays of Kara's submissive side became too tempting for the other amazons. Requests were made and Artemis granted a few trusted amazons permission to also capture and ravish Kara. She would always eventually be returned to Artemis, though. Kara couldn't be happier, she had only just discovered her submissive side and she was revelling in these newfound sensations.

She had thought she had to be so strong all the time to rule as queen, but she now knew how wrong she was. She enjoyed the knowledge that she could be taken and used at any time, the feeling of helplessness now making her pulse with excitement. She was happy to let the amazons that Artemis had vouched for kidnap her and take her prisoner, but Artemis herself was the only one who Kara truly thought of as her 'mistress'. Kara was utterly in awe of her second in command.

While her feelings were nowhere near the deep love and adoration she felt for her beloved Lena, she still felt a strong sense of passionate lust when in the redhead's possession, wanting to give herself to the powerful Amazon completely.

Artemis was just so skilled at manipulating her body, at building her arousal then making her burst with pleasure. She felt a small tingle anytime she saw Artemis entering a room, felt her heart beating harder at the excitement of being kidnapped and ravished once again.

It had even made Kara better at dominating her own slaves. She had learnt so much from Artemis

and now used the same techniques when kidnapping and dominating Sam, Lois or Vicki, or any of the other pleasures slaves that she might choose to take whenever she pleased. But best of all, it had strengthened her relationship with Lena. They were both completely in love, happy and content in their marriage.

Artemis would always capture them together, and being ravished at the same time was their favourite thing to do together. Lena was now allowed back in her lab, and with her newfound happiness she was inspired to make all sorts of devices, both magical and technological, to give the residents of Paradise Island unlimited pleasure.

Lena would frequently find herself snatched away from the lab, either by her wife, Artemis, or one of the other amazons Kara had given permission to kidnap and have their way with her. But when she wasn't being ravished,

SEX AND CHAOS

Lena was happy to be working on the betterment of all on the island. It seemed this golden age would never end. Kara had put all her troubles behind her, but unfortunately not all had forgotten about who currently languished in the island's dungeon...

Kara had just finished kidnapping and ravishing her beloved wife and they both collapsed to the bed, their naked bodies moist with a light red blush to their soft skin. Kara breathed heavily then smiled and rolled over on top of Lena, their bodies settling into each other, their legs entwining, their breasts pressing together. "I love you," She said softly as she leaned down to kiss her, smiling happily before their lips met.

"Mmmph..." Lena gave a soft whimper of pleasure through the gag Kara had tied tightly over her lips when she had stolen her away from her labwork. She adored these times with her powerful wife and Lena was immensely proud of the queen that Kara had become. As her gag was loosened, Lena pursed her lips in anticipation of the kiss she knew was coming. She and Kara could practically read each other's minds with how in sync their lovemaking had become.

Kara grinded into her, moaning against Lena's mouth with the long passionate kiss. Then she heard the door opening behind them. She didn't look up, she had let go of her paranoia, knowing that this surprise entry was likely Artemis. She felt her shoulder being gripped, and she was rolled off of Lena and onto her back. As she'd suspected it was Artemis, dressed in the brown leather minidress of a solider Amazon.

She knelt between both of them on the bed, using both hands to press a cloth down over their faces. They both made helpless moans as they writhed on the bed, looking up at her with a wide eyed inviting gaze. She smiled down at them, watching as their eyelids fluttered and drooped closed, a sight she had seen many times, but never tired of.

Once they were out, she tucked the cloth into the belt around her waist, then she unclipped the ropes coiled against a strap on the other side of the belt. She rolled them both over and pulled their wrists behind their back, then quickly bound them and looped cords several times around their torsos, above and below their breasts. She did the same with their legs, tying rope around their ankles and their soft, creamy thighs.

Once she was done with the rope, Artemis pulled a white cloth between both of their lips to gag them. There was no-one they could call out for help to anyway, but she always restrained and gagged them so they knew they were her captives, their movement and their speech controlled by her. Once she was done, Artemis hoisted Kara up on her shoulder, then she did the same with Lena, settling her on the opposite side.

She gave their juicy rumps a firm squeeze, then carried them out of the bedroom and out of the palace. She smiled and greeted the amazons she passed on the streets as she took them to her private chambers, happily showing off the prized slaves she had in her possession, their long legs and shapely rears catching the attention of every amazon. She didn't notice, however, that she was being followed. Moving stealthily at a distance was a small group of amazons led by Nubia, keeping track of where Artemis was going...

Artemis made a final thrust against Kara's backside, her hips slapping firmly into its soft shape. The stern amazon drove the strap-on deep into the captive queen's warm canal, burying it inside as she brought the shuddering blonde to orgasm. She was leaning down over her, one hand resting on her waist, the other on the top of her head, pushing Kara's face down between Lena's thighs.

Lena lay on her back with her legs bound at both ankles and tied to either bedpost, moaning at the sensations of Kara's tongue, making small writhing motions with her arms bound behind her back. As Artemis had ravished her, she had kept Kara's head firmly against Lena's most sensitive area, forcing her to pleasure the helpless beauty as she pumped the strap on in and out of her. Lena came to orgasm moments later, moaning loudly through her gag as Kara's tongue finally made her burst with a release of pleasure.

Artemis smiled, letting out deep moans herself as she felt the magical effects of the strap-on pleasuring her too. She made a final few pumps of her hips, grinding the strap inside of Kara's glistening wet opening, then she pulled it out and unstrapped it from her hips. In the next room she had run a bath, lines of wispy steam rose up from the warm water, the scented oils giving it a floral scent.

Artemis set the strap-on down then lifted Kara up onto her shoulder, carrying her to the bath. It was a large marble square built into the floor, big enough for Artemis to comfortably sit Kara down with the back of her head resting on the edge. She then scooped Lena up from the bed, sliding an arm under her back and her legs to cradle her lovingly to her chest.

She lay Lena down next to Kara, lowering her naked body into the warm waters. Then she began to bathe them, dipping her hands beneath the surface of the water and gently stroking their bodies.

She massaged their breasts and their legs, she kneaded any tension out of their shoulders. They were still moaning softly from the after effects of their powerful orgasms, the two helpless women shuddering at the strong, dominant touch of Artemis's hands.

She tended to them carefully, washing every inch of their supple nude forms before lifting them out of the water. She dried each of them off, then rubbed rose scented cream into their skin, making their bodies even more soft and deliciously smooth, the cream making her hands glide over them like silk.

Once they were properly bathed and moisturised, Artemis redressed them in their slave dresses. She was so adept at handling them, so strong and in control, guiding them forcibly into the skimpy fabric that clung to their sweetly scented bodies. She then laid them down on the bed and began to bind them, kneeling over them as she wrapped them in rope.

She tied their legs together and their wrists behind their back, then she gagged them with white cloths between their lips. Artemis knew how they liked to be left, and she settled them into a spooning position, with Kara behind Lena. She then gave them each a slow caress, running her hands up their legs then squeezing their breasts through their dresses as she said "I'll be back soon"

She leaned down and kissed each of them on their gagged lips, then she went to run a bath for herself, leaving them to enjoy each other's company. Almost immediately Kara began to grind against Lena; despite being pleasured by Artemis, she was still incredibly horny. Lena began pushing back with her shapely rump, rubbing it teasingly against Kara.

Lena moaned through her gag as she felt Kara nuzzling at her neck, pressing her gagged lips to her soft skin with wet kisses. Their muffled moans filled the room, then came a soft slapping sound as Kara began thrusting her hips against Lena's pleasantly plump bottom, dry humping her as they writhed against each other on the bed.

They were so lost in the pleasure of each others bodies, the two captive wives didn't even notice the door opening. It swung open silently, and Nubia sneaked up on the loving married couple. She had a chloroform soaked cloth in her hand, her nervous eyes glancing toward the bathroom where Artemis was bathing.

Only when her knee pressed on the bed did the two women finally stop their grinding. Nubia pounced on Lena first, quickly pressing the cloth over her mouth and nose as she loomed over both of them. Lena made a scared, muffled gasp, and began wriggling beneath the strong amazon. But in her bondage there was little she could do, and soon she felt that familiar dizziness washing over her.

She continued moaning desperately, her legs wriggling up and down as she tried to get away. Kara meanwhile was just watching this take place with keen interest, she assumed Nubia had been given permission to capture them both by Artemis, and she enjoyed being a submissive so greatly she simply waited in anticipation for her turn. Lena felt no such excitement, she was suspicious of the look she saw in Nubia's eyes. After being captured and kidnapped for real so many times, Lena could tell the difference between the "pleasure slave snatching" that Artemis and the other amazons practised, and an actual abduction with nefarious intent and she fought Nubia right up until she passed out.

Once she was out, Nubia turned her attention to Kara, leaving Lena sleeping peacefully on the sheets. Kara began to make helpless whimpering moans, playing her part of the innocent damsel. Nubia paused, then smiled as she realised the queen thought this was just a game, then she pressed the cloth down over her mouth and nose, lying down on top of Kara to pin her body to the bed.

That small wriggle Kara made now rubbed her body against Nubia's, the amazon's toned figure squashing down into her. She made a small muffled sigh and her eyes soon fluttered shut. Nubia carefully peeled the cloth up, assessing Kara's resting features. Then, she tucked the cloth away and slid off of her.

SEX AND CHAOS

Nubia lifted Kara up from the bed, getting her in a sitting position on the edge of the bed then hoisting the blonde up onto her shoulder. She quickly did the same with Lena, wrapping her arms around both sets of thighs and spanking the rumps resting on either side of her head. She made another cautious glance to the bathroom, but Artemis was completely unaware. With her captives drugged and slung over her shoulders, Nubia hurried out of the room, easily stealing them away.

Nubia took Kara and Lena to a hidden shelter past the forests of Paradise Island. It was a secluded spot where she could keep them for as long as she wanted. Her intentions were to force Kara to renounce the throne and abdicate to Diana. With her beloved wife Lena held captive as well, Nubia was confident her plan would work and Kara would have no choice but to surrender.

Waiting for her in the stone structure were the last of those loyal to Diana, all of them wanting their true queen to rise back to power. The bedroom was made up nicely, not as nicely as the palace, but the bed was large and the sheets were soft. The other amazons waited inside, watching as Nubia came in with the two captured damsels over her shoulders.

"I have them" She said as she shut the doors behind her. She then walked over to the bed and dumped Lena onto the sheets, her body making a small bounce before going still. "Excellent work" one of the amazons said as they moved closer to the bed, her eyes looking down lustfully at Lena's bound form, her slave dress having slid up just enough to show off a teasing glimpse of her rear. "Yes, now we can keep them here until they comply to our demands..." another amazon said as she too moved closer to the bed.

The three of them all began looking down at Lena as Nubia took Kara to a nearby wooden chair. She sat her down, facing the bed as one of the amazons said "While they're here we might as well have some fun..." The three of them all looked to Nubia and she gave them a small nod as she said "Go ahead"

They needed no other instruction, the three of them pouncing on Lena as they began groping and kissing her, untying her legs so they could spread her thighs to ravish her. While their bodies entangled on the bed, Nubia retrieved a small vial of smelling salts. She brought the vial under Kara's nose, drifting it slowly until the kryptonian began to rise from her slumber.

Kara's head tilted up from her chest, her eyes fluttering as she moaned softly through her gag.

As Kara's eyes opened she first saw Nubia standing beside her, then she looked across the room to see Lena being ravished on the bed. It wasn't an unusual sight for her to wake to after being captured, and as far as she knew, once they were done, she would be knocked out again and safely returned to Artemis.

A small shiver of excitement went through her as she watched the three amazons having their way with Lena; without the smelling salts her wife was waking up slower, her eyes still half closed with a sleepy glaze. In this sleepy state, Lena made small shudders at the hands and lips against her skin, her body waking to an overwhelming array of erotic sensations.

Kara made a helpless moan through her gag and looked up at Nubia, writhing sensually in her bondage with a wide eyed gaze that invited the amazon to ravish her as well. Nubia had been just about to make a threat, to demand she step down as queen. But seeing that look in Kara's eyes made her pause. She reached out, stroking a hand along Kara's cheek as she said softly "You truly have accepted your submissive side..."

To an amazon, there was no more enticing sight than a beautiful, submissive woman yearning to be taken and used, and Nubia couldn't deny her yearning to ravish the helpless blonde. Her hand stroked lower and she began squeezing Kara's breasts through the thin fabric of her slave dress, taking each soft mound in her hand and groping it firmly.

Her mission was forgotten now, all she wanted was Kara's body. She lifted her captive out of the chair and sat down in it herself, then she set Kara down in her lap. As soon as she was settled on her lap she began stroking and caressing the blonde's bound form, running her hands up along Kara's soft legs and her heaving bosom.

She leaned in and kissed at Kara's neck, then she took her breasts and made a small bite of her nipples through the dress, dampening the fabric with her saliva. Nubia moaned in pleasure against Kara's lips, and Kara moaned in return, trembling on the amazon's lap as she felt herself being utterly dominated.

"You love being submissive don't you..." Nubia whispered in Kara's ear, her hot breath making her shudder and gasp. As Kara began moaning in

SEX AND CHAOS

reply Nubia flipped her over, settling her face down across her knees. Her hand rose then slammed down on Kara's bottom as she began to spank her, making a loud slapping sound. Kara gasped, her hips twitching, then Nubia raised her hand and brought it down again.

It was intoxicating to hear her girlish gasps, and Nubia quickly settled into a steady rhythm, her hand rising and falling as she reddened the queen's plump behind, that soft juicy flesh jiggling with each hard smack. She spanked her for a short while, then brought her to the bed, untying her legs like they had done with Lena and taking a strap-on.

She plunged it deep into Kara's opening, pumping vigorously as she felt the queen shuddering beneath her. The amazons also quickly retrieved their own strap-ons, one pushing it between Lena's lips while the other bent her other and found her moist folds with the hard tip. Every woman was brought to orgasm over and over, their naked bodies entwining on the bed in a hedonistic display of pleasure.

Kara's newfound submissive nature had just been too much for them to resist, they each took their turn with her, switching between her and Lena as they were both thoroughly dominated. They were all exhausted once they were done, collapsing on the bed and sharing each others warmth.

Breathing heavily, Nubia took a cloth damp with chloroform, and used it to knock out both Lena and Kara, kissing and grinding into them until their eyes closed. She sighed as she peeled the cloth away, then she looked over to her allies on the bed with her as she said "We need to discuss our plan... I think this might've been a mistake..."

They talked it over and came to an agreement: Kara was a better ruler than Diana ever could be. Diana would never give herself to her subjects in the way Kara had, and if put back in power, she would almost certainly lock Kara away where she couldn't be enjoyed by them all.

With that erotic lovemaking session, Diana had lost the last few still loyal to her, with even Nubia now agreeing that Kara had to remain on the throne. They just had to return her to Artemis. As far as the queen knew this was all part of a game, no-one ever had to discover how close they had come to treason.

They agreed on their plan, then got dressed, they had been ravishing the helpless damsels for the better part of the day and it was now the late afternoon. They dressed Lena and Kara back in their slave dresses, then they securely tied them back up and gagged them. They also added blindfolds just in case the kidnapped beauties awoke while being transported; the amazon conspirators didn't want their captives to realise they had been taken and kept in this isolated shelter.

Nubia carried Kara while one of the other amazons carried Lena. Nubia had decided all of them should explain this to Artemis, to ensure they were all still trusted. They carried Lena and Kara back to Artemis's bedchambers, knocking respectfully at the door then entering. The redheaded amazon had been moments away from raising the alarm, she was pacing up and down angrily in her room.

She knew that other amazons would capture Lena and Kara sometimes, and she had assumed that's what had happened. But she hadn't given her permission to anyone today, and as soon as Nubia entered she exploded at her "What do you think you're doing?!" She marched over and pulled Kara off of Nubia's shoulder, lifting her up onto her own in a possessive manner.

Nubia bowed her head as did the other amazons and she said in a soft tone "I'm sorry Artemis. Please forgive me. I thought you left them on the bed to be taken. We were just helping further our queen's education in submission..."

Artemis eyed Nubia suspiciously, then she slid Kara off of her shoulder and down to her feet. She untied her gag then kissed Kara gently on the lips. She then slid down her blindfold and looked into her eyes as she said "Is this true? They were simply educating you?"

Kara smiled and nodded as she replied "Yes mistress. We were never in any real danger" Artemis kissed her again then said "Very well" She then retied the gag around Kara's lips and added "But you'll have to be punished for being away from me for so long." She hoisted Kara up onto her shoulder and gave her rump a firm smack, elliciting a squeal of surprise followed by an apologetic whimper from Kara. Then Artemis looked to Nubia and said "You're forgiven. But next time you will ask my permission or there will be consequences"

Nubia bowed her head again and said "Yes Artemis, thank you" Artemis walked up to the amazon holding Lena and commanded her to hand over the helpless damsel. She was moved onto Artemis's free shoulder and with a firm spank to Lena's plump tush she said "And you'll be punished as well, little one…"

Nubia and the three amazons quickly exited, looking to each other with relieved expressions at having narrowly gotten away with their lie. As Lena was carried to the bed she made a frustrated moan through her gag. She had wanted Artemis to ask her about Nubia's true intentions as well. She still strongly believed that Nubia and the other amazons had been intending to actually kidnap her and her wife, but with the gag sealed tightly over her lips, Lena couldn't accuse her.

"I'm going to have punish and ravish you both all night to make up this day that was stolen from me" Artemis said as she spanked both their bottoms at the same time. They both let out muffled gasps, then Artemis tossed them down on the soft sheets of her bad. With a small pout Lena realised it would be a while until she was able to share her suspicions, for now all she could do was moan helplessly as Artemis ravished her and Kara once again.

While Nubia had been kidnapping Kara and Lena, two other women on Paradise Island were busy capturing their own prize. Alex and Kelly technically belonged to Artemis now that they had been taken from Diana's possession, but as Artemis was always so busy training Kara and Lena, they were free to do as they pleased. This suited them just fine, Kelly loved living on this island with Alex, ravishing her at every opportunity. The two of them also loved ambushing and kidnapping Sam whenever they got the chance to catch her off guard.

That same day, they had found Sam lounging in her bedchambers. Giving her no time to react, they rushed in with chloroform and rope with mischievous smiles on their faces. Sam was grudgingly familiar with being the unwilling prey in the two vixen's kidnap games and she gave a small yelping "No!" and tried to flee, but she was easily tackled by Alex. Kelly and Alex then both held her down and kept a damp chloroform cloth over her mouth and nose, forcing Sam to inhale the chemical deeply and eventually succumb to the soporific fumes as she made small wriggles on the bed. They then kissed Sam on her plump lips, kissed each other passionately, then they began undressing her.

They stripped Sam of her soldier slave garb and redressed her in a pleasure slave dress, taking off her sandals to leave her feet bare. "That's better" Alex said as she felt up Sam's body in the silky slave dress. Kelly retrieved the ropes and handed a few to her lover, then they both began to tie Sam up.

Once she was nicely bound and gagged, Kelly hoisted Sam's limp form up onto her shoulder "Now let's get her back to our room and have some fun!" Kelly said as she gave Sam's bottom a firm pat. Alex reached out and squeezed it as well, then she leaned forward and kissed Kelly, moaning softly against her lips. The two women walked calmly out of the building Sam lived in, heading down the street with an excited anticipation at ravishing their captive.

There was an alley they always cut through after capturing Sam in her quarters, it led back to their own abode much faster. They slipped between the buildings and down the alley, Kelly making a slow stroke of Sam's luscious legs as they walked.

Suddenly they were both seized from behind, a pair of cloths pressed down firmly over their mouths and noses. Sam slipped off of Kelly's shoulder landing on the floor on her side with a soft thump. The two women tried fighting their attackers but the chloroform made them too weak, they wriggled and squirmed but they were held tightly from behind, one hand over their face with the cloth, and the other clinging around their waist to keep them in place.

Their moans grew softer and finally their eyes began to droop closed, both of them melting into the grip of the women holding them. Their eyes snapped shut at almost the same time and they were lowered to the floor. Standing over them were Mercy and Eve, both of them with sinister smiles on their faces.

"That was easy..." Mercy said with a cruel smirk, then they began tying up Kelly and Alex. They were concealed from view in the alley, able to bind, gag and blindfold the two women without anyone seeing them. At the other side of the alley a covered horse drawn cart was waiting. Eve hoisted Alex over her shoulder, and Mercy did the same with Kelly. They carried them to the cart, lifting up the covering on the back, then bundled the two women onto the cart.

They quickly put the covering back over them, hiding their captives. Now they could take the cart through town and no-one would ever know they were kidnapping the two women in the back. In the alley, Sam was beginning to return to her senses, she made sleepy blinks and looked up fearfully to see Mercy standing over her.

"You weren't a part of our plans..." Mercy said teasingly as she crouched down "...but the more the merrier" She then pressed a cloth over the helpless Sam's mouth and nose, forcing her back down into a deep sleep. With her other hand she began roughly groping Sam's breasts, pressing her fingers down into their soft shape and rolling them around in her hand.

She waited until Sam's eyes closed, then she lifted her up onto her shoulder, giving her behind a firm spank as she carried her down the alley. She loaded her up onto the cart with Alex and Kelly, putting the cover over them so they couldn't be seen.

"Let's get moving. They have an important role to play and we shouldn't keep our mistress waiting..." Mercy said cryptically as she sat up at the front of the cart with Eve. With a small flourish of the reigns the horses began to move, the cart rumbling along the streets as the two women discretely kidnapped the three helpless beauties.

As Eve and Mercy completed their kidnapping, Diana was being pulled deeper into the same sinister plot. She was still in the dark dungeon, but she now wore a black tiara, the item emitting a strong and foreboding dark magical energy.

She had just finished placing it on her head, then she looked to the hologram of Roulette and asked "How did you make this appear in my cell? Nothing from Man's World should be able to get through Theymiscara's magical defences." Roulette just smiled slyly and replied "That's not for you to be concerned with. You simply need to play your part in this plan and I will see you are returned to the throne. Can you do that? Obey me without question?"

Diana sighed and hung her head as she replied "Yes..." There was nothing she wouldn't do now, her anger toward Kara had only grown by the day the longer she stayed down here, languishing while up above the other amazons revelled in pleasure without her.

"Very good..." Roulette replied as she saw the look of anger in Diana's eyes, then she asked "And have you decided yet? Which of your sisters you will kidnap and give to me as tribute in exchange for my help?" A small smirk spread across Diana's lips as she raised her head and looked at Roulette to reply "Yes. I know exactly who, the one who took my position as second in command. I will give you Artemis...

CHAPTER 15

The Imposter

Chapter Summary: Kara and Lena go to Man's World on a diplomatic mission while Artemis decides to investigate what Diana and the other prisoners have been up to...

"I just think they're planning something, I don't have any proof yet but...mmpphhh..." Kara calmly came up behind her beloved slavewife and clamped a cloth over her mouth and nose. It muffled her words and Lena instantly felt the familiar scent of chloroform fill her lungs. Kara had one hand on the cloth and the other reaching round to gently grope and fondle Lena's breasts, squeezing her bosom through the thin silky fabric of her slavedress. "You have no need to worry, my love..." Kara said softly by Lena's ear as she kept the cloth in place, then she kissed her a few times on the neck, her lips pressing hungrily to Lena's supple skin as her other hand now moved down to fondle Lena's lusciously plump rumpcheeks "...you have nothing to fear, my darling Lena. I will always keep you safe."

Lena had been trying to voice her concerns about Diana, Eve and Mercy, but once again her fears were dismissed. She had been kidnapped so many times that Kara simply thought her beautiful damsel of a wife was being paranoid and that was nothing to be overly concerned about. Lena had been greatly enjoying how relaxed and at peace Kara had become recently, but in times like this she wished she was being more aware of the dangers surrounding them. The reason for Kara's newly found peace was in the bedroom with them. Artemis had just finished ravishing then bathing them both, and she pulled her leather amazon dress back into place as she said "The Amazons who will be accompanying you are waiting by the plane, your highness."

Kara felt Lena going limp in her arms, her eyes fluttering closed as she faded away "Good" she replied to Artemis "I need to leave for my diplomatic mission, and while I'm gone you're in charge" She lowered Lena's limp form down to the bed and pulled her wrists behind her back. She quickly wrapped her beautiful slavewife in white rope, binding Lena's limbs with a practised precision. She then pulled a white cloth tightly over the drugged beauty's lips to gag her. Just as Kara was tying the knot of the gag, the doors to the bedroom entered, and Nubia came in.

"Artemis. My queen." She said with small nods at them both. She had a white cloth in one hand and ropes in the other, and with a sultry smile she looked to Artemis and said "With your permission, I was hoping to capture and ravish these two..." Her eyes gleamed with lust as she looked at the temptingly scantily-clad forms of Kara and Lena but Artemis shook her head and replied "You'll have to wait. Our queen and sweet little Lena are both leaving on a diplomatic mission" Nubia sighed and hung her as she replied "Very well"

Kara hoisted Lena up onto her shoulder and gave Lena's bottom a firm squeeze and satisfied pat as she said "You can kidnap Lena and me as soon as we return. I'll be looking forward to it and I'm sure my gorgeous wife will be eagerly anticipating our captivity, as well." She gave Nubia a teasing smile then carried Lena out of the room. Once she was out of the palace, Kara flew up and over to the beach where her invisible jet and the accompanying Amazons were waiting. She could've flown all the way there herself, but she wanted to take the plane so she could have some fun with Lena on the journey there and back.

From the balcony, Artemis watched Kara flying toward her plane, and with a small sigh she turned back into the bedroom. With Kara and Lena gone she had nothing else to occupy her time, so she decided to find two of her other slaves to play with. She left the palace and went to the chambers of Alex and Kelly, it was only a short walk and she arrived with an eager lust.

However, as she pushed open the door to their bedroom, she found it empty. She paused in the doorway with a suspicious expression on her face. Alex and Kelly should've been here. Lena's suspicions about Mercy, Eve, and Diana suddenly came back to her, and she started to wonder if she should head down to the dungeons to question them.

As the plane was taking off, Roulette's sinister plot was continuing in the dungeons of Paradise Island. "That's it, just keep watching the pretty crystal..." Mercy was standing in front of both Alex and Kelly, waving a crystal necklace back and forth in front of them. They were on their knees with their wrists bound behind their backs. Kneeling behind them was Eve, and anytime they showed even the faintest resistance to their brainwashing she would reach round and press a cloth over their mouth and nose, forcing them to inhale the scent of chloroform, weakening them so they would be unable to fight the hypnosis.

As she chloroformed them, she groped their breasts firmly, smirking as they became completely entranced "You are under our complete control..." Mercy cooed softly as she continued swinging the crystal back and forth, watching as Alex and Kelly followed it mindlessly, their eyes drifting side to side. "You will be completely unaware of your brainwashing until you are instructed to obey... when we tell you to obey you will find yourselves helpless to resist. Do you understand?" Eve pressed the cloths to their mouths to weaken their minds for this final hypnotic suggestion, making them so sleepy that Mercy's words burrowed deep into their subconscious brains.

"Yes... I understand..." They both responded in a soft monotone voice, their mouths hanging open as their eyes drooped half closed. "Very good. Now sleep. Sleep deeply and let my words echo in your minds" Mercy said as she stopped swinging the crystal. Eve clamped down the cloths and held them there until both women sunk to the floor, their limp forms crumpling as they were rendered unconscious.

"That was too easy..." Mercy said with a smirk as she tucked the necklace away, standing over the two unconscious and now brainwashed women. "Don't be too pleased with yourself..." came a voice from the other side of the room, the holographic projection of Roulette had been watching the brainwashing and continued "...your methods aren't nearly as thorough as I would like, unfortunately we don't have time. That simple hypnosis technique won't be able to control them forever"

Standing beside Roulette was Wonder Woman, who interjected "It won't need to be forever. Soon I will control this island again, and they will obey me whether they like it or not. Now let's get on with this plan of yours, I've been in this dungeon for far too long" With that, she took one of the magical tiara's that Roulette had sent her, each one imbued with dark magic. As Diana settled the tiara on her head, it magically changed her appearance, making her look exactly like Artemis.

In the corner, Samantha was still helplessly bound and gagged, and she whimpered helplessly into her gag as she watched this transformation with trembling eyes. Diana took a second to assess her disguise, then she smiled and turned on Sam. "While I'm gone, I'll need you to stay here..." She said as she crouched down and placed the other tiara on Sam's head, then she teasingly added "...Wonder Woman." The tiara instantly changed Sam's appearance to look like Diana, anyone who came by the dungeon would now see her inside and would never realise the real Wonder Woman had escaped.

The representatives for the nations of Man's World had assembled in a large auditorium. They waited patiently, each one of them having a small placard in front of them with the name of their country. They were all sitting facing a podium, waiting for Kara's arrival. The doors opened and Kara came striding in, flanked by her Amazon guards. They made an intimidating display, the women fully armed and showing off their toned bodies in their leather dresses, the skirts resting around their firm thighs.

Kara was dressed in her superheroine attire, but she was no longer seen as a simple heroine, everyone in the room now knew her as the queen of the Amazons, and the ruler of Paradise Island. She had Lena resting over her shoulder, her beloved slavewife bound and gagged. She walked right up to the podium, stopping in front of the microphone and smiling as her eyes scanned across the room.

She gave Lena's juicy rump a firm pat then said "As you can see, Lena Luthor remains a captive and a pleasure slave of Themyscira. But that's not all she is..." Kara stroked Lena's thighs more lovingly as she continued "...we have recently married, and as she is now my wife; her claim to the Luthor fortune belongs to me." Kara paused to see if anyone would dare dispute her claim, her hand squeezing Lena's rounded bottom as she let the silence hang in the air, punctuated only by Lena's soft, gagged moans of pleasure with each squeeze and spank of her luscious cheeks by Kara's strong hand. She knew they had little choice but to let her have the vast Luthor fortune. No nation wanted the war to start again. Before the ceasefire, Themyscira had been easily decimating the military forces of every nation. Kara had all the power and she was enjoying revelling in it.

SEX AND CHAOS

"Using a part of this fortune, I will construct an embassy for Themyscira on Man's World. To ensure the peace between our two worlds continues..." The representatives seemed more hopeful at this comment, peace is what they all wanted, and diplomacy would be a lot easier with an embassy they could visit. But then Kara added "...and the recruitment of the women of Man's World will, of course, continue. Only now, with the embassy in place, women will be able to voluntarily surrender themselves to become pleasure slaves or soldier slaves." At this announcement the room became more tense and there was a chorus of angry grumbling as the representatives talked amongst themselves. Kara's 'recruitment' was just another word for kidnapping, all their countries had seen dozens of women captured and stolen away to be ravished on Paradise Island.

As they angrily talked amongst themselves Kara gently slid Lena off of her shoulder and set her shapely wife down on her soft bare feet in front of the podium. She turned Lena so she was facing the microphone then loosened her gag, pulling it down to rest at her neck. She was still thoroughly bound, so Kara had to keep her hands on Lena's hips to balance her. Lena made a small submissive glance over her shoulder, and Kara kissed her on the side of her neck for encouragement. She then turned her head back toward the microphone and stated "I want to make it clear that the Luthor fortune is to be given fully to my owner, my queen, and my wife, Kara Zor-El. As I am now her property, so too do all my assets belong to her. And I am eager to see the embassy which those funds will help build. This will help usher in a new age of peace between Themyscira and Man's World; the same type of harmony that I have found in my complete submission to the amazons of paradise island following my kidnap and captivity at their hands."

Lena felt Kara kissing her on the neck as she said softly by her ear "Well said, my love" She then turned her around and kissed her more deeply, proudly displaying her love for Lena in front of everyone in attendance. After the long kiss, she pressed a cloth over Lena's mouth and nose, forcing her into a deep sleep as she filled her lungs with chloroform. Lena passed out with a warm smile on her face, her eyes fluttering closed in Kara's embrace. Once she went limp, Kara pulled her gag back from her neck to being firmly sealed over her lips. She then hoisted Lena back stop her shoulder, stroking her long supple legs lovingly before giving her bottom a firm pat.

With Lena back in place, Kara moved closer to the podium again. She made a stern expression, glaring out at the assembled world leaders as she said "I can hear that many of you are displeased that my recruitment efforts will continue. There will be no negotiation on this issue. I know that all of you in this room were responsible for my beloved Lena's kidnapping by Lex Luthor, and as you can see, that plan came to nothing" She gave Lena's rump a firm pat to emphasise her point "Lena is back with me where she belongs, and any other plan you try to devise to undermine me or capture my beloved slavewife will fail just the same. If any of you ever make a move against my amazons or our slaves, and especially Lena, then I promise you the wrath of Themyscira will be swift and merciless"

Kara let her words hang in the air for a moment, her eyes scanning across the room, daring someone to challenge her. No-one spoke up and Kara made a satisfied nod before turning to leave. She began to step away from the podium when someone called out "What about Maxwell Lord?"

Wonder Woman murdered him and still hasn't answered for that crime! Have you forgotten we were not the ones who started this war?" Kara paused, her jaw tightening as she spun around angrily. She stepped back to the podium and yelled back "No amazon will ever answer to a man! And you should be hailing Wonder Woman as a hero for ridding the world of someone as abhorrent as Maxwell Lord. Now, if you have any further questions you can visit my embassy, I intend to have it constructed immediately" With that she turned and left the auditorium, refusing to answer any more questions. Her invisible jet was parked right outside the government building, and she boarded it along with her amazons. "Are we returning home my queen?" One of the amazons asked as the jet began to lift into the air. Kara slid Lena down to sit her on her lap as she took a seat and replied "No, not yet... I have one more stop to make first"

"You've got a visitor, Luthor!" The guard barked angrily as he slammed his baton against the metal bars. Lex was lying on his small bed wearing an orange jumpsuit, he had been staring at the ceiling trying to think of a way to escape his captivity, but now his head tilted up with a curious expression. It wasn't visiting hours, so whoever they had let in here had to be someone special. He could hear their footsteps approaching, and he rose up from the bed, standing close to the bars with his arms crossed. She came into view and his eyes narrowed with an angry glare as he said "What do you want?"

Kara had left her amazons on the plane, but she had brought Lena with her just to gloat. Lena was slumped over her shoulder, Kara's arm wrapped tightly around her thighs to keep her in place. "I came to see you one last time..." Kara said with a teasing smirk as she patted Lena's rump possessively "...I wanted to let you know that while you've been rotting in prison, I have made Lena my wife. And, as she is now my wife, the entire Luthor estate belongs to me, a Kryptonian"

Luthor seethed angrily and slammed his hands against the bars, his eyes trembling with rage as he growled "This isn't over!" Kara let out an amused laugh at his anger and patted Lena's bottom again as she replied "Oh, but it is over, Lex. You're never getting out of prison, and as the queen of Themyscira, no nation dares oppose me. Your plan to use Lena against me failed, and this will be the last time you see either one of us" She gave Lena's behind another firm pat, keeping that teasing smile on her face as she turned and began walking away. Luthor continued yelling after her but she just ignored him, he was in the past now and she was solely focused on her future with Lena.

Back on the plane, she settled Lena on her lap again, nestling her in close and gently groping her. After a few minutes, Lena's eyes began to flutter open, they were hazy at first, then she came to her senses. She looked up at Kara and made a loving muffled sigh through her gag, her bound form making a small writhing motion on her lap. Kara smiled at the sensual wriggling motions Lena made, and she carefully slipped the gag from her lips. She then leaned down and kissed her deeply, her tongue invading the confines of Lena's mouth. After the long kiss, Kara squeezed Lena's breasts a final time then lifted her head back up. "I want to apologise for being so possessive of you during this trip, my love. I just can't help wanting to show you off and gloat over my ownership of you after they tried so hard to keep us apart..."

Before Kara could continue apologising, Lena lifted up on her lap and kissed her, silencing her words. She peeled her lips away and looked into Kara's eyes as she said "I love it when you're possessive of me, Kara. I am your pleasure slave, your slave wife. I love being reminded that you own me and, regardless of which of your subjects you may share me with, I truly belong only to you. You have nothing to apologise for. As far as I'm concerned, there is nothing I would rather be than your prized possession." Kara smiled and leaned down to kiss Lena, her arms wrapping around her and squeezing her bound form tightly.

They both let out moans of pleasure against the others mouth, then after a few moments Kara pulled her mouth away. She gently fondled Lena as she smiled down at her and said "Coming back to Man's World made me think of how this all started... being kidnapped and enslaved by Wonder Woman was the best thing that ever happened to either one of us..." Hearing Kara mention Wonder Woman reminded Lena of her suspicions, and she opened her mouth to tell Kara. But Kara was already in the process of gagging her, and before Lena could say anything a thick white cloth was pulled between her lips. Kara then stood up, cradling Lena in her arms as she carried her to the back of the plane. At the back was a private section with a bed where she could ravish her precious slavewife in peace.

Back on Themyscira, Roulette's plan was in motion. Alex and Kelly had been returned to their bedchambers. Using the same covered cart they had been kidnapped in, Eve and Mercy took them back to their bed without anyone seeing. They laid Kelly down with her back propped up on the headboard, then they tied up Alex, using lengths of white rope to tightly bind her. Once she was bound, they gagged her with a white cloth between her lips and placed her in Kelly's lap. Mercy leaned in close to them and whispered "Once you hear the door close you will awake from your trance. You will have no memory of what has happened to you, and you will act perfectly normal until you are told to obey."

Eve and Mercy smirked mischievously at each other then hurried out of the room to continue the plan. As soon as the door slammed shut, both Alex and Kelly began to awake as instructed. Alex let out a muffled moan through her gag and Kelly a deep sigh. Their eyes fluttered open, neither one could remember anything past kidnapping Sam. But seeing Alex's sensual form bound and gagged on her lap was too much for Kelly to resist. Her lingering questions were pushed to the back of her mind as she began kissing and groping Alex. She laid her down on the bed and began grinding into her, stroking her with her hands she began to undress her helpless slave.

SEX AND CHAOS

As Kelly began to ravish Alex, they were both still being searched for by Artemis. She had looked all over the island for them, not wanting to believe the suspicions about Diana could be true.

Finally, she relented and began making her way to the dungeons, feeling a strange apprehension as she arrived. She didn't know it, but Eve and Mercy had only just beaten her there, and as she slowly descended the stone steps into the dungeon she could hear movement. She reached the lowest level and opened the steel door to the cell. Stepping inside, she saw Diana bound and gagged, the former ruler of Paradise Island now sobbing helplessly in the arms of Eve and Mercy.

Artemis was immediately suspicious, it wasn't like Diana to be so pitiful, especially not in the clutches of Eve and Mercy. "What's going on in here? Diana is a prisoner of Themyscira, but you two have no right to bind or gag her. Why have you done this?" Artemis said angrily as she stepped into the dark prison cell, putting her hands on her hips with a stern glare. Eve and Mercy just smirked at her, both of them groping Diana who continued whimpering through her gag. Then Artemis heard a reply, coming from a corner of the room, behind her and to the right "To show you what fate awaits you..."

Artemis recognised the voice instantly, for it was shockingly familiar to her own. She spun round to see an exact doppelganger of herself. She had no idea it was Diana wearing the tiara and she simply stared at this sinister reflection in stunned silence. Then her doppelganger lunged at her, tackling into her as they began wrestling on the ground. They rolled side to side as they both tried to overpower the other, their strong well toned bodies tensing as they both let out frustrated grunts.

The real Artemis was almost pinned down on her back, then she managed to get her foot to the chest of her attacker. She kicked her back, making the fake Artemis stumble backward and slam into a wall. Artemis scrambled to her feet, charging at the doppelganger then punching her hard in the stomach. The fake groaned and clutched her midsection as he bent over, and as she did Artemis noticed the dark aura surrounding the tiara she was wearing. She grabbed it from her head and tore it off, then she let out a shocked gasp as the illusion fell "Diana?" She said as her eyes widened, then she was grabbed from behind by Eve and Mercy. She would've been able to be beat either one in a fair fight, but they both gripped an arm each and managed to hold on. Artemis struggled as Diana quickly put the tiara back on. Diana then punched Artemis in the stomach, three times in quick succession. Artemis let out a breathless wheeze and dropped to her knees, trembling as she struggled for air.

"You're using dark magic, Diana... whatever you're planning... if you don't stop, you will doom us all..." Artemis groaned, making a small weak struggle as Eve and Mercy kept their hold of her. "I don't need advice from a traitor. You should be more concerned about your own fate" Diana said coldly as she retrieved some lengths of thin white rope. She placed them down in front of Artemis then said "Strip her" Working together, the three women forcibly removed Artemis's warrior attire, stripping her down to just her skimpy undergarments. They then tied her wrists behind her back and wrapped up her legs, tying each knot as tight as they could make it. "Let me go" Artemis moaned as she wriggled in her bondage, her half naked form tensing against the ropes but unable to break free.

"You're not going anywhere, my dear sister. I'm handing you over to Roulette" Diana said as they finished tying Artemis. She began to prepare a cloth, making it damp with chloroform as Artemis moaned "No! You can't!" She made another frustrated writhing motion on the floor, showing fear for the first time as her voice trembled "Please Diana, I beg you, do not do this. We are amazons! Sisters! Do not turn on me like this! Do not put me in bondage and hand me over into the possession of that foul woman!" Diana finished with the cloth, the white fabric now soaked with the sleepy chemical. She stood in front of Artemis and paused, an internal conflict showing in her troubled expression. Then she thought of having Kara and Lena back in her clutches, and her desire to own them again was too strong for her to resist. She crouched down and pressed the cloth firmly over Artemis's mouth and nose, keeping it in place and forcing her to inhale the chloroform.

"No! Mmmmpphhh!!" Artemis's desperate plea was cut off, and soon her eyes began to flutter closed. Her terrified expression softened as her features lost all tension, her eyelids drooping as her body went limp. With a weak sigh her eyes snapped closed and she slumped down to the floor.

SEX AND CHAOS

Diana peeled the cloth away, then used a longer piece of white fabric to tie between Artemis's lips.

With the gag in place she scooped Artemis up from the floor, hoisting her up and resting her listless body atop her shoulder. She carried her to a corner of the dungeon that Roulette had designated. She set her down in the corner and stepped back, then a moment later there was a flash of white light and Artemis was magically teleported away. Diana sighed, knowing she had gone past the point of no return. Then she dressed in Artemis's leather armour to complete her disguise. "Good luck..." Eve said with a sly smile as Diana headed to the door, then as she left Mercy added "You will soon have all you desire..."

Kara entered her bedchambers with Lena over her shoulder. She was glad to be home on Paradise Island; she had accomplished everything she had wanted on her trip. She set Lena down on her feet in front of the bed, then she gently laid her precious wife down on it. She began kissing along Lena's body as she untied her, then the two of them kissed passionately. Kara started to grind into Lena, pushing her into the soft sheets. Then she heard movement behind her, she rose up from the bed and turned around to see someone entering the room. It was Artemis, moving quieter than she normally would. "Artemis, has everything been alright on the island in my absence?" Kara said with a warm smile. Artemis smiled back and stepped slowly toward her as she replied "Yes my queen. Everything has been going exactly as it should..."

Diana was moments away from pouncing on Kara and tying her up, but then another women came down the hall, eagerly calling out "You're back, my queen! I assume you haven't forgotten about our agreement?" Diana let out a small frustrated sigh as Nubia entered, she would now have to postpone her plan. Kara nodded and replied "Of course, I'm all yours. Completely helpless..." She made a sultry smile at Nubia then turned to Lena who, after Kara quickly unbound her, was now sitting up on the bed "For your good behaviour, my love, you can have some free time to yourself. Until Nubia decides to capture you as well, of course. Nubia do you...mmmppphhh..."

As she spoke Nubia came up behind her, wrapping one arm around her midsection, pinning Kara's arms to her sides, and using her other hand to press a chloroformed cloth over her mouth and nose. "I agree..." Nubia whispered softly in Kara's ear before kissing her on the neck, then as she was drugging Kara she looked to Lena and, with a wink, said "You may spend some time in your lab if you wish, cutie. In a few hours I will send some of my slaves to kidnap you so you can join the fun" Lena watched happily as Kara's eyes drooped closed, knowing how important it was for her wife to occasionally be submissive. Nubia groped Kara firmly, squeezing her breasts until she passed out. She then turned her limp form around, kissed her deeply, then hoisted her up onto her shoulder, giving Kara's beefy rump a satisfied spank and squeeze to both cheeks. Nubia then reached forward and, with a casual flick of her hand, knocked the sandals off of Kara's limp feet, leaving them bare, as an amazon slave's feet were always expected to be. Having already changed into the skimpy slave dress Artemis always expected her to be in during her "training sessions", Kara was now the perfect picture of a submissive amazonian slave girl.

Lena slid off of the bed and began walking to the door, but she noticed Artemis was still standing by the doorway with her arms crossed, a small frustrated frown on her face. As Lena walked past her she noticed the tiara she was wearing seemed to be emitting a strange energy, it made a sinking sensation deep in her stomach and Lena paused to stare at it. Artemis noticed her staring and gave her rump a firm spank, then she pinched her juicy bottom as well as she said "Be on your way, Lena!" With a shocked gasp, Lena hurried down the hall, rubbing her sore behind.

Diana watched Lena leaving then looked over to Nubia who was laying Kara down on the bed, getting ready to bind and gag her prize. She stepped out and closed the doors to give them some privacy, then let out an angry moan. Lena had clearly noticed something about her tiara, but she couldn't capture the troublesome slavewife now, not until Nubia had kidnapped Lena, as planned. If she took Lena before Nubia was able to snatch up and ravish her, then the gorgeous concubine's disappearance would be noticed immediately. Diana grudgingly accepted that she would have to wait for their arrangement to be over, then act swiftly and capture Lena before the troublesome and clever damsel raised her concerns. She just hoped she would get her chance soon, Lena's suspicions were becoming dangerous, and the brilliant beauty needed to be captured and silenced.

SEX AND CHAOS

Lena's luscious rump still had a faint red mark from where Artemis had spanked her, and she knew there was something off about the amazon's behaviour. Artemis had never been so cruel with her; she had never teased or pinched Lena in such a bullying way. Even when disciplining her, the stern amazon had always been firm, yet respectful. Lena was now more suspicious than ever and she hurried down the halls of the palace toward her lab, the soles of her bare feet slapping softly against the marble stone floor. She turned a corner and was suddenly grabbed by two women.

Before she could even see who they were, a damp cloth was pressed firmly over her face. She let out a gasp of shock, inhaling the chloroform deeply. Everything went fuzzy and she passed out, sinking into the arms of her attackers. She was quickly bound, gagged, slung over one of their shoulders, and carried away...

When Lena awoke, she was lying on a bed in the pleasure slave quarters of Paradise Island, bound securely. She sat up, her eyes fluttering as she saw Lois and Vicki sitting on the bed with her. "Mmmph?" Lois reached forward and gently undid Lena's gag to allow her to speak freely. "Why did you kidnap me and bring me here? I have very important business to attend to in my lab!" Lena said in a sleepy mumble as she stomped her bound little bare feet in frustration. Lois and Vicki looked to each other with concerned expressions then Lois replied "We know you think something sinister is going on and we want to help. Artemis has been acting strangely today and yesterday we saw Alex and Kelly being kidnapped by Eve and Mercy. We tried to report it, but today they showed up like nothing was wrong. We decided that we had to kidnap you because we think they might try to capture you next."

"What about Sam, has anyone seen her?" Lena asked worriedly, to which Vicki shook her head and replied "Nope, she's completely disappeared, and we all could be next if we don't find out what's going on here. No-one else will listen to us as we're just pleasure slaves. Can you tell Kara about what's happening?" Lena sighed with a small pout as she replied "I can't right now. I'll have to wait until Nubia has finished having her way with us, then try to tell Kara. Nubia said she'll be sending her slaves to collect me soon" Lois and Vicki exchanged a mischievous look as Vicki said "So we have some time alone with you until then?" Lena nodded innocently, unaware of the slightly sinister designs of her current captors.

The two women hadn't had the chance to ravish the most desired pleasure slave on the island, and the golden opportunity of having Lena bound and helpless before them was too much to resist.

They both pounced on her, kissing and groping her as they quickly stripped her of her silky white dress. Lena made a small roll of her eyes, knowing she was a prize impossible to resist.

Then she began shuddering and moaning at the actions of the women, their lips and their hands were all over her, sending tingles of pleasure through her body. Lois and Vicki undressed as well, the three gorgeous women now completely naked. They continued stroking and kissing Lena for a short while, their nude bodies pressing into hers. Then they grabbed a pair of strap-ons and began to ravish the helpless damsel, Vicki pushing the hard rod between Lena's lips and Lois taking her from behind. They all moaned loudly in an erotic release, enjoying this burst of pleasure before they had to confront the sinister forces at play on Paradise Island.

TO BE CONTINUED...

AUTHOR NOTE

Thank you for reading this story, I hope you enjoyed it as much as i did writing it for you. The concluding part of the story will be in the next edition of this book attached to it as a series, hopefully, it would have been released by the time you are reading this. I will really love your feedback so i will have my eyes on my email inbox, so, therefore, please kindly use the comment section of where you purchased this book from to place your reviews, suggestion and ratings for this book for it will help me improve the forth coming stories that are yet to be released. You can contact me the author via my email (viaoptimisticdaily@gmail.com).